CHAPTER

1

It was mid-May at an eastern Connecticut state university. Dark clouds slowly moved into the area as moderate rain covered the rural campus. Exams were over, and most students were anxious to get home. Across the street at a popular college campus café, a well-dressed forty-year-old man named Dickie scanned the names of professors from the university's online directory. Dickie waited in his black BMW, hoping to target a young student as his next prey. When he finally saw the perfect one, his hunt began as he shadowed his victim inside the café. He spotted the redhead sitting at one of the high-top tables at the front window facing the main road. Without waiting for the host to seat him, Dickie moved swiftly to a vacant table adjacent to the student. He smiled and said, "Hi," passing by the student, who returned the smile. Dickie sat at the table with his back to the wall, providing him a view of his target and the front entrance.

Dickie was dressed in a designer suit with a coordinated tie, giving him a well-groomed professional appearance. However, no one would describe Dickie as good-looking. He stood about five feet, ten inches tall, with a protruding belly hanging over his belt. He had narrow shoulders and receding dark hair and wore black-rimmed glasses that partially covered his bushy eyebrows.

The waitress first stopped at the high-top table to take a soft drink order from the student before turning to Dickie, who asked for a dry martini with three olives. As he sat there waiting for his martini, he couldn't help stealing several glances in the direction of the student, hoping to make eye contact. His body tingled each time he stared at the student.

Minutes later, another student entered the café and walked toward the redhead sitting at the high-top table. He looked Middle Eastern with dark hair and brown skin. He sat opposite the redhead as they both greeted each other. Dickie was disappointed that his hope of connecting with the redhead might not happen now that the other student had arrived. Nevertheless, he continued eavesdropping, hoping the situation would change.

"Hey, Tav. How did you do on your exams?" asked the redhead.

"I thought I did well, JD. The computer theory exam was a breeze. I finished before anyone else. I think I aced it. The algorithms exam was the one that worried me, but I'm sure I did pretty good on that one too. I was done early but looked over my answers to a few questions before leaving. How did you do?"

"My accounting exam wasn't as hard as I thought it would be. I'm psyched my exams are over. I can't wait to get home for the summer."

"Listen, JD. I want to apologize for not being able to give you a ride. I know I promised you I would, but my advisor asked if I could stay on campus to assist him with a research project today. He wanted me at his office in an hour, and I told him I'd be there. I'll be a part of his project that will last a couple of weeks to complete. I forgot all about giving you a lift home."

"That's okay, Tav. I know you were counting on working with him on the project. I'm happy for you. I'll find a ride home. After my mom picks up my sister, she'll come to get me. So, no worries, my friend." Even though disappointed in not getting the ride, JD didn't show it.

The waitress dropped off a Pepsi for JD. She also asked Tav for an order, which he politely declined because he was leaving. The waitress then turned to the table where Dickie sat and dropped off the martini. "What else can I get you, hon?"

"Give me a second." Dickie pretended to glance at the menu while straining to hear the conversation behind the waitress. He thought he heard

Tav say he was leaving. If so, his plan for an opportunity to meet the redhead just improved.

He turned back to the waitress. "I'll have a cheeseburger, medium, with lettuce and tomato and an order of fries."

Dickie carefully tipped the martini to his lips while listening to Tav say he had to head back to campus. With Tav about to leave, it triggered a chill up Dickie's spine as he squirmed a bit in his chair, planning his next move. His brow showed tiny beads of sweat while Dickie prepared to take advantage of this opportunity. As he watched Tav leave the restaurant, Dickie got up from his seat and approached the student.

"Hi. I'm Professor McGivens. I believe you were one of my students last year."

JD looked at the older man, trying to remember him. "I don't think I was in your class."

"You didn't take my poli-sci class last year?"

"No. I'm a business major and haven't taken any poli-sci classes."

"Ah, you look very much like one of my past students. Maybe it's just the red hair. Anyway, how do you think you did on your exams?"

"I think I did good, including on the last exam I had this morning. I'm just glad all my exams are over, and I can go home for the summer."

"Where's home?"

"Southbrook, Massachusetts."

"Nice town. What time are your parents picking you up?"

JD hesitated, knowing it wasn't going to happen soon. "My dad is working out of state today, and my mom is picking up my sister at a prep school in New Hampshire. As luck would have it, my ride home just canceled on me a few minutes ago. So, I have to call my mom and tell her to pick me up either later tonight or tomorrow sometime."

With his fingers crossed, Dickie proposed his offer. "Well, I'm heading to Boston in about forty-five minutes. I'll have to make a quick stop at my place on the way to pick up my overnight bag, but if you're interested, I'd be happy to drop you off on my way to Boston."

"For real?" asked JD.

"For real. It's a long drive. I could use some company."

"That would be great. I'm all packed. I just need to go back to my room and get my backpack. I could run to the dorm and be back in about a half-hour. Is that okay?"

Looking at his watch, Dickie answered, "Well, I have a couple of phone calls to make first. How about we meet in front of the student union, say in forty-five minutes?"

"Yeah, that would be great. Thanks. I'll be waiting out front of the student union before then. I don't want to miss the ride."

"Great. I'm driving a black BMW. See you then."

JD bolted out of the café. He waited for traffic to pass, then ran across the street and up the campus hill toward the dormitories. Back at his table, Dickie sat back in his chair with a grin on his face. McGivens was the name he took from the school's directory listing of professors while he waited in his car outside the café. Sipping his martini, Dickie's heart began beating against his chest in anticipation. Although he sometimes shared his prey with his cousin, Randy Flemming, he wanted this kid all to himself. He thought back to times when similar plans failed before his cousin taught him tricks to use, like playing roles and telling lies. The professors Dickie had in college never impressed him. They had inflated views of themselves and favored pretty girls over male students. However, now pretending to be one of them helped gain a young student's trust.

Dickie didn't really have to make any calls, as he told the student. He only needed time to eat the burger and fries he ordered because he was starving. While waiting for his meal, excitement built inside him—he felt butterflies fluttering in his stomach just thinking about his encounter with the redhead. He didn't want to be late for his rendezvous, so when his meal arrived, Dickie asked the waitress for the bill and quickly gobbled down his meal.

An hour later, Dickie drove his BMW up the entrance ramp and merged into traffic on I-84 East toward Boston. The unsuspecting young teenager was sitting contently in the passenger's seat. Light rain fell, causing the heavy traffic to slow down.

"By the way, what is your name?" asked Dickie.

"I'm Josh Davis, but my friends call me JD. I appreciate the ride, Professor."

"What classes did you take this semester?"

"Accounting II, statistics, business communication, and some required classes like English. I did great in all my classes, and I felt the exams went fine for me."

JD was a handsome kid, five feet, eight inches tall, weighing one hundred and forty pounds. He had freckles on his nose and upper cheeks. His dad was an engineer, and his mom a teacher. The two continued to talk about life on campus and their plans during the summer break. Then, as Dickie neared the Massachusetts border, he noticed his exit up ahead.

"I'm going to take the next exit to make a quick stop at home for my overnight bags and grab a quick sandwich. I hope you don't mind, JD. I make great subs. Are you hungry?"

"No, I don't mind, and I am hungry. I only had a Pepsi all day."

Dickie took the upcoming exit and headed for his family's summer retreat home nestled deep in the woods. Unfortunately, it began raining much heavier, forcing him to slow to twenty-five miles an hour. His wipers were at high speed as the rain intensified, making it difficult to see the road ahead of him. Then an oncoming vehicle with its high beams glaring made it much worse for Dickie to see. Nervously, Dickie grasped the steering wheel even tighter. He searched for the streetlamp that was his landmark for turning onto his street. He was practically at a crawl when he finally caught sight of the streetlamp up ahead. As he approached the intersection, he eyed the broken street sign and made the turn. Finally, Dickie relaxed a bit and loosened his grip on the steering wheel.

"We are almost there, JD. We'll grab a quick sandwich, and I'll have you home in no time." Dickie fantasized about what he had in store for the naive teenager. JD only thought about getting home and spending time with his family and friends. He had no idea what horror awaited him.

CHAPTER

2

It was the start of a new work week following Thanksgiving. ATF Supervisory Special Agent Sam Caviello arrived early and sat at his desk at the Hartford, Connecticut, field office. ATF was the acronym for the Bureau of Alcohol, Tobacco, Firearms, and Explosives, the law enforcement agency responsible for enforcing federal firearms, arson, and explosives laws.

The agency began way back during Prohibition as the Alcohol Tax Unit. Its most famous agent was Eliot Ness, whose job, along with his team of just thirty-four agents, was to eradicate illegal alcohol operations by violent organized criminals, the most notorious being Al Capone. In addition, the agency worked closely with local and state authorities to prevent and prosecute violent criminals and felons who illegally possess, or use firearms in the commission of violent crimes, including the distribution of illegal drugs. ATF agents also assist local and state authorities in arson investigations and prevent the unlawful manufacture, sale, purchase, and use of explosives and destructive devices.

Although he enjoyed being in charge, Sam still yearned to be in the field investigating crimes, not sitting behind a desk reviewing reports and putting up with deadlines. It could be monotonous at times, but he still loved the job. It was a career filled with excitement and personal satisfaction in serving the general public. Every day brought new challenges.

After sitting behind a desk for hours reviewing reports, Sam needed a coffee break and fresh air. So he walked across the street to the corner café, inhaling the fresh air as the sun shined brightly on a clear day in November. At the café counter, he ordered a coffee with cream, no sugar, and a grilled English muffin.

Sitting at a window table and sipping his coffee, Sam read the morning paper starting with the sports page. His thoughts strayed from the newspaper back to Thanksgiving Day. He thought of his son spending Thanksgiving dinner with his mom and a stranger while he had a takeout turkey dinner alone at home. Divorced but still on friendly terms with his ex-wife, Ann, she had always invited him to have Thanksgiving dinner with her and their son, Drew. However, this year he never got the invite. Drew had called him a few days in advance to explain that his mom had been dating a guy for a few months, and she invited him to dinner instead. Although happy that Ann was dating, Sam felt left out from being with his son. It would have been nice if his son decided to have dinner with him since the ex was dining with her date. He was pleased for Ann to have someone in her life and thought maybe it was time for him to start dating again. The problem was his job took up most of his time. He didn't go to bars or dating sites to meet women. The only place he might meet women was at the gym, but no one there ever got his attention for dating.

His thoughts were interrupted when his cell phone vibrated. The call was from Terry Baker, the Sergeant in charge of the Hartford County's State Police Drug Task Force.

"How are you, Terry?"

"Hey, Sam. I'm good, thanks. I'm glad I reached you. Have you decided on an agent to assign to our task force? We could use another firearms guy. Our undercover had already purchased cocaine from a local dealer, and he placed another order to buy a kilo. The dealer claims he could deliver. If we can negotiate a deal and the guy agrees, we plan a buy-bust when he delivers the goods. Our concern is the dealer always carries a gun and brings a couple of armed associates for backup. We can use as much help as we can get for an arrest."

"I have decided who to assign to your team. I'll inform the agent this morning and get back to you. When you set a date for the bust, let me know. I'll get whatever agents are available to help out."

"Perfect. I appreciate it, Sam. Thanks."

When Sam returned to the office, he asked Agent Rick Ziglar, known as Ziggy to his colleagues, to join him in his office. Ziggy, an ex-Marine Corps infantry officer, worked well with local and state cops. He had a great sense of humor and made those around him laugh with his stockpile of jokes.

Ziggy entered Sam's office, sat down, and asked, "Where did you go? I was looking for you."

"I had to get out of the office. So I walked across the street to get a cup of coffee."

Flustered, Zig threw up his arms. "You should have told me. I would have gone with you."

"Sorry, I thought you were busy on the phone."

"Did you read the story in yesterday's paper about the guy who broke into the zoo and stole Otto, the zoo's prized baby panda bear?" Sam shook his head no. "A day later, the police caught the guy, but they questioned whether they should charge him with breaking and entering or grand theft Otto."

"Oh, like grand theft auto. I get it, but it's not that funny. You've had better. Anyway, I wanted to see you because Terry Baker asked me to assign another agent to his task force unit since Toby transferred to South Carolina. I've decided to assign you."

With a frown on his face and shaking his head in protest, Ziggy argued, "Sam, I'm still working on the preparations for a trial on that gun case. I don't have time to get involved with the task force."

"I know. I told Baker that you wouldn't be available to join the unit for a couple of weeks."

"I don't know, Sam. Both my sons, Michael and Chris, play fall and winter sports. I prefer to be close by the high school so I could attend some of their practices and scheduled games."

"Come on, Zig, you should be able to work your schedule around that. You enjoy working with the state and local guys, and it'll help establish new contacts. Plus, most task force work is after normal work hours. So you should have no problem arranging your schedule around seeing your sons' afternoon games or practice sessions. When you finish up with your current court case, you'll be free to join them. I know you'll thank me later for this assignment."

Ziggy knew Sam was right. The two of them were not only colleagues but friends, and he knew Sam wouldn't stick him with a lousy assignment. "Okay, I know this is a good detail that will result in gun case referrals for me. I'll get in touch with Terry to let him know that I'll join the unit as soon as I finish the case I'm working on."

"Thanks, Zig. In the next day or two, you and I could go to the task force office to meet the guys in the unit." The office phone rang. The administrative assistant answered the phone and told Sam that Agent Macheski was calling for him.

As Ziggy left the office, Sam answered the call. "Boss, one of my informants just called to tell me a Jamaican, Devon Tillman, is in town dealing coke, and he's always armed. I'm in the Narcotics Unit at the Hartford PD with Sergeant Chris Lansing. We ran a record check on Tillman and learned he has a long rap sheet and was wanted by the NYPD for assault and dealing drugs. New York confirmed Tillman is wanted for felony assault in the first degree. They claimed Tillman pistol-whipped a victim and is a person of interest in two other separate assaults. They faxed a copy of the warrant and a photo of Tillman to us at the PD."

Sam asked, "Does Tillman live here now, or is he just dealing in Hartford before heading back to New York or wherever?"

"My CI told me Tillman was bunking at his sister's apartment in the North End but will probably be heading back to Bridgeport tonight with his brother-in-law. That's where they both live. The CI said he doesn't know the brother-in-law other than he goes by the name Jubba and drives an older silver Honda Civic with a loud exhaust. The Narcotics Unit has the address of Tillman's sister, and Jubba's Honda Civic was spotted parked on the street outside her apartment."

"So, what's your plan?" asked Sam.

"We're setting up surveillance on the apartment, hoping Tillman and Jubba leave soon. I'm with a crew from the Narcotics Unit and Agents Sanchez and Clarkson. I also spoke with Attorney Murphy, who advised that we don't have probable cause to enter the sister's apartment without confirming Tillman is in there. However, he made it clear to arrest Tillman if he leaves the apartment."

"Okay, keep me updated. I have to finish up a few things here. When I do, I'll come out and join you."

As it got close to five in the afternoon, Sam decided to call Pete to let him know he'd join them in about twenty minutes. After clearing his desk, he locked up his files and set the office alarm. Sam took the elevator to the garage level to get his government ride. Then, from the secured trunk of his car, he grabbed his ballistic vest, two additional loaded magazines, and sneakers to replace his shoes in case they had to chase the suspect. While driving to the location, he contacted Pete. "What's your 20?"

Pete gave Sam the address and then said they were parked diagonally across the street from the apartment in the parking lot of Mary's convenience store.

"Be there in ten."

Sam spotted Pete's vehicle several minutes later and pulled up behind him. He left his car and slid into the back seat of Pete's sedan. Hartford PD's sergeant, Chris Lansing, was sitting in the front passenger's seat.

"What's the status, Pete?" asked Sam.

Pete pointed out the silver Honda parked diagonally across the street in front of a five-story redbrick apartment building. "We ran the license plate on the Honda. It came back registered to Alvina Dixon of Bridgeport, Connecticut. A background check on her disclosed two arrests: shoplifting and the other for breach of peace. Alvina has a brother, Lloyd, who we believe is Jubba. Lloyd Dixon has a felony record for possession of a stolen vehicle and possession with intent to distribute cocaine."

"Who else is part of the surveillance other than Sanchez and Clarkson?"

"There are two black-and-white patrol cars, one parked at each end of the street. Sanchez and Clarkson are in one car, and two drug unit guys are in their car. If the subjects leave the apartment, we positioned the patrol cars in each direction Jubba might take when he drives off. No matter which way he goes, there will be a black-and-white to block the street to stop them. We and the other covering cars will fall in behind Jubba's vehicle."

"What do we do if Tillman and Jubba don't come out and are in for the night?"

"We can wait him out and take him in the morning," responded Pete.

Sam knew a lengthy surveillance would mean a shift change for the locals that could complicate the operation. He suggested calling the informant and having him knock on the apartment door to make a buy from Tillman. "It's not important if he makes the buy as long as he sees Tillman inside. That gives us the probable cause to enter the apartment to make the arrest."

Sergeant Lansing piped in. "I agree, Pete. If Tillman doesn't leave soon, it's better to try to get him before long instead of spending the whole night waiting."

Acquiescing, Pete called the informant but had to leave a message for a callback when the call went directly to voicemail. Just before six, Pete tried again, but again, no luck.

Twenty minutes later, two guys exited the apartment building and headed toward the Honda. While looking through their binoculars, both Pete and Lansing agreed that Tillman had entered the passenger side of the Honda. The Honda's headlights came on, and it departed, heading south. Lansing radioed both patrol cars that the target vehicle was heading south. Pete already had his car in gear, waiting until the Honda passed his position, and then moved out to follow behind it. As Pete drove behind the Honda, his cell phone rang. He glanced at the number calling, pressed the answer button, and said to the informant, "Disregard, call me in an hour."

Up the road, a patrol car with its lights flashing pulled out and blocked the street, causing the Honda to stop. Pete and one of the detective's vehicles with emergency lights flashing pulled to the rear of the Honda, boxing it in.

Pete, Sam, and Lansing exited their ride with guns drawn. They saw Tillman sliding out of the Honda and began running. All three ran after him, yelling, "Police, stop!"

In his mid-fifties and a chain-smoker, Lansing lagged behind Pete. On the other hand, Sam, in much better shape and wearing sneakers, was only about twenty-five yards behind Tillman. Sam continued to yell for Tillman to stop.

While breathing heavily and tiring some, Sam still gained on Tillman. His adrenaline was flowing on high octane while he began sensing a cautionary flash of trouble ahead. His body trembled with a stinging sensation down his spine. It was a sign Sam frequently felt as a warning of a looming threat. He grew extra guarded as he watched Tillman run around the back of the nearest house and toward a wooden fence. A section of the fence was separated and leaning into the neighboring backyard, leaving a wide gap to run through. Tillman raced toward the fence and tried leaping through the narrow opening but tripped on a bottom cross-section and fell hard to the ground.

Sam cautiously moved toward the fence, aiming his gun at Tillman with his finger off the trigger. Not knowing what the suspect would do next, Sam shouted, "Stay down, don't fucking move!"

Tillman disregarded the command, stood up, with his hands slightly raised, and slowly turned to face his pursuer. Now alone with his gun pointing at Tillman's chest, Sam had only one thought. *He has a gun.*

Still breathing heavily but with a firm, steady grip on his gun, Sam placed his finger on the trigger, saying, "Put your hands higher, or you're a dead man."

Tillman briefly hesitated before reaching into his waistband for his gun. This action was nerve-racking for Sam, so he pulled slightly on the trigger, ready to shoot to kill. But, for a moment, Sam had an out-of-body reaction, like the scene wasn't real, only a terrible dream, as he witnessed Tillman desperately searching his waistband for his gun—but there was no gun. Tillman realized his gun must have dropped from his waist when he fell, but it was too dark for him to see it on the ground. Although Sam recognized Tillman was frantic, looking for his gun on the ground, Sam still maintained the pressure on the trigger until Pete and Chris Lansing came into view with their weapons pointing at Tillman. Then, unexpectedly, spotlights from the two neighborhood homes lit up the rear of the backyard, with neighbors peering out their rear windows. Having no choice seeing three guns pointed at him, Tillman raised his hands high and yelled, "Don't shoot! I'm unarmed!"

Sam breathed a comforting sigh of relief as he released the pressure on the trigger and shouted, "Keep your hands up and slowly turn around."

As Tillman turned, Sam maneuvered his way through the opening in the fence. He stepped on something hard on the ground as he did and shouted, "Pete, cover him."

"I got him in my sights, Sam. If he does anything stupid, he'll be on the ground permanently."

Sam placed his firearm in its holster and handcuffed Tillman behind his back. Sam guided Tillman through the fence, where Pete and Lansing took control of him. Sam took out his mini flashlight and searched the ground beneath him.

"Gun on the ground!" Sam shouted loud enough for the neighbors to hear.

Sam's heart still pounded rapidly on his chest, thinking how lucky it was that the gun had fallen out of Tillman's waistband. He was so relieved he didn't have to pull the trigger and kill Tillman, especially with an audience looking on from the two neighboring homes.

Sam briefly looked up at those watching from the windows and now the back porches of the two homes, knowing he was on a stage with cell phone cameras filming the event. He tried putting his thoughts aside as he took out a pen from his pocket and stuck it in the gun's trigger guard to pick it up without placing his fingerprints on it. Then, he held it high for all the cameras to capture.

"Pete, do you have latex on you?" asked Sam.

"Yeah, give me a second." Pete put on a pair of latex gloves as Sam handed him Tillman's gun to secure it as evidence. The weapon would eventually be examined for prints and traced, hoping to determine how Tillman acquired it. Most likely, it was a stolen gun.

As Pete escorted Tillman from the scene, Sergeant Lansing, seeing the growing audience in the backyard, called out, "Police business. Get back in your homes."

Tillman was brought back to where the police stopped the Honda. Jubba was cuffed and held by the detectives. One detective reported Jubba's driver's license identified him as Lloyd Dixon. "We also found a loaded handgun under the driver's seat, six small packets of white powder in his jacket, and three dozen more packets in a metal candy container in the glove box."

With three ATF agents and three police detectives to handle the two suspects and evidence, Sam, still feeling the adrenaline encompassing his body from his encounter with Tillman, called it a night and asked Pete to take charge of the operation. He thanked the local officers for their assistance and asked if one of them to drive him back to his car.

Sam then drove home, where he hoped to come back down to earth and relax. However, Sam couldn't help thinking back to the events of the evening. It was troubling that he was so close to pulling the trigger and shooting Tillman dead. If that had happened, Sam knew someone would have second-guessed him for shooting an unarmed man, even though Tillman's gun was within his reach. It was a daunting situation where you only had a split second to decide—an unsettling decision to make. In hindsight, Sam credited the numerous shoot/don't shoot practice scenarios he had participated in during his Special Response Team training. The training ingrained the practice for agents to distinctively act as taught, which was to confirm the seriousness of the threat before doing what agents hoped they would never have to do—kill someone. However, as his thoughts about the night's encounter lingered, Sam knew he would struggle for hours before dozing off to sleep.

CHAPTER
3

Andy Richardson was home in Queens, NYC, spending the Christmas holiday break with his family after completing his first semester exams at Bushnell College in Hartford, Connecticut. He planned to spend Christmas with his mom, Marci, his dad, John, and his sister, Mara, before traveling to Boston to celebrate New Year's Eve with his high school buddies, Keith Miller and Todd Gilchrist, who attended Boston University.

Keith and Todd urged Andy to drive to Boston with them the day after Christmas. However, his mom's annual mammogram revealed suspected tumors in both breasts, so he remained home to support her until the biopsy results came back after Christmas. To add to the family worries, Andy's dad got furloughed from his job due to cutbacks at the plant. In addition, Andy lost the use of his car. Three days before, his sister borrowed his car, and while driving on an icy road, she slid into a guardrail. Although Andy was happy his sister didn't get hurt, he now had no car to drive to Boston.

He considered his options on how he intended to get to Boston to meet up with his friends. Since he no longer had a car, he planned to take the bus to Hartford, drop off his following-semester school essentials at his dormitory, and attempt to find a student there who might be traveling to, or most of the way, to Boston. If that failed, he might have to hitchhike. After all, before he had a car, he and his friends hitchhiked dozens of times.

Although he had never hitched such a long distance, Andy was older now and convinced he could do it if he had to.

His mom and dad arrived back home from the hospital after the biopsy later than anticipated. They ordered out for a pizza and sub sandwiches so his mom wouldn't have to cook. They tried to enjoy dinner while waiting for a call from her doctor with the biopsy results. Andy, his dad, and Mara avoided talking about the biopsy or money issues while they ate dinner. The doctor finally called after dinner, informing Marci the lumps were benign, but the doctor recommended periodic monitoring to check for any changes. That was great news for the family and allowed Andy to focus on his trip to Boston without worrying about his mom. He gave his mom a big hug and a kiss.

"Great news, Mom. I'm so happy everything is okay. I'm going to my room to pack for my trip to Hartford and Boston. Then I'll shower and go to bed. I have an early-morning wake-up."

*   *   *

The weather looked bleak as Sam looked out his office window. Wednesday began with the sun shining until dark clouds rolled in, bringing light rain. Sam was looking forward to the upcoming long New Year's weekend.

Looking at his watch, he saw the time was only three in the afternoon. He was alone in the office. Most of his staff took vacation time between Christmas and New Year's, and those working were in the field, probably close to home. At first, Sam planned to stay in the office to cover the phone calls until five o'clock but decided he'd lock up the office and head home a little earlier. He cleared his desk and locked the files. Just as Sam was about to put the office phone on answering service, the phone rang. After getting only one call all day, it amazed him that the phone would ring just as he was on his way out.

"Sam, this is Steve Roberts. We just approved a Special Response Team callout, and the operational plan is being faxed to you as we speak. Group supervisor, Jeff Doherty, is in the office with me and will fill you in with more details shortly. The team will execute a search warrant on the residence of the local leader of a white supremacist group. We will need every team member available. Doherty plans on having a briefing at his group's office Friday morning at ten with the raid scheduled for early Saturday morning."

Sam shook his head in disappointment.

"I know this is short notice to work on the holiday weekend, but the informant contacted Doherty only moments ago with information that the group plans on crashing a peaceful planned protest rally armed with guns. The informant knows the leader stashed several firearms at his place for possible use against those participating in the protest on Saturday afternoon. I've already notified Agent Altimari to contact the rest of the team to save you some time. You and Ziglar could check into a Boston hotel tomorrow night rather than face the Boston commuter traffic on a Friday morning. Doherty will make reservations at a nearby hotel for you two."

Roberts handed the phone to Doherty. "How are ya, Sam? Did you get the fax I sent on the operational plan yet?"

"Let me check in the fax room. Be right back." The fax was just coming through the fax machine. He grabbed the pages and went back to his desk. "Okay, I have it. Why don't you go over the plan while I read along?" said Sam, the SRT leader.

As Sam studied the plan before him, Doherty went over the details, including the probable expectations and assignments. Doherty agreed to Sam's minor adjustments and then said he would call him back with the hotel name and address within the hour. Sam then searched for Ziglar's number on his cell and called him, knowing he wouldn't be happy when told the bad news.

Ziggy answered the phone after five rings. "Ziggy, buddy, it's Sam. I don't have good news for you. Before you complain, I'm only the messenger, and I have to be there too. I received a call from the ASAC requesting we be in Boston Friday morning for a briefing on an SRT callout early Saturday morning. So we'll leave for Boston tomorrow."

"Bullshit! You gotta be kidding me! I have a doctor's appointment tomorrow afternoon at two. Not to mention my sons are playing ball Saturday afternoon at the high school."

"Sorry, Zig. Do you think I'm happy about this? No freaking way. We plan to hit the home of a white supremacist group leader. You can still make your doctor's appointment tomorrow. Meet me at my apartment tomorrow around five, and we'll ride up together. With luck, we might make it back home in time for you to watch your kids play on Saturday afternoon."

CHAPTER

4

At sunrise, Andy made sure he packed everything for his trip. He then had a quick breakfast and kissed his mom. "Don't worry about me. I promise once I get to Hartford, I'll call you and then again when I get to Boston."

"Please be careful and have a good time with your friends. I know you are looking forward to seeing them. Don't worry about me. I'm fine. Call me every day so that I know you are all right."

Andy loaded his backpack and a small duffle bag into his dad's car while waving goodbye to his mom and sister. His dad then drove him to the bus station in Queens Village. When they arrived there, his dad hugged him and handed him an envelope.

"Be careful, son. Call your mom every day like she asked you to. She'll be worrying about you if you don't call. Here is a little extra cash to cover some of your expenses."

When boarding the bus, Andy didn't fail to notice the older woman eyeing him as he took a seat on the bus. Although he was only five feet, nine inches tall, he was a good-looking nineteen-year-old with thick bushy blond hair, widely set blue eyes, and a slender but toned muscular body. His smooth complexion and peach-fuzz facial hair made him look younger than his age.

Andy slept most of the way to Hartford. Once the bus pulled into the terminal, Andy grabbed a cab to Bushnell College, a fifteen-minute ride from the bus station. When he arrived at the college, he realized it was already after one o'clock. Light rain started to fall. The cab couldn't drive up to the dormitory, so Andy had to walk in the rain to his dorm room. Once there, he unloaded what he had and then went up and down his dormitory halls, asking anyone still at school if they were heading toward Boston, with no luck. He thought maybe someone still at school would be heading in that direction, but most students had already left after exams. Most of the students left on campus were foreign or grad students.

When back in his room, Andy counted all the money he had saved for his time in Boston.

Typically, his parents would have given him sufficient additional funds to cover all his expenses, but money was tight now that his dad wasn't working. The little money his dad gave was already used for the bus and taxi to Hartford. Doing a little calculation in his head, he figured he needed most of the money he had and then some while in Boston. He needed to come up with a plan, but first, he called home and talked for longer than he wanted with his mom and dad before checking the bulletin boards in his dorm for rides toward Boston. Not finding any, he left his dorm to check the bulletin boards and halls in the neighboring dormitories. He asked any student he saw on his way if they, or anyone they knew, planned on driving to or near Boston. The last student he saw said he was only going as far as Tolland, only about twenty-two miles.

"Is that in the direction of Boston on the interstate?" asked Andy.

"Yes. It's off I-84 toward Boston. I can give you a ride that far if you want," answered Lucas Collins.

"Are you leaving right now?"

"No. I have to meet with a friend for a while. I could meet you at the north entrance of the student parking lot at five."

"Okay. Thanks, Lucas. I'll see you at five." Andy was disappointed but figured he wouldn't find anyone this late traveling near Boston. If he hitch-hiked, he knew it would take longer to get to Boston, but he'd feel more comfortable having additional money to spend there. Back in his dorm room, he called Todd to let him know his status.

"Hey, Andy, are you on your way?"

"I'm still in Hartford and short on money, so I decided to hitchhike. My best guess for arriving in Boston would be between eight and nine tonight. I'll call you when I'm close."

Andy then charged his iPhone while he waited to meet Lucas Collins. Forty-five minutes later, he grabbed his cell phone and blue backpack and headed to the student parking lot. Unfortunately, the rain started again and came down much heavier. Andy covered his floppy hair with his New York Yankees baseball cap while moaning about having to hitchhike to Boston in the rain. He arrived at the student parking lot on time, but Lucas Collins wasn't there. The rain subsided while he waited twenty minutes before Lucas finally showed up.

Andy didn't know Collins, but while driving on the interstate, they talked about school, their studies, and their plans for the holiday weekend. It took nearly thirty minutes to get to the exit where Collins dropped Andy off on I-84 in Tolland. It was almost six o'clock. The rain had eased to a mist with dense fog moving in. Andy hurried to the nearby overpass to get cover from the weather.

CHAPTER
5

Dickie, who previously used the name Professor McGivens, shivered as he stepped into the brisk night air and walked toward his BMW 535i. He had left work a little early, as he often did, to catch up on errands before the upcoming holiday weekend. He planned to stop at his favorite watering hole for a martini and meet up with his cousin, Randy Flemming, who had called and said he had something lined up for them.

Driving across the Connecticut River's bridge from Hartford to East Hartford, he navigated to the Back Room. The Back Room was just that, the back room of a bar and grill called the Main Street Tavern, located on the south side of town. Upon entering the tavern's parking lot, he noticed Flemming's pickup truck was already there. He parked his BMW in the rear lot and entered the pub through the back entrance.

As Dickie entered the bar, he first surveyed the room for any prospects before spotting Flemming at the bar. It was generally busy during the afternoon happy hour, thanks to reduced drink prices and complimentary hors d'oeuvres. Still, it wasn't that crowded, probably due to the weather and the upcoming holiday weekend. He hopped on the vacant barstool next to Flemming.

"Hey, Randy, how are ya doing? It looks like ya need another drink. Your glass is empty."

"Dickie! You're late, cousin! I've been waiting for almost an hour for you to arrive and buy me a drink. After all, you're the guy with the big bucks."

"You're dreaming. I have to work for a living like everybody else."

"Yeah, right. Your old man has one of the most successful construction companies in the state. Who are you kidding?"

"Yeah, yeah. My father might be loaded, but that doesn't mean I am. Tell me what you've lined up. I'm horny as hell and need relief. It's been a while."

"I've been watching this young girl who is an utterly stunning beauty. She has this beautiful crop of curly blond hair and dazzling blue eyes. She's thin but shapely with nice boobs for a fifteen-year-old."

Dickie shook his head negatively while Randy spoke. "Shit, Randy. You know I'm not into girls. That's not who I thought you had lined up for us."

"Listen, Dickie. Just try this once. You might like it. Come on. It'll be something new. You said you were horny as hell. You're still going to get off, you know."

Dickie was only half listening to Randy. He fantasized all day at work about hooking up with someone for the weekend. He thought back to when he first experienced sexual pleasure. Although not blessed with good looks or physique, Dickie was educated, well-spoken, and well-groomed. His father always encouraged him to play sports and date girls. However, when he tried to get friendly with a couple of girls he liked at his school, they rebuffed him or laughed in his face. Being chubby and shy as a kid, girls avoided him, called him names, or just walked away from him. His dad, a bigger, rugged, and more physical type, always pushed him to stand up to the bullies. He pressured Dickie to join a gym to get in shape and eat less junk food to lose weight. Dickie remembered getting bullied by the school's tough guys and felt intimidated around good-looking, athletic kids who had no trouble getting dates with the girls.

Dickie's closest school friend, Jared, was shy like him but an absolute brainer. They became buddies and did homework together at each other's homes. When Dickie needed help with his studies, Jared was willing to tutor him, especially in math and science. Going through puberty, they talked about how girls avoided the two of them. They became absorbed in learning more about sex, and the more they discovered, the more they wanted to experiment with it. First, they began by touching themselves, which ultimately led to mutual stimulation. Dickie enjoyed the pleasurable feeling and wanted to experience it more often, not only with Jared but with other boys.

"Dickie, are you still with me? You seemed to have drifted off in space, not hearing a thing I said."

"Oh, I don't know, Randy. I'm not sure about being with a girl. I'll let you know tomorrow."

Dickie thought Randy wanted to meet because he had set something up for a fun evening, but it wasn't the case. So, since his dad asked him to check on the family's summer retreat home, Dickie decided to head there and get that done.

"Randy, I'm heading to my dad's place. I'll think about what you said about the girl, but don't get your hopes up. I'll let you know."

"Dickie, you gotta experiment a little, ya know. Anyway, I have another prospect I've been watching. I'll let you know if it's a possibility. By the way, my backhoe is still at your dad's place. So when do you want to plant those trees?"

"I'll call you when we can do it. I gotta go. See ya, cousin." Dickie paid for the drinks before heading for the exit. As he did, a good-looking young kid who appeared too young to be in a bar walked in and passed by him. Dickie instantly felt his emotional urges rising and turned to watch the kid saunter toward the rear of the room and take a seat at a seemingly vacant booth. Not able to tell if anyone else was in the booth, Dickie decided to take a look before someone else did. As he approached to greet the young kid, he noticed someone was sitting across from him, and both were in a fun-loving discussion holding hands. Disappointed, he turned and decided it wasn't his night.

He exited the bar and hustled to his BMW as it started to rain. He took a deep breath as he pushed the keyless entry button to his two-year-old Beamer and slid into the driver's seat. He started her up, placed it into drive, and sped out of the parking lot. His speed picked up as he headed toward the entrance ramp for I-84 East. Entering the ramp, he stepped on the gas and merged into traffic.

Passing through Manchester, he glanced at the speedometer and noticed the needle holding steady at eighty-two miles per hour. Feeling a little high, he wanted to push the pedal to the floor but decided to slow it down to seventy. He didn't want to press his luck and get pulled over by a state trooper.

His thoughts were on enjoying a night full of sexual bliss where everything and anything goes. He passed through the town of Vernon and entered the town of Tolland.

CHAPTER
6

Dense fog on the interstate caused Dickie to slow to forty miles an hour. Approaching the Tolland exit, he noticed a figure up ahead under an overpass, so he clicked on his high beams, which didn't help to see much better through the dense fog. Not able to make out what appeared to be a young kid hitchhiking, Dickie lightly tapped his brakes to slow down as he got closer for a better look at the person. Slowly entering the underpass, he saw a young kid wearing a baseball cap covering his bushy blond hair waving.

Dickie abruptly slammed on his brakes. Although he knew he would be exiting the highway only a few miles up the road, he wasn't about to miss this opportunity. He shifted into reverse to back up to the youngster while still in the traffic lane. A car in the back of him had to brake hard to avoid ramming the backside of his vehicle. The driver behind him blasted the horn and repeatedly flashed his high beams in apparent anger. Ignoring the other car, Dickie rolled the passenger window down to get a better look at the hitchhiker.

"Where are you heading, kid?"

The hitchhiker leaned forward into the open window and answered, "Boston."

"Well, you're in luck. I'm heading there myself. Hop in."

Andy Richardson ignored the driver behind him, who flashed his high beams in his face, threw his backpack into the BMW, and slid into the front seat. *What luck*, Andy thought. *Somebody up there is watching over me.* His concerns about being alone on the dreary fog-filled highway began to subside. He couldn't help but smile as he thought about the good times he would have this weekend with his friends in Boston.

Dickie was annoyed by the flashing high beams coming from the car behind him. While spinning his wheels to get away, he rolled down his window, stuck out his arm, and gave his middle finger up high so the driver behind him could see it. Distancing himself from the car, Dickie finally calmed down and changed the radio station from classical music to pop to put his new young friend more at ease. When he glanced over and saw the kid tapping his fingers on his right knee in unison with the music, Dickie felt the excitement building inside as he anticipated a very sensual evening at his place. The fog was suddenly thickening, so he slowed down, not wanting to miss his exit not far up ahead.

Dickie turned to the kid and said, "I live just off the highway at the next exit. I hope you don't mind me taking a quick detour to pick up my bags for my weekend in Boston. The bags are packed. Besides, I'm starving and can make sandwiches for both of us. We could eat them there or on the way to Boston."

"No problem. I'm a little hungry myself."

Dickie could feel his heart pumping against his chest. The buzz he felt from his drinking put him in a feverish mood of anticipation for what was to come. His grip on the steering wheel was uncomfortably tight as he turned onto the exit for rural Route 59, heading toward where he planned on a night of fulfilled pleasure.

*   *   *

It was still misty, with fog increasing on the interstate, but fortunately, the amount of traffic lessened. Agents Caviello and Ziglar were driving on I-84 eastbound on the way to the briefing in Boston. The two agents focused their conversation on politics and sports rather than the upcoming early-morning raid they were to take part in on Saturday morning.

"It's been a while since we took in a basketball game at the civic center. The women's team is hosting Notre Dame in a couple of weeks. We should get Jennifer and Pete to join us again and go to the game," suggested Ziggy.

"I'm up for that, Zig. A week later, they'll be playing South Florida on campus. That should be a great game. Maybe we should try to get tickets for that game too."

"So, Sam, since we're bomb agents, you should know what they call a dog with brass balls?"

Sam shrugged his shoulders in ignorance.

"They call him Sparky," answered Ziggy.

It didn't even crack a smile from Sam. "Oh man, that wasn't one of your best, Zig."

Sam's government sedan, commonly referred to as his G-ride, passed the Vernon town line while slowing down because of the worsening fog. He wanted to maintain a safe distance from the car in front of him. As he approached the exit for the town of Tolland, Sam noticed the driver in front of him tapped its brake lights, so he tapped his to slow down. Passing the exit, Sam saw the car suddenly stop in the traffic lane and then back up toward him. He slammed on his brakes to avoid an accident.

"What the hell is this guy doing?" questioned Sam.

"Looks like a kid is hitchhiking under the overpass," answered Ziggy.

Sam pounced on the horn several times and flashed his high beams. As he did, the hitchhiker turned to face him with a startled look of concern. Sam and Ziggy clearly saw the surprised teenager with his full head of blond hair sticking out under his New York Yankees baseball cap. The kid threw his backpack inside the car and jumped in. The BMW then spun its wheels and fishtail as it sped away. Sam and Ziggy both commented on the BMW's license plate that read "DICKH 1."

"What an asshole," remarked Sam.

"Did you get a look at the license plate?" asked Ziggy.

"Yeah, it's a vanity plate."

"Ha, you know what that plate must stand for? Dickhead one," joked Ziggy.

They both laughed as Sam pulled out into traffic, not noticing that the BMW driver had given him the finger out his window. It didn't take long before Sam followed right behind the BMW again.

"I'm going to give this dickhead a lot of room." Sam released the pressure on the gas pedal to lengthen the gap between the two cars.

Both vehicles settled down to a reasonable speed, considering the dense fog on the road. Several minutes later, the two agents noticed the BMW's right taillight signal for a right turn, and before long, it took the exit just before the Massachusetts border a short distance ahead.

"That's weird. This guy picks up a hitchhiker and takes an exit only a few miles down the road. You think it's likely the driver and the kid live in the same rural town?" asked Sam.

"Beats me. If the kid doesn't live there, the driver is not taking him where he wants to go," replied Ziggy.

CHAPTER
7

A short distance after taking the exit, Dickie took a right turn and headed east for about two miles. He had to slow to a turtle's pace as it became nearly impossible to see through the rapidly thickening fog, and he could no longer make out the lane divider on the road. His fingers were tired from the tight grip on the steering wheel while concentrating on staying in the proper lane. Up ahead, he finally could make out the glow of a streetlamp. When he came upon it, he turned left and smiled when he noticed the broken street sign, confirming this was his street. He headed toward the S-curve in the road. He slowly turned around the first part of the sharp curve and then the next that got him close enough to see the mailbox marked number 17. There he turned onto the dirt driveway of his dad's summer home. "We'll stop here for a few minutes, Andy. Then we'll be on our way."

"It's very dark here." Andy couldn't see a thing and got a little nervous. He held his hand on the door handle in case he had to jump out and run for his life. But, when he spotted a light up ahead, his hand released his grip, and his worry diminished. "I thought the driveway was going to go on forever. Isn't it a little scary living out here in the woods? There are no neighbors nearby."

"I admit it's a bit remote, but there is a lake not far from here where many owners in the neighborhood fish, water-ski, and paddle canoes around the lake. In the summer, we often have family get-togethers and parties. It can get quite lively around here. We're coming up on the house now."

Andy could see the light shining from the house. He was relieved. The butterflies in his stomach started to settle, and he began to breathe normally again. "I was a little nervous not being able to see anything with the fog. It reminds me of a horror movie I saw a couple of years ago. It was about a scary dark forest that if you went into it, you never came back out."

"Well, you don't have to worry about not coming out of the woods here. It's completely safe." Dickie parked in front of the cape's attached two-car garage. The floodlight above the garage doors lit up the driveway. He used the remote to open up one of the garage doors. "Let's head inside, and I'll make some sandwiches, grab my bag, and we'll get you to Boston."

"Okay, sounds good because I'm starving."

Once inside the house, Andy felt more relaxed. He commented on the interior. "Wow, Professor, this is nice. Did you fix this place up yourself? The kitchen looks brand new."

"No, I didn't do any work here. We had the help of an interior decorator, but thanks for the compliment. I hope you don't mind if I turn on some music. It helps me relax while working in the kitchen, especially after driving through that damn fog. I'm still trying to loosen up my fingers and relax my back, which feels tight. Sit down and make yourself at home. I'll open up a can of Coke for you."

Soft music began to play as Dickie returned to the kitchen. He filled a small bowl of pretzels and opened a can of Coke that he shook a bit before putting it on the table. "Sit down and relax. Enjoy some pretzels and Coke while I prepare the subs. That's when you'll taste the best sub sandwiches you ever had. I have the finest old-country ham, imported Italian cheese, peppers, heirloom tomatoes, and Italian lettuce. Then, I sprinkle on salt and pepper and some Spanish olive oil. They are scrumptious, and you are going to love them!"

"I'm getting hungrier just listening to you!" said the teenager.

Andy took off his coat and wrapped it around the back of the chair as he sat down. He grabbed a couple of pretzels and pressed the cold can of Coke to his lips. He was thirstier than he realized and poured half the contents down his throat.

He continued munching on the pretzels and downed the rest of the Coke. It wasn't long after that Andy started to feel drowsy and light-headed. He could hear the professor talking, but his voice sounded more distant, like coming through an echo chamber. So close to passing out, Andy struggled to snap out of his stupor and stay alert. He rubbed his eyes and lightly slapped his cheeks to no avail.

What the hell is going on? Andy thought to himself. He felt trapped between sleep and a nightmare. He knew something was wrong and turned to face the professor for help but was shocked by what he saw. "What? Oh, God, no. Get away from me! Please, Professor."

Dickie stood there up close and naked from the waist down, only inches from Andy.

"Come on, Andy. Let's have a little fun tonight before we drive to Boston. You please me, and I'll do the same for you."

Andy was close to vomiting. His adrenaline was pumping at full speed, his heart was racing, and all he wanted was to escape, but his body was too sluggish. Dickie grabbed Andy's head, trying to push it toward his naked body.

"No! Let me go, please!" he screamed while trying to push the professor away. Andy tried standing, but Dickie pushed his head down to the tabletop while the chair fell back to the floor. Dickie had Andy's body bent over at the waist. Then, while holding Andy's head down on the table, Dickie got behind him, reached around Andy's waist with his free hand, unbuckled his belt, and pushed down his pants and underwear.

"Please, Professor, I don't want to do this. Let me go! Please!"

Andy tried to resist, but he was too weak to raise his head pinned to the table. Dickie pushed up against Andy. Andy knew what was coming next. He struggled but couldn't muster the strength to break away. His face was distorted in pain as tears rolled down his face.

He thought of his dad, wishing he was there to protect him. He was scared and wanted to pass out until it was over. As the professor's weight bore against his backside, Andy knew he would never live this down. The invasion continued for only a few minutes, but it seemed like an eternity.

"Oh, that was good, kid. We'll enjoy more of the same later." Dickie spanked Andy's rear end mumbling something Andy couldn't make out. Dickie then straightened up the chair and forced Andy back into a sitting position on it.

Andy's eyes, blurred from his tears, could only see the outline of his assailant walking into the living room. He heard the music switch from soft pop to classical and the sound of the professor humming and making indistinguishable sounds while his arms were waving in the air like he was conducting an orchestra. His body motions mimicked a dance, a dance of joy. With his back to Andy at the kitchen counter, Dickie pulled up his trousers lying on the floor next to the refrigerator. With continued humming, he began preparing the sandwiches.

Andy realized this deranged monster wouldn't morph into Mr. Nice Guy. After what he did, there was no way he would casually drive him to Boston as if nothing had happened. Andy knew this beast wasn't through with him yet, and this was his last stop. He had to get up and escape, or he was dead meat. It took all his mental and physical strength to reach down and pull up his pants. Andy quietly grabbed his coat and his hat from the table. Although his sight was still blurry, he silently lifted himself off the chair and drowsily tiptoed toward the living room door. It was now or never. His hands searched for the doorknob, but the door wouldn't pull open when he turned it. He searched above for a deadbolt knob and softly unlocked it. Back to the doorknob, he grasped and slowly turned it to open the door, then quietly snuck out.

Dickie finished preparing a sub while swaying with lustful passion, almost as if he was dancing in rhythm to erotic music.

"Ah, the maestro has finished his gastronomical wonder!" he shouted.

Dickie was flying high, fantasizing about fulfilling his sexual appetite with the kid. He thought back to similar times with his cousin Randy and his uncle, back to his much younger days. How intense and stimulating it had felt. How much he had enjoyed it and sought more of the pleasure it gave him. His eyes rolled back as he became suspended in euphoria until suddenly, he felt a cold breeze against the back of his neck that took him out of his trance.

Wondering where the frosty air was coming from, he turned to face the kid. His eyes widened, and the veins in his neck bulged with anger. The kid was gone. He froze momentarily in disbelief. *What the hell? I put enough drops of the drug in the Coke to put the kid in la-la land for hours.* Stunned that the kid was gone, his eyes refocused from the empty chair to the open front door.

"How did that kid get up and walk out of the house?" whispered Dickie.

Terrified that the kid managed to escape, he rushed to the door and flicked on the spotlight to light up the whole front yard. He scanned the area until he spotted the kid stumbling to the ground, picking himself up, and disappearing into the woods. Dickie knew the kid would head to the main road. He couldn't let that happen, anxiously thinking, *I can't let him get to the road and wave someone down for help. I gotta stop him.*

Panic set in as he rushed to the kitchen, opened the cabinet's center drawer and grabbed a flashlight. He then hurried out of the garage to his car. Dirt and stones flew from the car's spinning wheels as he quickly gunned his car down the driveway, stopping about halfway down. After shutting the car off, he exited and rushed into the woods with his flashlight beam lighting the way. He moved quickly but noisily, breaking branches and crunching leaves as he advanced to the area where he thought the kid might have reached.

Stopping for a moment, he flipped off the flashlight and listened for the sound of the kid's movement. The only sound he heard was a vehicle driving by on the road. It was rare to have much traffic in the area at this hour, but he was concerned one could pass by if the kid made it to the road. Out of shape and deep in worry, Dickie breathed heavily with sweat rolling down his back. He didn't move a muscle and remained still. It was cold, and his body began to shiver. He realized he had run out of the house without a coat. He was miffed at himself, thinking about what trouble he would face if the kid escaped.

Hearing leaves swooshing and branches snapping to his right, Dickie sensed the kid was close. He stared in the direction of the sound until he saw a moving silhouette and pointed his flashlight in that direction. When Dickie turned the light on, Andy froze as the light hit his eyes, like a deer caught in the headlight beams of an oncoming car. The two stared at each other only for seconds before Andy shuffled forward in the direction of the road with all the energy he could muster. A branch clipped the top of his head, catching hold of his baseball cap, but Andy kept moving forward without it. It baffled Dickie that the kid could move at all. Shaking his head in disbelief, Dickie aimed his flashlight at the ground to light up his path as he tried to cut off Andy's sluggish, off-balance movement.

Dickie upped his pace and closed to within a few feet behind the slow-moving youngster. He was so close he could hear Andy's heavy breathing. As he got closer behind, he raised his flashlight high to club the kid's head, whispering, "I've got you now, kid. You'll be sorry you ran."

*   *   *

Marci Richardson looked at the clock for the fifth time in the last twenty minutes. It was after eight o'clock, and she could barely contain her anxiety. She looked at her husband, John, and asked with a concerned voice, "Why hasn't Andy called? I'm concerned about him. He promised to call as soon as he got to Boston."

John joined Marci sitting on the edge of the bed and rubbed her back.

"I'm sure he's okay. You know he has been under a lot of stress lately, between exams and worrying about you. I think he just forgot to call in the excitement of seeing his friends and having a good time at some college party."

"Can we call his friends instead of trying him for the third time? Maybe Todd or Keith will answer their phone."

John asked Marci for her cell phone. Marci's hands trembled while she handed him her cell. John scrolled through the contact list to Todd's name and hit the call button. The number rang seven times before Todd answered.

"Todd, this is John Richardson. Marci and I haven't heard from Andy as of yet. Is he there with you, or have you heard from him?"

"No, he is not here yet, and I called him about thirty minutes ago but only got his voicemail. Maybe he hit some traffic or stopped for some food on the way. I'll remind him to call you as soon as he gets here, or do you want him to text you?"

"No, no, please call as soon as he gets there or when you hear from him. We just want to make sure he is all right. It doesn't matter what time it is. Please call us."

He turned to Marci as he ended the call. "Todd promised to call us as soon as he hears from Andy. He said Andy's ride to Boston could have hit some traffic on the way. So let's get to bed early. You had a trying day and look exhausted."

"I don't think I'll sleep a wink until we hear from him. Andy said he'd call, and he's not answering our calls. Why wouldn't he at least answer his phone for chrissake?"

"I wish I knew. Maybe Andy's cell phone lost its charge, and he can't call until he gets to Todd's campus dorm. Let's get ready for bed and try to get some sleep, please."

He tried to change the subject, but Marci was only thinking about Andy. Marci knew that John was concerned about Andy too, but he handled it in his own way. She spotted him downing two shots of bourbon just before joining her in the bedroom. They each changed into sleepwear and went early to bed. They talked for a short time before the bourbon helped put John to sleep. Marci continued tossing in bed for an hour before dozing off. The bedroom was silent, other than the ticking of the alarm clock.

Ring! Ring! Marci vaulted to a sitting position when she heard her cell phone ring. Her anxiety accelerated, and her stomach felt like it contracted in knots. She stretched for the phone but juggled it and dropped it to the floor.

"Dammit!" She felt for the phone on the floor until finally grasping it. "Andy, is that you?"

"Mrs. Richardson, this is Keith Miller. I was with friends when Mr. Richardson called Todd. At the time, I didn't think much about Andy not being here yet. I figured it might take him some time to get to Boston, then find his way to BU from where he got dropped off. I called his cell earlier and left messages without hearing back from him. I kind of lost track of time and haven't been with Todd the whole time. I thought maybe Andy had called him, but I'm with Todd now and, as you know, he hasn't heard from Andy either."

"Andy promised to call us as soon as he got to Boston. It's not like him not to call, especially since we left messages. I'm worried, and I don't know what to do."

Keith remained silent for a moment. He was unsure how to respond to a friend's distressed mother. "Mrs. Richardson, Andy is a smart guy. I'm sure everything is okay, and he'll get here soon." Marci thanked him for calling and hung up with disappointment in her voice.

John, now awake, asked, "No luck, huh?"

She frowned with tears in her eyes. "No. Keith called Andy's cell earlier and only got voicemail. If we don't hear anything soon, maybe we should call the police."

"Let's wait till morning. In the meantime, try getting back to sleep. We can tackle this head-on tomorrow, even if we have to drive to Boston." John placed his arm around Marci as they both placed their heads on the pillow. Marci closed her eyes, knowing she would spend most of the night watching the alarm clock and waiting for the phone to ring. As a mother, she knew something terrible had happened to her son.

CHAPTER
8

As Dickie's hand swung down hard for Andy's head, he tripped on a small tree stump and fell flat on his chest, causing a sharp pain to his rib cage. His flashlight dropped from his hand and rolled a few feet in front of him. Pausing to regain his breath, he struggled to get up while pushing his glasses up from the tip of his nose. He grabbed the flashlight and staggered in Andy's direction.

"Andy, stop! I'm sorry. I won't hurt you. I promise I'll drive you right to Boston." Dickie vented his anger with a softer tone, trying to get Andy to stop, but followed up his cry to the kid by whispering, "No way, kid. I'm not driving you anywhere."

Angry, tired, and gasping for air, Dickie increased his pace, ignoring the ache in his rib cage. Branches constantly slapped against his face and body. He was obsessed with catching his prey. He saw Andy was close, staggering toward the end of the woods line. He thought of grabbing the kid's collar and pulling him to the ground. Once within reach, he extended his arm to grab hold of Andy's coat collar. The tip of his fingers touched it. He stretched his arm out farther. *Grab it, goddamn it!* He grasped the collar and yanked it. Andy felt the pull on his collar, but it ended when he heard a whipping sound and Dickie crying out, "Ow! That hurt!"

Dickie was whacked across the face by a large tree branch, knocking him back off his feet as his glasses flew off his face. Hurting from the smack in the face, he struggled to turn over on his stomach and reach for his flashlight. While searching for his glasses, he shouted, "Andy, come on, buddy! Please, don't tell anybody! I'm sorry. I thought you wanted to have fun with me. I promise I'll take you right to Boston. Come on, please, Andy!"

It took a moment for Andy to regain his posture from nearly falling backward. He struggled moving forward and managed to stumble and fall out of the woods onto the grassy shoulder of the road. Andy was dazed and out of breath but aware of the need to get up and call for help. "Where's my phone?" he whispered while patting his outer pockets in search of his phone until he finally felt it. He pulled the phone from his pocket, knowing the call he had to make. *Hurry up, dammit.*

His hands trembled while looking back toward the woods for his predator. With his eyes blurry from the cold, damp air, it was difficult for him to unlock his phone.

C'mon, c'mon! Andy told himself. He could hear the sounds of leaves scattering in the nearby woods, knowing the professor was getting closer. He desperately wiped his eyes until he could make out the numbers on the phone. Finally, Andy entered the password and uttered, "Got it!" He glanced toward the woods and saw the professor. Nervously shaking with fear, Andy quickly got to his feet, made a call, and listened as it started to ring.

Waiting for someone to answer his call, Andy glanced back at the woods while backing into the road. He spotted the evil beast step out of the woods and walking toward him. The heavy fog still surrounded them. His call rang a fourth time as he anxiously watched his stalker moving toward him. Then, unexpectedly, he heard the sound of a car approaching. He turned toward the sound and saw headlight beams from a vehicle coming around the curve heading toward him.

Oh, thank God, he thought as Andy lifted his arms high, waving for the vehicle to stop. He moved farther into the road, waving and screaming, "Help, stop! Please stop! Help!" His screams prevented him from hearing a female voice answering his call.

"911, what's your emergency?"

Dickie stopped dead in his tracks. He was in a complete state of panic as he moved back behind the brush and watched the approaching vehicle with its blurred headlights heading toward Andy.

Andy stared at the oncoming lights, waving his arms and yelling for help. Then abruptly, his moment of joy suddenly turned to fear as the vehicle kept coming straight at him without slowing. His arms were still in the air but no longer waving, and his legs became paralyzed as he whispered to himself, *"Oh, shit. He doesn't see me."*

Dickie, frozen in place, gazed as the vehicle's headlights bore down on Andy and lit him up like a Christmas tree. Within seconds, tires squealed, and the sound of a thud from the vehicle hitting Andy was heard. The impact sent Andy sailing into the road's grassy shoulder.

Dickie's mouth dropped open as he retreated farther back into the dark of the woods and softly muttered, "Holy shit. The freaking truck hit him." His eyes became fixed on the driver of a pickup truck. The fog was thick, but he was close enough to see the driver cover his face with his hands. He didn't hear any other vehicles close by. The driver sat there doing nothing before making a feeble attempt to shine a flashlight outside the driver-side window. It looked as if the driver didn't want to find whatever he hit since the beam was shining too high from the ground.

Suddenly, Dickie could hear another vehicle. He could see headlight beams coming from the opposite direction toward the truck. The truck driver quickly drove off and disappeared around the next curve, passing the oncoming vehicle. Dickie ducked behind the brush as the other driver went by, not slowing or noticing anything awry. While his whole body was shaking in a state of distress, Dickie wasn't sure what he should do.

Should I go down and check on him? Could he even still be alive? He had questions without answers. He wanted to leave the scene and head home, but something inside him urged him not to leave anything to chance.

His mind was rapidly going haywire with options. Although trembling, not only from the cold but also from fear, he knew it was a considerable risk going down to check on the kid. If anyone saw him leaning over a dead body, they'd call the police. But he couldn't chance that the kid might still be alive. If someone found him, he might talk about what happened to him. Dickie thought through every possibility. If the kid were found dead, the police would investigate why the kid was in front of his father's property, and if they examined the body, they'd know the kid was drugged and assaulted.

He couldn't decide. He was like a frightened little boy with his body shaking unmercifully. *Maybe I should clean the house up and head home or go to my father's house to establish an alibi—Nah, he'd only interrogate me for showing up unexpectedly at this hour.*

After much consternation, he concluded there was only one safe choice. He listened for any vehicles approaching. Not hearing a sound, he rushed to the body. He heard soft moans coming from the injured kid as he got close. *Shit, he's alive.* Without hesitation, he quickly pulled the kid up by his armpits and dragged him into the woods to hide him from any other traffic.

Once hidden from the road, Dickie felt some relief, asking, *Now what?* Pausing before struggling to pick the kid up over his shoulder, he thought to himself, *Shit, this isn't easy, Dickie. Time to lose some weight and get in shape. Ha. Fat chance.*

He carried Andy about twenty feet before dropping him to the ground. Dickie had to pause to catch his breath. But doing so, Andy became more vocal, trying to yell for help with a voice too weak to be heard. Dickie looked down at him, breathing heavily and shaking his head in disgust. "Shut up, kid. Nobody can hear you." He hoisted the kid up again and continued his labored walk to the driveway.

Once there, he put Andy on the ground to catch his breath again. He lumbered several yards up to his car and rolled it to where he had placed Andy on the turf. Placing the flashlight onto the passenger seat, he pulled the trunk handle and got out of the car.

As he moved toward Andy, he saw the kid was trying to get up. "Again? For chrissake, kid. How could you still move?" Dickie thought Randy won't believe this. Something must be wrong with the drink formula.

He opened the passenger door of his car, retrieved his flashlight from the front seat, and angrily struck Andy on the head. Andy collapsed to the ground without a sound.

"You deserve that, kid. You were stupid for running away and getting yourself hurt. We could have had fun."

Dickie squeezed the flashlight into his back pocket, grabbed Andy's arms, and dragged him to the rear of the car. While doing so, the flashlight, not placed deep enough into his rear pocket, fell onto a cushion of leaves on the side of the driveway. Dickie's heavy breathing, still labored from dragging Andy's body, caused him not to hear the soft landing of the flashlight. Struggling again to lift Andy's body, he managed to shove the kid into the trunk and slam the lid shut. His hands felt wet, and thinking it was sweat, not blood, he rubbed them dry on his trousers.

He got into his car and sat there staring into space to catch his breath and think about what to do next. He realized what he had to do, but he had never done it alone and wasn't about to start now. He put the gear in reverse and backed up to the house. Noticing the backhoe was still in the backyard, Dickie pulled out his phone and called Randy. *Randy knows what to do.*

CHAPTER
9

Zake Barnes was ready to head home after a long, hard day at work as a maintenance mechanic. As usual, he dropped by his favorite pub near the company to have dinner and a few beers before calling it a day. Zake was in no hurry to get home to an empty house. He had been married and divorced twice, in no small part because he was usually drunk when he got home to his wife.

As a regular, he was well known by Vinnie, the Pub's owner and bartender, who would often give Zake a beer on the house before he left for home. Sometimes Zake's coworkers would also stop at the pub, and they would end up drinking way past dinnertime. Zake arrived for happy hour just before five that afternoon. None of his coworkers were there, so he spent most of the time chatting with Vinnie. The pub was just about the only social time Zake had these days since life for him had become somewhat dull and undoubtedly lonely. As he gulped down the last drops of his fourth beer, this one with a whiskey chaser, he waved over the bartender. "Vinny, unless you're going to pour me a free beer, I'm leaving."

"I already gave you one ten minutes ago. Besides, you've had enough for the ride home. They say it will be tough going with heavy fog on the highway. So take it easy, Zake."

Zake noticed the time was past seven o'clock. "Okay, Vin. I'm out of here. See you soon, and oh, yeah, thanks for the beer."

As he walked to the ten-year-old gray pickup truck that looked older than him, Zake lit up a joint and took a long drag. Zake was on the thin side at five feet, ten inches tall, and weighed only 135 pounds soaking wet. His face had a semblance of a mustache and fuzzy goatee. He took another long drag on the weed and climbed into the truck. He drove to the entrance ramp to I-84 and carefully merged into traffic.

"Wow," he said to himself. "Vinny wasn't kidding. I could hardly see the road through all this fog. But, hey, fog, I want you to know, I'm a little foggy myself, ha, ha."

His drive home in the fog was from hell. After flicking his second spent joint out the truck window, Zake tried to focus and get his bearings as he got closer to his exit. He slowed down to thirty miles an hour until he saw his exit and pressed further on the brakes to avoid missing it. Realizing he was a little tipsy, he tried not hitting anything along the way. Unfortunately, the fog worsened, reducing visibility to about twenty-five yards. He slowed to twenty miles per hour on the back roads while talking to himself to stay awake.

"Where's that friggin' streetlight? I can't find my way home unless I see it. Where, oh, where are you?"

Slowing down to a snail's pace, he finally saw the streetlamp marking the spot where he had to turn. He turned onto the curvy back road and saw the fog clearing a bit ahead, so he accelerated some as he approached the upcoming S-curve. He felt he could still cut the corner on the curves if he didn't see any oncoming headlight beams. It was a game he often played with himself. Not seeing any oncoming headlights, Zake stepped on the gas a little more while cutting the corner around the bend. When he rounded the second curve, the fog unexpectedly became denser, making it difficult to see if he was even in the right lane.

After Zake rubbed his eyes to clear his blurred vision, he saw a figure appear on the road before him. "What the hell is that?"

He slammed on his brakes, but the alcohol severely diminished his reaction time. He hit the brakes too late as he heard and felt a thud from his truck hitting whatever was on the road. He stopped and momentarily rubbed his eyes again before finally opening the driver-side window. Zake peered out to see what he hit. With the heavy fog and no moonlight, it was pitch black with dense fog, making it impossible to see anything off the side of the road. Zake felt panic building inside of him. He was frightened that it might have been a person he hit. It was a dilemma for him because he knew he couldn't call for help in his state of intoxication.

Reaching under the seat for his flashlight, he directed the beam toward the grass shoulder along the left side of the road. He couldn't see, or didn't want to see, anything since his flashlight beam aimed higher than the ground. "Nothing there. Probably just a deer or some other animal searching for food." His search of the shoulder lasted only several seconds.

"Yep, it was a freaking deer, not a person, Zake, you dumb ass. Deer run out into the road all the time out here, for Pete's sake."

He sat there convincing himself of what he hit when he saw headlight beams heading toward him from the next curve in front of him. He was already halfway into the wrong side of the road, so he put the truck in gear, drove back into the right lane, and passed the oncoming vehicle as they rounded the curve in different directions.

"Oh, man! What did I just do? Was I dreaming or what? I hope it was a deer. Yes, that's it, baby boy, it was just a deer," he blabbered, talking to his truck as he continued to drive on.

As he neared his cottage, he became disturbed that the impact may have damaged his old truck. "I hope you're okay, baby boy. Daddy's going to check you out in a few minutes."

He needed to keep the old pickup in good shape. It was his only means of transportation to and from work. At this time of night, the traffic on this road was very light, since most homes in the area were summer cottages separated by heavy woods. He turned into his driveway another mile up the road, still jittery over the accident.

He sat in the truck for a few minutes to calm down before walking to his cottage. He unlocked the front door and flipped on the outside floodlight switch to light up the driveway and his truck. He returned to his pickup and examined the front driver's side for damage. The chrome frame around the headlight was missing. There were spider cracks in the headlight, and the side of the front fender had minor damage. A closer look showed reddish spots around the headlight and fender. He fetched an old white T-shirt from the interior cab and wiped down the damaged area. Being upset with himself, Zake again persuaded himself it had to be a deer, not a person. *Maybe I'm so drunk I'm just hallucinating the whole thing, and it never really happened*, he thought.

For a moment, and only a moment, he thought of calling for help, but realized it would likely get him into serious trouble. His stomach didn't feel so good. It tightened and churned, making gurgling sounds. He became nauseous, feeling he would throw up, so he staggered to the cottage and flopped onto his bed. Again, his stomach was cramped with sounds of indigestion. The thoughts of the accident continued to cause uneasiness within his entire body. He tried to shake it off as he tossed from one side of the bed to the other. He then abruptly got out of bed and quickly made it to the bathroom, where he sprayed the commode with vomit. He knelt before the toilet until he expelled the last chuck. He labored to get up and throw cold water on his face before stumbling back to bed. Zake reasoned he'd check out the accident scene in the morning daylight, and if he found nothing there, he would feel comfortable blaming the incident on his drug-induced hallucination. It didn't take long before he passed out.

CHAPTER
10

The following morning, Sam and Ziggy met at the hotel café for breakfast before heading to the federal building for the briefing. Ziggy continued complaining about working on a holiday weekend, but he accepted the sacrifices he had to make as part of the job.

Ziggy, only five feet, six inches tall, weighing no more than one-hundred-and forty-five pounds, was in great shape and easygoing but a little headstrong. But, as a former Marine Corps captain who commanded a rifle company in Operation Desert Storm, he didn't take crap from anyone.

"Not for nothing, Sam, but too many morons volunteer for gigs at headquarters and later become field division bosses. Too many are empty suits who don't know shit about actually getting the job done out here in the field."

"Unfortunately, most talented agents aren't interested in becoming part of management. Like me, they prefer fieldwork instead of working behind a desk eight hours a day. Most agents have settled with a family and don't want to move several times to become the agent in charge."

While they had their breakfast, Sam recalled that idiot in the BMW who almost backed right into them on the highway. "That asshole almost caused an accident, and you know how that triggers a ton of paperwork, not to mention an internal investigation."

"Yeah, he would have wrecked the G-ride, but that would have been a blessing in disguise! We wouldn't get to Boston and have to work this weekend," Ziggy said jokingly.

"Hah! Wishful thinking, Zig. We still had your car at my place not far from there."

"Speaking of accidents, remember when we pursued that guy, Coleman, who had thrown a Molotov cocktail into a barbershop because the owner was screwing his wife?"

"I remember Zig. What about it?"

"We were chasing that asshole in Torrington and were about to take that sharp curve in the road . . ."

"Is there a point to this story, Zig?" Sam interrupted, knowing where Ziggy was going with it.

"Well, I was moving at a good clip, and out of nowhere, you yelled for me to hit the brakes."

"And?"

"Don't you remember? The guy we were chasing got hit by a tractor-trailer truck just around the bend. If I had taken that corner at the speed I was going, we both would have been toast. I know you couldn't have seen the accident around the corner, but you never told me why you had me stop."

Sam paused, taking a moment to recall what he had said in the past. "Didn't I tell you? I thought a kid was about to dart out in front of us."

Sam never shared that he got weird feelings that warned of looming dangers hoping that the 'kid darting out to the road' story was how he had previously explained why he yelled out to stop.

Ziggy laughed. "You're full of shit, Sam. I don't remember you saying anything like that! Tell me how you knew what was around that corner."

"I didn't know! I just felt you were going too fast for the curve. Come on. It's late. We should get going."

Sam quickly got up to avoid the issue and dropped his share of the bill on the table. "I need to hit the men's room, so I'll meet you at the checkout counter in a few minutes."

They arrived early at the ATF office. Ziggy went to one of the groups to say hi to friends while Sam sat in the empty conference room waiting for the start of the briefing. While waiting, he thought back to Ziggy's inquiry about how he knew about an accident beyond the curve in the road. Sam could never explain how he knew about threats or how he found things or people. It was too far-fetched for anyone to understand. No one would believe it, and he didn't understand himself. Sam's thoughts were interrupted as agents entered the conference room.

Jeff Doherty greeted everyone, apologizing for working the holiday weekend. He then began to outline the operational plan for the raid. It took nearly three hours to go through it all and make the team assignments. Jeff had passed out photos of the suspect, his criminal record, and his residence to the team members. He also added that a pit bull stood guard, chained to a shed in the backyard. Once the briefing ended, Jeff, the Special Response Team leader, Ron Altimari, and Sam, the team supervisor, headed north of Boston to Lowell for a drive-by of the suspect's residence.

The suspect, Michael Blake, was a repeat violent offender at protest rallies. He and his followers opposed those who rallied for government laws that gave minorities parity. He and his kind harassed and spoke out against protesters and others who didn't look like them. As a felon, Blake served time for assault and battery, possession and sale of fentanyl, domestic violence, breach of peace, and interfering with the police. He was a violent tough guy who stood about six feet tall and weighed about two hundred and thirty pounds with a potbelly hanging over his belt. He was fifty-four years old, with long gray hair usually tied in a ponytail, and was a walking, breathing advertisement for tattoos.

As a white supremacist leader, Blake distributed white nationalism literature and led his group in opposition to minority protest rallies. If necessary, Blake's group would intimidate and threaten the leaders who organized the demonstrations. Their action would often lead to violence, including beatings and shootings.

The agents drove by Blake's residence a couple of times to study the lay of the land. As they passed by, they observed the pit bull guarding the shed at the back of the house. Sam felt it was always better to survey the actual target location versus viewing only photos. He didn't see anything that would change the raid plan. Since the team had an early-morning pre-raid briefing scheduled at the Lowell Police Department not far from the suspect's house, they decided to call it a day and head home, or in Sam's case, to the hotel.

Back at the hotel, Sam once again thought back to Ziggy's inquiry about how he knew about an accident beyond the curve in the road. Thinking back to when he first experienced those strange feelings, Sam considered them a curse. However, after experiencing similar sensations and the subsequent outcomes, Sam realized they were not a curse but a warning of an impending threat. So, he researched the phenomena and came to accept them as extrasensory revelations. It turned out Sam didn't only experience them prior to threats but also when he tried to find something or someone. In those situations, the sensations guided him to who or what he sought. It took time for Sam to grasp the meaning of the feelings, but he finally realized they were a gift. However, since he couldn't explain how or why he had this gift, he decided to keep it a secret. Besides, who would believe him?

Throughout his teenage years, Sam experienced these mysterious sensations, or whatever they were. It wasn't until he finished college and became a federal agent that he realized their remarkable value. As an investigator, it gave him a heightened awareness of unseen threats and guidance in finding clues, such as critical evidence or suspects that helped solve crimes. He accepted what he had acquired and took advantage of the ability even though he couldn't explain it.

He tried shaking the thoughts from his mind. It never did him any good. Finally, he showered and went to bed but couldn't help trying to unravel the mystery of how he came to possess this phenomenon. It always brought him back to when he was very sick as a young child. Too young and ill to remember that critical night, Sam's only knowledge of it was told to him by his older brother, Jim. Jim often repeated he and their mom rushed to the hospital when the doctor caring for Sam called and said he might not make it through the night. For as long as Sam could remember, Jim always joked about it, but maybe he wasn't kidding. Like it was yesterday, Sam recalls what his brother told him. "When mom and I arrived at the hospital, the doctor told her you had passed away. Mom cried and nearly fainted. It took her a few minutes to recover before she entered your room. Mom nervously went to your bedside, where you looked like you were just sleeping. Then, with tears in her eyes, mom leaned over you and kissed your forehead. Like the sleeping princess, you opened your eyes and said, 'Mom.' It was like magic. Mom's kiss woke you from the dead."

CHAPTER
11

Marci Richardson was up before six the next morning, checked her cell phone, and saw no messages or calls. Aware that John had barely slept through the night, she grabbed the cell phone from the nightstand and quietly made her way to the bathroom without disturbing him. Feeling queasy, jittery, and having a dry mouth, Marci decided to take diazepam to calm her anxiety. She wandered to the kitchen to prepare breakfast and saw no messages on their phone's answering machine. When opening a cabinet door for a coffee bag, she just stared into space with agonizing thoughts about her son. She closed her eyes, wet from tears, and tried to put unpleasant thoughts out of her mind. When Marci finally reached for the coffee, she realized it was the wrong cabinet door. She opened the right door, grabbed the coffee bag, and prepared coffee in the percolator. Marci couldn't concentrate on anything except Andy's well-being.

The noise of kitchen utensils clanking and the smell of fresh coffee brewing woke John from his sleep. He got out of bed, made a quick stop in the bathroom to wash his face, and went to the kitchen. He saw Marci staring out the kitchen window deep in worry, so he put his arms around her, saying, "Good morning, hon. Did you get any sleep at all?"

"Maybe an hour. I felt sick to my stomach and got up twice, thinking I would vomit. No one called John. I know something terrible has happened to him. A mother knows. If he were okay, he would have called us. We need to call the police. I can't stand not knowing."

"Okay, I'll make a final call to Todd and Keith first, just in case Andy got in late and didn't want to wake us."

Marci handed him her phone. As he pressed the call button, John squeezed her hand, whispering, "Please, sit down and try to calm yourself."

Todd answered the call on the sixth ring. John didn't wait for his hello. "Todd, this is John Richardson. Any word from Andy?"

In bed and not fully awake, Todd answered with sleepiness in his voice. "Oh, Mr. Richardson. No, I'm sorry, I have not heard from Andy. So you haven't heard from him either?"

"No, we haven't. We're worried that something happened to him on his way to Boston. Could he have called Keith or another friend?"

"Keith is here sleeping on the recliner, and I know he hasn't heard from Andy. I can't think of anyone else Andy knows in Boston or any other place he would go to other than here."

"Andy was in Hartford yesterday around two in the afternoon. He should have arrived at the Boston bus station by four or five at the latest." There was no response. "Are you still there, Todd?"

"Yes, I'm here . . . uh, but are you sure Andy was taking a bus? He called us after three yesterday and said he would hitchhike and most likely get to Boston around nine or later."

"Hitchhike! I gave him money for a bus! I don't understand why he would hitchhike?"

"I don't know, Mr. Richardson. Maybe he wanted to save money. I hope everything is all right. Is there anything we can do here?"

"I can't think of anything. We're going crazy with worry. Marci and I are going to call the police. We may need to give them your cell number and Keith's too. If you hear from Andy or anything about him, please call us right away." He hung up, trying to understand why his son would thumb to Boston. "Should we call the police in Boston or Hartford?"

Anxious to find out anything, Marci said, "Call the Hartford Police."

"Yeah, maybe Hartford can coordinate with Boston and the state police."

John's call got transferred twice before the deputy chief of investigations transferred his call again. Finally, his call went to voicemail for Lieutenant Marcus Nelson in the missing persons unit. The message reported no one was in the office and to leave a message for a callback.

"This is John Richardson from Queens, New York. Our son Andy is missing. He is a student at Bushnell College in Hartford. My wife and I last spoke with him yesterday around two in the afternoon while he was on campus. He was leaving for Boston to meet friends who attend Boston University. Andy was supposed to call us when he got to Boston, but he didn't, and his friends have not heard from him either. My wife and I are afraid something happened to him. Please call us back as soon as possible."

John left his number and hung up. He looked at the clock and saw it was only six-thirty.

"There was no answer, only voicemail for a lieutenant in the missing person unit. Maybe their shift doesn't start until seven. Let's have coffee and wait for them to call back."

Thirty-five minutes later, the phone rang. "Hello, this is John Richardson."

"Mr. Richardson, this is Lieutenant Marcus Nelson. I received your message about your son, and I assure you our department will do everything we can to find out what happened to him."

A little nervous, John started to give the officer background information he felt was needed, but it was jumbled and confusing.

"Mr. Richardson, please stop. I know you and your wife are worried and want answers. By law, I'm required to complete a missing person report. It is very detailed but will provide us with everything we need to investigate. I'll walk you through it step-by-step, basically asking for who, what, where, when, why, and how. I'll need the names and telephone numbers of all persons with relevant information. When we complete that, my office will make the initial inquiries with other police departments and hospitals and get back to you when we have something meaningful to report. We will move as quickly as possible."

After John answered all the questions, he thanked the lieutenant and hung up the phone. He looked at Marci while shaking his head. "Why would Andy be hitchhiking? I'm upset he didn't take the bus. I gave him money to cover his round-trip bus fare. I don't understand."

Hearing her son hitchhiked, Marci feared she was right that something terrible had happened to him.

CHAPTER
12

Zake tossed and turned in bed, trying to get the accident out of his mind. He had an uneasy feeling he hit a person rather than a deer. He got out of bed and took two ibuprofen capsules for his acute tension headache. On his way back to bed, he stared out his bedroom window, watching snow fluttering from the gusty wind as it covered the hood of his pickup truck like a blanket of cotton. It mesmerized him for a minute or two before he sank into his bed again, where he dozed off around two in the morning.

The alarm sounded at five-thirty. Zake hit the snooze button at least three times before finally forcing himself to get up. He prepared a pot of coffee, took a quick shower, and skipped trimming his goatee. After pouring coffee into his thermos, he left for work. Zake looked older than his age of forty-four. His face had premature wrinkles around his droopy eyes and the sides of his lips, probably from his heavy smoking of cigarettes and pot and daily doses of alcohol. Dressed in old torn jeans and a worn-out burgundy sweatshirt, he walked outside to his pickup, now covered with at least four inches of snow. It irritated him while he talked to himself.

"I'm tired, a nervous wreck, and got little sleep. Now, I hafta put up with wipin' off all this snow. I feel like shit and should call in sick, but I need the overtime."

Knowing he would drive past the accident site, his anxiety caused his stomach to churn with nervous queasiness while his heart pounded in his chest in fear of what he might find lying on the side of the road. He grabbed a snow-removal brush from inside the truck and cleared the windshield and the front of the pickup as best he could. Next, he concentrated his efforts on cleaning the damaged section near the truck's headlight to ensure there were no visible blood spots. When he finished polishing the damaged fender, Zake realized maybe the snow was a good thing after all. The ground would be covered and hide any sign of an accident. Either way, he would stick with his story, figuring no one was that stupid to be walking in the middle of the road on a night like that.

Zake climbed into the driver's seat, put the shift in reverse, and backed out of the driveway onto Old Hollow Brook Road. He kept his fingers crossed and made sure he drove the speed limit. As he rounded the curve in the road and came upon the accident site, he pulled off to the side of the snow-covered road. He looked out over the shoulder as far as he could see. Seeing nothing, he opened the door and slid out onto the pavement. Still apprehensive, he slowly walked along the shoulder, inspecting the area where he hazily remembered hitting something. He stopped his inspection when he heard a vehicle approach and saw it pull into the back of his truck.

"Oh shit, no. Just what I need now. A state cop," he whispered.

The state trooper engaged the blue emergency lights, exited the cruiser, and marched toward Zake. The African American trooper towered over Zake. He was about six feet, four inches tall, with an athletic build, and in his mid-thirties.

"Anything I can help you with, sir?" asked Trooper Curtis Simmons.

"No, sir, I, uh, was cumin' home from work last night drivin' real slow because of the heavy fog. When I took the curve, sumthin came out onto the road and hit my truck. It scared the shit out of me. I stopped and looked around but saw nut'in. I got out of the truck and used a flashlight but din' see anythin'. I'm not sure what it was. I figga it was a small deer that ran back into the woods after it hit my fender."

Trooper Simmons asked, "Did you call the police for assistance?"

Zake thought for a moment before answering. "Uh, no. I kinda thought it was betta to wait till mornin.' I was gonna, but din' think you guys, I mean, you know, the local guys, worked here at night."

Trooper Simmons responded, "You should have called. What if it had been a person you hit, and they needed medical attention?"

"Yeah, uh, I guess you're right, maybe I shoulda called, but I'm pretty sure it was just a deer that ran into the woods."

"Had you been drinking or taken any drugs before getting behind the wheel last night?"

"No, no, I was drivin' home from work and just stopped to grab a quick bite at a burger joint on the way."

The trooper turned to focus on Zake's truck. "Is this the truck you were driving last night?"

"Yes, sir, that's my baby boy. I mean my, my truck," Zake nervously mumbled.

The trooper walked to the front of the truck to get a closer look. He noticed the headlight frame was missing, and the area around it was wiped clean. "Looks like you wiped the fender area clean."

"Yes, sir. My truck got covered with snow this mornin,' so I cleaned it off. You know, the windshield, the hood, fenders, and headlights."

Suspicious, Simmons asked for Zake's driver's license and registration. The trooper then returned to his cruiser and radioed for an MVD registration check and a wants and warrants inquiry. There were no pending warrants on Zake. Only a DUI arrest from two years earlier. The motor vehicle registration matched the documents Zake had given him.

"Zake, I'm going to need your full name, date of birth, address, and home and cell phone numbers. Also, your employer's name, address, and phone number."

Zake, shaking timidly and avoiding eye contact with the trooper, answered the questions the best he could but not in the same order they were asked.

Simmons then told Zake he could go but be careful driving to work.

He waited for Zake to depart and then walked about forty yards along the snow-covered shoulder, inspecting the area. He found nothing suspicious. Simmons was heading into work early after a day off. His first item of the day was to submit a report of the encounter with Zake Barnes to the shift supervisor.

CHAPTER
13

It was five-thirty on a chilly Saturday morning three days before New Year's Day. A tan-colored van drove slowly along a narrow neighborhood street in a small suburb of Lowell, Massachusetts. Inside the van, Sam whispered to Agent Doherty, "Jeff, find a good loud song to rouse up and energize the guys napping in the back."

Doherty scanned through his phone and found one of his old-time favorites, 'Born to Run,' by Bruce Springsteen, and began streaming it through the van's audio system. In the back of the van were eleven members of the ATF Special Response Team, including Sam. Roused up by the music, the team readied themselves for entry into the home of a known violent criminal. Supervisor Jeff Doherty was seated in the front passenger seat directing the agent driving the van. He held a federal search warrant for the home of the local leader of the MAPA, the Massachusetts Patriot Assembly.

Following behind the van were two nondescript sedans. One sedan held two Boston ATF agents and two local police detectives. The ATF agents wore ballistic vests under raid jackets embossed with the gold-colored letters "ATF" and its badge on the front of the jacket and "POLICE" in large letters on the back. The second sedan contained four additional Boston ATF agents similarly dressed. The six agents and two detectives made up the search team that would enter the home only after the tactical team entered and rendered the home safe by securing all persons inside and preventing the destruction of evidence.

Behind the two sedans were two marked black-and-white police cruisers. The first contained two officers, a lieutenant in the front passenger seat and a uniformed officer driving. The second cruiser had only the driver, a uniformed officer. The lieutenant was there to provide local officer supervision and, perhaps more importantly, to call for medical or additional police assistance if needed. The uniformed officers were responsible for neighborhood traffic control.

Doherty silenced the music as the van slowly took the last turn onto Duxhall Avenue, heading toward the target residence. He had the van stop a short distance from the home to allow for a quick view of the house to ensure there were no surprises like additional vehicles in the driveway that could require changes to the raid plan. The dwelling and property appeared to be the same as they expected.

The home was a small grey cape with the front door opening into a small foyer, with stairs straight ahead leading to two second-floor bedrooms and a shared bathroom. The living room was to the right of the entry, and to the left was a dining room. The kitchen and guest bathroom were at the rear of the home. Also, in the back was a door leading to the basement and another leading to the backyard.

A confidential source had provided the agents with the layout of the home. There was no attached garage but only a small shed in the backyard where a pit bull kept guard. The dog was a potential threat, so the team had brought a rifle equipped with tranquilizer projectiles to neutralize it. Parked in the dirt driveway along the side of the home were two vehicles, one owned by the suspect, Michael Blake, and the other by a female believed to be his girlfriend. The federal search warrant covered the search of the house, the shed, and any vehicles found at the location. Sam's observations did not detect any immediate issues, so he gave the signal to execute the warrant.

As planned, the SRT van pulled into the driveway, blocking the two vehicles parked there. The two unmarked sedans parked in the van's rear while the two marked units were positioned on the street to control traffic, one east and one west of the target home.

The pit bull started to bark as soon as the van entered the driveway. "Just what we need. Not only is the dog waking up the suspect, but it's waking up the whole neighborhood. Let's move. Everyone out the door and in position!" shouted Sam.

The side door slid open, and Sam jumped out along with the agent carrying the battering ram. The rest of the tactical team followed behind, dressed in dark blue fatigues, vests, helmets, and traditional SWAT gear. The team moved in unison to the front door, where Sam knocked and shouted, "Police, with a search warrant!" Seconds later, the battering ram hit the front door with a loud bang. The door flew open as the team moved inside with their guns drawn. Sam followed behind them.

Michael Blake, startled by the loud noise at the front door, rolled away from his girlfriend, screeching, "What the fuck was that?"

Sam, yelling, "Police, with a search warrant!" followed the first two agents up the stairs where they believed Michael Blake would be sleeping. Two agents advanced to clear the living room and the kitchen, while two moved to clear the dining area and bathroom. Once the agents cleared the kitchen, they proceeded to clear the basement.

Still drowsy and thinking someone was breaking into his home, Blake reached for the end table drawer where he kept his gun. He nervously searched for the drawer handle, managed to open it, and clumsily grabbed the grip of his nine-millimeter pistol. Agent Susan Walker entered the room with her flashlight aimed more to the right of Blake at his girlfriend, who began screaming. Sam, closely behind Walker, focused his light on Blake and saw him pulling out a gun. Sam yelled, "Police, drop the gun!" while pushing Walker out of danger. Blake got off one round that just missed Sam's left ear. Sam quickly dove on Blake, slamming his gun-wielding arm against the end table. Blake's wrist and arm hit the edge of the table with such force it made a cracking sound, causing him to drop the gun to the floor as he yelled out in pain. "What the fuck? I thought someone was breaking into my home."

"Yeah, right, asshole, we identified ourselves as police. You just tried to kill a federal officer. That will add years to your jail time," yelled Sam.

"I think you broke my fucking arm."

"Tough shit. Now get out of bed and on your knees with your hands on top of your head. I said now, dammit!"

Sam kicked Blake's gun out to agent Martell who entered the room behind him. Blake's girlfriend, kneeling utterly nude on the floor, was shaking and vehemently screaming, "Leave him alone!"

With adrenaline flowing high and feeling pressure on his chest from the tense situation, Sam shouted to agent Walker, "Get some clothes on her, cuff her, and get her downstairs. I can't stand the screaming."

He then turned to agent Martell, who had cleared the other bedroom, and said, "Turn on the lights so we can see and cuff this asshole and take him downstairs. I want to check the closets."

"What about my arm? I think it's broken," complained Blake.

"Well, that wouldn't have happened if you didn't reach for your gun, stupid."

"I need some clothes. I'm bare-ass naked here."

"We'll get to it when we're ready." Sam turned to agent Martell. "Get a robe or sheet for him and take him downstairs.

After clearing the closet, Sam saw Jeff Doherty enter the bedroom. He knew Jeff came up to inquire about the gunshot. "Blake went for a gun and fired at us when we entered the room. Fortunately, he missed and got his arm broken for being an asshole. Everything's under control now."

Wearing a communication earpiece and mic, Sam called to his assistant leader. "Ron, this is Sam. Give me a status check."

"All is clear except the shed. I'm heading out there now with Deena and Ziggy, who has the tranquilizer gun."

"Roger that. Have the rest of the team maintain control of the suspects until the shed is cleared" After checking all the closets and other potential hiding areas upstairs, Sam headed downstairs with Jeff.

Out by the shed, the pit bull continued barking up a storm. Altimari shouted to Ziggy. "We're not going to put up with him, Zig. Put him to sleep."

Ziggy walked closer to the pit bull and fired one tranquilizer round into the dog's body. The pit bull squealed and continued to growl and bark, but the dog's growling simmered to a whimper until it finally laid down and fell asleep.

After using bolt cutters to open the lock on the shed door, two agents entered the shed and saw two Harley-Davidson motorcycles, better known as hogs, a lawnmower, tools, and two locked steel cabinets. Following the two agents inside the shed, Altimari told them to cut the locks on the cabinets.

Ziggy snapped the locks apart using bolt cutters and opened the cabinet doors. Inside the cabinets, they found several guns and ammunition.

"Maintain security here until the search team takes over, and keep an eye on the pit bull. We don't want him waking up and taking a bite out of somebody's ass."

Sam ensured all rooms in the house, including the basement, were cleared and secured, with the only two occupants under control inside the house. He then asked Doherty to call the search team to enter and begin their search. The agents and police detectives marched through the front door carrying evidence-collection paraphernalia to search the premises. The tactical team stood by to provide backup and assistance to the search team if needed.

Sam had the police lieutenant call an EMT unit to examine Blake's arm to determine the need for medical attention. The search team discovered several guns on the property, including a handgun with the serial number obliterated, hidden under the upstairs bathroom sink. In addition, they seized two twelve-gauge shotguns, both with the barrels sawed off in violation of federal law, six semiautomatic pistols, and ten boxes of ammunition in the locked steel cabinets in the shed. Agents also found forty-two small packets of white powder, which tested positive for cocaine, located inside a suitcase in a bedroom closet. The agents also seized Blake's cell phone and laptop computer as evidence in hopes they would contain the names and numbers of other MAPA members.

Hearing what the agents seized, it was evident by the look on Blake's face he knew he was facing significant prison time. Federal laws prohibited felons from possessing firearms and were punitive to drug traffickers who use guns in their illegal enterprises.

Blake preached to the agents and police officers, "Hey, you're all white guys. Somebody has to speak for us. I just want guys like us not to get shoved aside in this country. The government is forcing all the companies to hire minorities even if whites are more qualified. Pretty soon, we'll be the minorities. Anyway, I'm just holding those guns for friends. They're not mine."

"We're not interested in what or how you think. Tell it to the judge when he sentences you," said Sam indignantly.

"Most of those guns are mine, not Michael's. I have an FID card," claimed Blake's girlfriend, identified as Mara Markin.

Doherty responded to her claim. "A Massachusetts firearms identification card is only good for purchasing and owning long guns. Sawed-off shotguns are illegal for anyone to possess. So if you're claiming they are yours, we'll charge you for possessing illegal guns. Besides, the law presumed that any guns found in Michael's home and under his control belonged to him. I expect most will come back as stolen."

Not long later, the EMTs arrived and examined Blake's arm and said it could be fractured.

"Could you guys bring him to Mass General? We arrested him, so he'll remain handcuffed and in our custody. Our agents will ride with you for security purposes. Once treated and released, we'll transport him to the federal courthouse for arraignment," said Sam.

Once the search at Blake's property was complete and the evidence collected, Doherty arranged for the house and shed to be secured.

As the team entered the van to leave the property, Sam noticed a couple of the team members adding another sticker to a metal panel in the back of the van. They wrote the date and operation name on the sticker representing another 'notch' for the team.

Sam released the tactical team members to travel back to their respective offices. Doherty provided copies of the search documents and receipts to the detectives for their records and invited them to join him for coffee.

"Sam, remember, I want to get back to Connecticut to catch my son's game. Can we skip the coffee break?" asked Ziggy.

"Oh, Ziggy buddy, anything for you."

Sam and Doherty agreed to discuss the after-action reports when they were back at their respective offices.

With a happy look on his face, Ziggy slid into the passenger side of Sam's car. It was just after ten o'clock. "This wasn't as bad as I expected. I could get to see my boys play ball later today. That beats having to deal with assholes like Blake any day."

"So, Zig, does that mean you don't want to stop on the way to have lunch and a cold beer?" asked Sam.

"No way. But let's get back to that new pub we tried a couple of weeks ago? Their happy hour was great, and those lovely ladies were checking me out."

"You are so full of shit, Ziggy. They were looking at me, not you," said Sam jokingly. They both cracked up laughing and were happy the early-morning raid went off well with all the agents going home safe.

CHAPTER
14

On Saturday morning, the phone rang at the Richardson's household. Marci moved quickly to answer it.

"Mrs. Richardson, this is Lieutenant Marcus Nelson from the Hartford Police calling regarding your son, Andy."

Marci put her cell on speaker so her husband could hear as well.

Nelson continued, "I contacted the director of campus security at Bushnell College and asked his officers to canvass the dormitories and interview anyone who saw or talked to your son on the day he went missing. In addition, I had my staff contact hospitals in Hartford and the towns along I-84 toward Boston. We also contacted the Connecticut and Massachusetts state police to determine if there were any reported accidents or incidents involving your son or anyone fitting his description in areas from Hartford to Boston and near Boston University. So far, no hospitals in Connecticut have reported any treatment to your son or anyone matching his description. In addition, the Connecticut State Police advised us earlier this morning there have been no reported incidents along I-84 regarding your son or anyone fitting his description. I will let you know when I hear back from the Massachusetts authorities."

Nelson added, "I'd like to have recent photos of your son so we can share them with other law enforcement agencies and prepare a missing person flyer."

"Is it okay for us to bring them to you today? It would be nice to meet with you in person. We can be there in about three hours," asked Marci.

"Great, just ask to be escorted to my office at the front desk. We are doing everything we can and as quickly as possible to find your son. I'll see you in a few hours."

Three and half hours later, Marci and John Richardson entered the Hartford Police Department and got escorted to the office of Lieutenant Nelson.

"Let me introduce you to one of my top investigators, Detective Kalisha Jenkins. She is a ten-year veteran police officer and has proven that she can get the job done."

Marci opened a large envelope and handed Jenkins three color photographs of her son, saying, "These photos are the latest ones I can find. One was from last year, and the other two from within the last six months."

Detective Jenkins reviewed the photos and then asked Marci and John a series of questions, confirming Andy's age, date of birth, height, weight, eye and hair color, school address, and cell phone number.

Taking notes as the Richardson's answered her questions, Jenkins asked, "Does your son have any enemies, or had he had any recent confrontations that you are aware of, either from home or at school?"

"No. Andy would have told us if he did," replied John.

Jenkins continued, "We will need a list of the names of Andy's friends and roommates at school, what Andy was wearing when you last saw him, what he might have been carrying with him, and anything else you could remember. The Massachusetts state police have not reported back as yet. We need to get a missing person bulletin sent to all New England police departments and the FBI as soon as possible. We expect to have this completed within twenty-four hours. Don't hesitate to call us anytime. I assure you that we will keep you updated with any pertinent information we receive."

*   *   *

Randy Flemming made a right turn at the mailbox marked 17 and drove up the dirt driveway much later than Dickie Harrington wanted. Dickie was in a dreadful panic the night before when he had called Randy for help. Randy parked in front of the garage doors and beeped the horn. A moment later, Dickie came from around the corner of the garage and waved for Flemming to follow him.

"Dickie, what's got you so wound up, man? I thought you might have been havin' a heart attack. Look at you. You're sweatin' bullets and shakin' like a leaf."

"I picked up a kid last night, brought him here to the house, and gave him our special Coke mix. I had a moment of fun with him, but he bolted out the front door when I turned my back. How was that possible?"

"Did you put enough in the Coke?"

"I thought I put in enough to put him in a deep stupor, but he was able to fight it off."

"If you're talkin' about a young, healthy boy, you might need a strong dose. Now that cute slim chick I mentioned at the bar yesterday might need less. I still think you oughta give it a try with her. I promise you will enjoy it just as much. Anyway, what's so urgent that you begged me to come here last night?"

Dickie had Randy follow him to the other side of the basement bulkhead door, where a blue plastic tarp lay on the ground. "What's that?" asked Randy.

"The kid tried to run for help, but I got lucky. When he ran out into the road trying to wave down a pickup truck, the driver didn't see him in the fog and hit him. The driver must have shit his pants because he drove off and left the kid there."

"Dickie, you've used the backhoe before. So why do you need me?"

"I'm not good at that yet. You use the backhoe for your job and can get the work done in half the time. Anyway, I need help to carry the kid out into the woods. He's dead weight."

Randy stood there in thought. *Dickie acts like a kid half the time. I expected more from a guy with his education.* "Dickie, my boy, I'll help you on one condition. You have to join me with the chick I told you about."

"Come on, Randy. You know my feeling about girls."

"Well, that's what it's gonna take to get my help. I'm not big on girls either, but a little variety doesn't hurt. It feels the same, man. Just close your eyes and pretend it's a boy."

Dickie shied away from girls when he was younger. Even when he tried being friendly with girls, they either laughed him off or ignored him altogether. Dickie remembered when he got caught not paying attention to the teacher who called on him to answer a question. All the kids would stare at him as he mumbled a reply that had nothing to do with the question. That always triggered laughter from the students, especially the girls, who whispered "stupid" to each other. Even during gym classes, kids made fun of him for not performing simple physical tasks. The girls on the other side of the gym would laugh the loudest. Also, when the jocks bullied and called him names, the girls with the guys generally instigated the bullying.

"Hey, Dickie, wake up. You went out in space there for a second. What the hell were you thinkin' of, cousin?"

"Nothing. Just thinking of being with a girl. I'm not sure I'm up for it."

"Well, what's it gonna be? I'll help you if you agree to havin' fun together with the girl."

"Is that the only way you're going to help me?"

"Yep. Otherwise, I'm outta here. You're on your own."

Although not happy about it, Dickie conceded. Randy climbed onto the backhoe, started it up, and asked Dickie to point out where to dig the hole. It took Randy about fifteen minutes to finish. He then helped Dickie drag the blue tarp to the spot.

"You want to say the last rites before we roll him in, Dickie?"

"Nah. Let's just throw him in."

"You want to throw the tarp on top of him or use some plastic?"

"No. It's my dad's tarp. He might wonder what happened to it. The kid won't feel anything. Besides, he pissed me off by running away. I had to chase him through the woods. Branches were hitting me in the face. I fell a couple of times, and I thought I broke a rib. It broke my glasses too. Screw him."

Unrolling the tarp, Randy grabbed the kid's backpack as the body rolled into the hole. "Hey, nice backpack. No sense buryin' that too. I can use one of these."

"No, no, Randy. It's filled with the kid's clothes and underwear and stuff. You don't want anyone finding his stuff with you."

"Yeah, I guess you're right. Okay, big guy, jump up on the backhoe and push the dirt into the hole."

"No, Randy, you do it."

"You have to learn, cousin. You'll probably do this again, so get up on the hoe and do your thing."

Dickie reluctantly climbed onto the backhoe. With Randy calling out instructions, Dickie slowly pushed loads of dirt onto Andy Richardson's body while cursing the kid under his breath. *You shouldn't have run from here, kid. Now you have to stay here forever.*

CHAPTER
15

S am took an extra day off after New Year's and arrived at the office early. He first called Jeff Doherty to ensure both their statements and reports from the raid were complete and compatible before transmitting them to his boss.

Agent Ziglar was working from home and would meet Sam later at the state police task force to assist in another undercover buy of cocaine. Two other Hartford agents were still on vacation, which gave Sam time to finish loads of paperwork and get the gear he needed to bring with him in case the drug buy was a go. Once that was complete, he texted Ziggy that he'd meet him at the task force office.

After one in the afternoon, Sam drove to the task force office. Having been to the unit's office several times, he quickly found the hidden driveway to the office. All makes of unmarked police cars were parked in the driveway and on the lawn. As he found a space to park, Ziggy radioed he was about five minutes out, so Sam waited so they could enter the office together.

When Ziggy arrived, they entered the office through the back entrance, passed the kitchen break area, and made their way to Sergeant Baker's office. Sam lightly tapped on the open door and entered as Baker waved them in.

"Hey, Terry, the paperwork on your desk looks higher than mine. I hope we're not interrupting your concentration," said Sam.

"No. I'm just working on the operational plan for tonight's drug buy."

"I needed to get out from behind my desk, so I decided to come and help out and have you introduce Ziggy as a new member of the unit."

"So, you're joining us on the operation tonight?" asked Baker.

"I am."

"Well, let's go meet the crew."

Sam and Ziggy followed Baker into the open living room area used as the squad room. Baker introduced them to seven task force members representing offices from Newington, Hartford, New Britain, Rocky Hill, East Hartford, Manchester, Enfield, and the three state troopers. After the introductions, Sam and Ziggy fielded questions about ATF.

When the conversation settled, Sam and Ziggy sat at an empty desk and discussed how the game went for Ziggy's kids the afternoon they returned from the raid. While they chatted, Sam noticed Sergeant Baker posting a missing person flyer on the bulletin board that caught his eye. He walked over to take a closer look at the photo in the flyer.

"Ziggy, come over here and take a look at this."

Ziggy walked over to join Sam, where he studied the photo. "Isn't this the kid we saw hitchhiking in Tolland? He got into the BMW with the license plate DICKH 1?"

"How could I forget the dickhead plate? It certainly looks like the same kid, and it says here he had a Yankee cap, same as the kid we saw that day."

Sam read from the poster, "His name is Andrew Richardson, a Bushnell College student. He went missing while hitchhiking between Hartford and Boston. This is the same kid, Zig. What gets me is the kid was hitching to Boston, but the BMW took the exit a few miles up the road. Remember?"

Baker, who was still close nearby, interrupted, "That just came in. You know that kid?"

Sam recapped what he and Ziggy saw on their drive to Boston. "This kid looked right at us when I hit the horn. This has to be the same kid. He got into a BMW with the license plate DICKH 1."

"Well, let's run a check on that plate," responded Sergeant Baker.

They went into Baker's office and watched as he sat at his computer and punched in the license plate. When the record appeared on the computer screen, Baker reported, "The record shows it's a black BMW four-door sedan, registered to Richard Harrington, white male, age forty-two, five-eleven, two hundred and ten pounds, and residing at 1418 Westbrook Road, West Glasterbury. I'll print out a copy of his license. Now, let's see if he has a record—uh, nope, no criminal record, but it shows we did an employment background check at the request of the chief of staff, governor's office. Ha, good luck with that."

After receiving the printouts of the information Baker gave him, Sam took Ziggy aside and said, "With Harrington possibly working at the governor's office, we need to use discretion. Let's keep this quiet until I can do a little more background on this guy. I'll contact the Hartford PD to let them know what we have. Don't mention it to anyone, not even to your wife."

"Are you kidding? If I said anything to her, the whole neighborhood would know about it within an hour."

Sam walked back to the bulletin board and took photos of the poster and the one above it describing another Connecticut student missing.

Twenty minutes later, Baker returned to the squad room, looking discouraged as he announced, "I just heard from Acevedo. The buy is off for tonight. Ace heard from the CI that Tato had to take care of another matter tonight but promised he would have the kilo in a few days."

CHAPTER
16

The next morning, Sam called Lieutenant Marcus Nelson, the contact person listed on the missing person flyer. The call went straight to voicemail. Sam left a message to call back regarding a lead on the missing kid, Andy Richardson.

Sam was intent on finding more about Richard Harrington. He was surprised that Harrington might be working at the statehouse. Also, he was somewhat taken aback by Sergeant Baker's comment, "Good luck with that," a reference he took to mean Baker didn't want any part of an investigation that could involve politicians.

Sam reflected on how best to run a more discreet but thorough background on Harrington without going through police channels. He knew he didn't have sufficient information to claim Harrington was responsible for the missing Richardson kid. Still, he intended to find out more while waiting for a response from Lieutenant Nelson.

The more Sam thought about it, the more questions he had. Why did Harrington, who lives in West Glasterbury, pick up a kid hitchhiking to Boston and then take an exit a few miles up the road? He certainly wasn't taking a shortcut to Boston. So, where was Harrington taking the kid?

Sam sat back in his office chair, deliberating about finding out more about where Harrington works. Then, he remembered he had a casual acquaintance who worked at the statehouse and decided to contact her. He didn't have her direct work number, so he called the main number and asked to be connected to Brenda Hayes. The phone rang several times before a female voice answered. Sam asked for Hayes and got put on hold.

After a long wait, a voice answered, "This is Brenda Hayes."

"Brenda, this is Sam Caviello. How are you?"

She sounded like she'd had taken too many phone calls already or had to put his name to a face before she replied, "I'm fine, Sam. What can I do for you?"

"I need information on a guy who I believe works at the statehouse, but I don't want to discuss it on the phone. I prefer to meet with you privately."

If she didn't put two and two together, he reminded her that he was a federal investigator and needed the information on the QT.

"What kind of information are you looking to get, Sam?"

"I'm not looking for a name, address, date of birth, and such. I have that already. I'd like to find out how this guy got a state job, what kind of reputation he has at work, and things you don't find in typical background records."

"Who are you referring to, then?" she asked.

Sam hesitated before answering. "This has to remain confidential between you and me."

He sensed she was impatient. "Well, if you can tell me who it is, I can at least tell you if I even know the guy."

"His name is Richard Harrington."

"Well, I know who he is, but I don't know much about him. I met him maybe three or four times."

"I understand, but you may be able to provide some insight about him that I don't have. I'm looking for anything that tells me a little about what kind of person he is. For example, is he liked or disliked among his coworkers, who his friends are, and so on. Tell me what you do know, or what you've heard, or anything, even the slightest thing that may not seem relevant or important to you, but it may be relevant to me. And I prefer not to discuss it on the phone. Give it some thought, and maybe we could meet for a few minutes at a coffee shop on your way home?"

"Hang on, and let me check my schedule. Better yet, give me your number, and I'll call you back by the end of the day."

Sam gave her his cell number and thanked her for any help she could provide.

It was nearly two in the afternoon, so Sam went across the street to the café for lunch. He ordered coffee and a small ham and turkey sub sandwich with cheese, lettuce, tomato, and light on the oil. He sat alone, staring out the front window as the traffic flowed by on the busy Main Street. His thoughts were on the kid who had gone missing. He wondered why the BMW driver took the exit for a rural town instead of staying on the interstate to Boston. Sam figured if there was foul play, it probably happened that night in that rural town.

Not hearing back from Lieutenant Nelson's office, Sam decided to call again. A female voice answered, who identified herself as Detective Kalisha Jenkins. "I was just about to call you. Unfortunately, our unit was in a training session until a few minutes ago. Lieutenant Nelson is meeting with the chief and should be back in the office soon. Can you come to his office now?"

"I can be there in about thirty minutes." Sam finished his lunch and returned to his office. He informed his assistant Peg that he would be at HPD and out of the office for the rest of the day. "Call me only if anything important needs my attention."

Sam was lucky to find an open parking space in the small front parking lot at the PD. Sam identified himself at the desk officer's window and informed the officer he had an appointment with Lieutenant Nelson. He took a seat and waited for someone to escort him to the lieutenant's office.

Ten minutes later, a side door opened, and a female walked out and greeted Sam. "Hi, I'm Detective Kalisha Jenkins. You must be Sam Caviello."

"Yes, that's me. Here's my identification."

Jenkins escorted Sam up to Lieutenant Nelson's office on the third floor, where she introduced him to the lieutenant and Detective Tom Griffen.

When all were seated, Lieutenant Nelson said he was anxious to hear what Sam had to say since they had no leads regarding Andy Richardson's disappearance.

Sam briefed them on what he and agent Ziglar saw on their way to Boston when the car in front of them stopped to pick up a hitchhiker.

"When I sounded my horn in anger, the hitchhiker turned to face me with my high beams lighting up his face. I'm sure it's the Richardson kid. He was wearing a Yankees baseball cap and carrying a blue backpack. I followed the car for only a few miles before it took the exit just before the Mass border."

In a pleading tone, Jenkins asked, "Please tell us you got the license plate number."

"I did. It was a black BMW four-door sedan with a Connecticut license plate DICKH 1."

Nelson asked Detective Griffen to run the plate.

"No need, Lieutenant," interrupted Sam. "It's registered to Richard Harrington, a white male, forty-two years old, of West Glasterbury. He doesn't have a criminal record, but the state police conducted an employment background check at the request of the governor's chief of staff. I've been in touch with someone I know who works at the statehouse for additional background on Harrington. I'm expecting a call back from her. Hopefully, she has some information on Harrington that I don't have."

"Well, this is the only positive lead that has come to our attention. Thanks for letting us know. We'll do some background on Harrington, then talk to him, and see what he has to say."

Just then, Sam's phone sounded. He didn't recognize the number but answered it.

"Hi, Sam, it's Brenda. I'm leaving work early so that I can meet you in about thirty minutes in South Windsor at the Starbucks across from the athletic club on Buckley Street."

"Okay, that works. I'll see you there."

"That was my source from the statehouse. I'm going to meet her in South Windsor. Hopefully, she'll have something we can use." Sam and the lieutenant agreed to meet the next day again after learning more about Harrington.

Sam walked into the coffee shop thirty-five minutes later and noticed Brenda seated at a rear table. He waved to get her attention and slid into the seat across from her.

"I don't have much for you. Richard Harrington is the son of Forster Harrington, the owner of the Harrington Construction Company, perhaps the largest construction company in the state. He's a big contributor to not only the governor's campaign but several high-ranking legislators. I only met Richard a few times through a friend who works with him in the same office. My friend told me Harrington is just an average worker, not very social, and keeps to himself. Plus, Harrington often leaves work early, especially toward the end of the week. That's about it. I didn't want to probe too much since you want this handled discreetly."

"Absolutely. I want to keep a tight lid on it because it may be nothing. I don't want it leaked that the feds are interested in Harrington when he may not have done anything wrong. Thanks for meeting me, and what you told me helps. I appreciate it. Can I get you a coffee, or something to eat, anything?"

"Oh no, thanks, Sam. I've got to get home and make dinner. It was nice seeing you again. If I hear anything more, casually, of course, I'll let you know."

Hayes then got up to leave, but as she walked toward the exit, she turned and walked back to the table where Sam was still sitting. "I just remembered that Harrington's sister, Rachel Peterson, also works at the statehouse for Representative Clark Edwards."

"Do you know Rachel or anything about her that would be useful in learning more about her brother?"

"I only met her at functions. So I don't know much about her, other than her father was a campaign donor to Representative Clark Edwards, which is probably why she and her brother got a job at the statehouse."

"With the last name of Peterson, I assume she is married. Do you know anything about her husband?"

"No, wait, one of my associates is either a friend or acquaintance of Peterson. When I get a chance, I'll ask him, discreetly, what he knows about him. If I find out anything, I'll get back to you."

Sam felt he was making progress in his inquiry. Knowing Harrington's father was influential in state political circles further convinced Sam that any queries about Richard would necessitate discretion. He was anxious to get this information to Lieutenant Nelson in the morning. He called his office for messages, and there were none. He drove to his apartment, thinking he needed to propose a joint Hartford PD-ATF investigation into the Richardson matter. ATF didn't have jurisdiction in kidnapping and murder cases, but he wanted to remain working on this case. His gut told him Harrington was behind the kid's disappearance, and he didn't want to get pushed out of the investigation since there was no apparent ATF violation so far. He intended to help solve this puzzle and was confident that he would.

CHAPTER
17

Sam left for work later than usual the following day. On his way to Hart-ford, Sam called Lieutenant Nelson's office to schedule a meeting. Detective Jenkins answered the call. "Good morning, Kalisha. It's Sam Caviello. Is the lieutenant available to meet?"

"The lieutenant won't be in until after eleven o'clock. You can still come in now, and I'll take whatever information you have."

"I need to stop at my office first. I can wait until the lieutenant arrives. Can you call me when he can meet?"

"I will. I have your number. Talk to you later."

While sitting at his office desk, he checked his messages and reviewed pending reports, but his mind drifted to the missing Richardson kid. It puzzled him that Harrington didn't drop the kid off at the exit he took so the kid could continue to hitchhike to Boston. Then, while deep in thought, the ring from his cell phone startled him. He recognized the call was from Brenda Hayes, so he quickly answered the call.

"Hi, Sam, I just wanted to let you know that I had a casual conversation with a colleague who knows Rachel Peterson's husband, Ron. He knows him through a mutual friend, and the three of them played golf together in a couple of tournaments. Peterson invited them to the Harrington family cookout last summer. My colleague said it was a very elaborate catered event, including great food, top-shelf drinks, music, and hobnobbing with VIP guests. They have a large cape located in the woods, either in Uniondale or Woodhaven. He drove up with his friend and didn't remember exactly how to get there, but it was just off I-84 before you hit the Massachusetts border. I hope it's something that helps. I didn't want to ask too many questions."

"That helps a great deal. Thanks, Brenda. I owe you big time." The information Brenda gave him answered why Harrington took that exit. Sam was more convinced something happened to that kid there, and most likely at the hands of Harrington. He needed to find and scope out Harrington's summer home.

He retrieved a Connecticut map from his desk and studied where the two towns were in relationship to the exit. Uniondale was the first town off the exit. He decided to drive to the Uniondale town hall to check if the property records listed Harrington's home. His cell rang again at ten-thirty. He answered the call from Lieutenant Nelson's office.

"Sam, this is Kalisha. The lieutenant is on his way to the office. He should be here in about fifteen minutes if you want to stop over."

"Thanks for letting me know. I'll head over there in a few minutes."

First, Sam called the state police barracks in Tolland to determine what trooper covered Uniondale. He found out Curtis Simmons was the resident trooper, but he was unavailable. Sam left his name and cell number for Simmons to call him back. In Connecticut, many small rural towns contract with the state police to provide a police presence in the lightly populated towns. The state police assign one or more resident troopers to cover towns without a police department. Some of these towns add a small cadre of trained local police officers or part-time constables supervised by the resident troopers.

Sam met with the lieutenant and the two detectives a half-hour later.

"Did you find anything else on Harrington from your source at the statehouse?" asked Nelson.

"Yes. Richard is the son of Forster Harrington of the Harrington Construction and Excavation Company. From what I gathered so far,

Forster Harrington is a large contributor to the political campaigns of the governor and ranking legislators. He probably used his influence to get his son a job in the office of the governor's chief of staff. Harrington's daughter, Rachel Peterson, also works at the statehouse."

"Just what we need. An investigation that potentially involves politicians. Anything else, Sam?" asked Lieutenant Nelson. Before Sam had a chance to answer, Detective Jenkins interrupted with her questions.

"If Harrington lives in West Glasterbury, why did he take an exit in eastern Connecticut? Also, were you able to see who was driving the BMW?"

Sam responded. "I've learned that the Harrington family has a summer home in the area near Uniondale or Woodhaven. So, I assume that's the reason he took that exit. Do I know for sure that Richard Harrington was driving that night? I don't, but chances are it was him? He is not married and has no children. His sister is married, and they have their own vehicles. The BMW belongs to Harrington, and I can't believe he would loan such an expensive car to someone else. I confirmed he didn't report his car stolen. When I leave here, I'm heading up to the town hall closest to where Harrington took the exit to check with the clerk's office to determine exactly where Harrington has property in the area. After verifying the location, I'll do a drive-by and take a few photos."

"I'd like to send a detective with you," suggested Nelson.

"This has to be very low-profile, and I prefer to do it alone. I don't want the town clerk to think we are investigating Forster Harrington. I'll tell them I'm conducting an employment background check. I know the rural towns in that area don't have full-time police departments. A resident trooper covers them. I called for the trooper who covers that area, but he was unavailable, so I left a message to have him call me back. When he does, I'll call you to have one of your detectives join me to meet with him. Maybe he knows the Harrington family and can tell us something about them."

Nelson replied, "Detective Jenkins will give you her cell number. While you and Kalisha meet with the trooper, Detective Griffen and I will contact

Richard Harrington. Hopefully, he'll talk to us and tell us what happened after he picked up Richardson hitchhiking."

Sam pulled out another flyer of a missing kid the state police posted next to the Richardson flyer. "While I look for Harrington's property, can one of your detectives obtain more information and background on this kid, Josh Davis? He's another college student missing, and I'd like to know if there is a possible link between Harrington and this Davis kid."

"Hmm, that name sounds familiar. Let me check my records." Nelson checked his computer for the list of missing person investigations. "I thought so. We did a preliminary investigation on Davis. He was attending school in Connecticut when he went missing. Unfortunately, the detective who did the preliminary check transferred out of the unit. When you get a chance, Tom, would you pull the file on Davis and review its status? Sam, after you and Kalisha interview the trooper, let's meet again to brainstorm where we go from there."

"Will do. I think it's important we keep this investigation to ourselves to prevent it from leaking out because of the suspect's father, who has political connections. Right now, the only ones who know about Harrington's connection to the Richardson kid are you three, me, and the ATF agent who was with me the night he picked up the Richardson kid."

Lieutenant Nelson replied, "I agree, but if at some point the investigation points solidly to Harrington, I'll need to inform the chief."

"If it gets to that point, I'd like to discuss establishing a joint HPD-ATF investigation. Of course, I'd have to get the federal prosecutor involved and my boss," responded Sam.

"That's something we should consider, a full-scale joint investigation and not waste more time finding out what happened to these kids."

CHAPTER
18

am left the Hartford PD. and headed east on I-84. It took him forty
minutes to get to the exit Harrington took that fog-filled evening. He
followed his navigation to the Uniondale town hall. It was a small redbrick building that could have been a post office at one time. It only had
one primary floor with offices on the basement level. He walked into the
town clerk's office and cleared his throat to get the clerk's attention. "Hi,
I'm looking to locate properties owned by persons with the last name of
Harrington."

The clerk, an older woman with all gray hair, wore glasses hanging at
the tip of her nose. "That could take some time. Are you an attorney or real
estate agent?"

Sam identified himself as a federal agent and told her he would be
willing to search the files.

"All the records are on our computer. Is this person someone we should
be concerned about?" the clerk asked.

"No, no, I'm just doing an employment background check on a job
applicant, and I'm looking for the address of a reference for the applicant
who supposedly lives in the area. I don't have the address, but I was told
they live either in Uniondale or Woodhaven."

The clerk asked Sam to follow her into an adjoining office. She sat at a desk in front of a computer and did a property search by name. Reading the computer screen, she pointed out two properties listed under the name Harrington."

Sam glanced at the screen before asking her to print out both listings and the plot plan showing the property lines. Sam noticed one of the names listed was Forster Harrington. Sam was careful not to hint which Harrington property interested him, in case she knew the owner. She printed the results of her search and handed them to Sam.

One property at 17 Old Hollow Brook Road listed Forster T. Harrington as the owner. The second property listed Michael G. Harrington as the property owner. He thanked the clerk for her assistance and left the office with the copies in hand.

Outside the clerk's office, Sam glanced at the directory of the town hall offices to find the location of the resident state trooper's office. He headed to the basement level, where he saw the lights in the office were off, and no one responded to ringing the outside buzzer at the locked door. Sam left the town hall and drove to 17 Old Hollow Brook Road using his phone's navigation. Fifteen minutes later, he made a left turn onto Hollow Brook Road. A portion of the wooden street sign was missing, with the remaining section only reading 'low Brook Road.' Following the road a short distance, Sam approached an S-curve sign and steered around the first curve before rounding the next, which led him to a mailbox marked 17. He pulled over onto the road's shoulder across from the mailbox and scanned the general area. He noticed an eight to ten-foot-wide grass shoulder on each side of the road with some snow cover in spots. The dirt driveway at the mailbox lacked any snow. He snapped photos, including of the mailbox and driveway.

Ensuring there were no other cars on the road, Sam drove up the driveway to look at the house and take a few photos before leaving the area. He estimated the driveway at about eighty yards long, with heavy woods on both sides, before approaching the clearing to the house. The house was a large gray cape-style home with an attached two-car garage. A small backhoe was sticking out from the rear corner of the house. Sam took several photos of the place and the backhoe before driving back down the driveway.

As he left the driveway, a police vehicle came around the curve in the opposite direction. When they passed each other, the officer gave Sam a guarded look. Sam watched his rearview mirror, and as he suspected, the officer made a turnaround in Harrington's driveway, flipped on his blue emergency lights, and quickly approached Sam's car from behind. Sam pulled over onto the shoulder, opened his window, and reached for the printed sheet he received from the town clerk with Michael Harrington's name. He didn't want to reveal he was looking for Forster Harrington's property in case the officer knew him.

The young officer approached Sam's open window. "Can I help you, sir?"

"Yes, as a matter of fact, you can, Officer. I'm looking for a Michael Harrington. I was told he lives in Uniondale."

The officer curtly said, "I've never heard of him."

"I was told he lived in this area, so I drove to the house back there and knocked on the door, but no one was home. I thought maybe they were at work, so I'd try back later."

"Don't bother. There is no Michael Harrington at that address."

"Okay, I guess I got the wrong information. Do you know where Michael Harrington resides?"

The officer, apparently annoyed, answered that he didn't know.

Sam thanked him for letting him know and was about to roll up the window and leave.

"I'm going to need some identification. Your license and registration," demanded the officer.

Sam noticed the name F. Asckis embroidered above the badge on the officer's jacket and that he was a Woodhaven officer. He smirked at the officer's name, thinking maybe that's how he got his job.

"So, Officer, you're a little out of your jurisdiction, are you not?"

"I saw you were coming out the driveway, and since you don't live there, it is my job as a police officer to investigate suspicious activity."

"How did you know I didn't live there?"

"You just told me you were looking for a guy named Michael Harrington," replied the officer.

"But you didn't know that until you pulled me over."

"Well, I know who lives there, and it's not you," the officer rudely responded.

Not wanting to get further hassled, Sam pulled out his credentials and badge. "I'm a federal agent. Here's my identification, Officer Asskiss."

The officer angrily responded, "It's pronounced Ache'is, and why is a fed looking for Harrington?"

"That's the business of the federal government, Officer. I'm not at liberty to discuss the government's business with you. Thanks for letting me know Michael Harrington doesn't live there. So, if there is nothing further, I have work to do, and I'm sure you do as well, serving the good people of Woodhaven. I believe we are now in the town of Uniondale."

Sam put his vehicle in gear and started to roll up the window.

"Well, just because you're a fed doesn't mean you can go on other people's property without permission."

"As a federal officer, I don't need your permission to conduct federal business regardless of where it takes me." Sam closed his window and drove away.

Officer Asckis was pissed as he watched Sam drive off. He wrote down Sam's license plate number and the make of his vehicle. He then got into his cruiser and drove up to the Harrington residence. Once at the house, the officer walked around, checking all the doors and windows to ensure they were secure. He then made a call on his cell phone.

"Harrington Construction and Excavation, may I help you?" asked the female answering the call.

"Yes, this is Fred Asckis, Woodhaven Police Department, calling for Mr. Harrington."

The female asked for the nature of the call, and Asckis replied that he had information regarding Harrington's property in Uniondale.

A moment later, Forster Harrington answered. "Fred, I only have a minute. What's going on? Something happened at my place?"

"I was driving by your property and spotted a car coming out of the driveway. I pulled the driver over. It turned out to be a federal agent who claimed to be looking for a Michael Harrington at your address."

"That's it?" asked Harrington.

"I thought it was suspicious that a federal agent was on your property. So I drove up to the house to make sure everything was secure. Just trying to look after things here at your property as you requested."

"Do you know if there is a Michael Harrington living in the area?"

"I never heard of him."

"Well, do me a favor and find out. If there isn't, then I might be concerned. If there is, then someone gave the guy the wrong address. Get back to me when you find out. I got to run."

Harrington hung up before Asckis could say another word.

CHAPTER
19

While driving back to Hartford, Sam answered a call. "Agent Caviello, this is Trooper Curtis Simmons. How can I help you?"

"Thanks for returning my call, Curtis. I'm not sure you can help me, but I wanted to describe an incident along I-84 eastbound in Tolland and ask if you remember anything on that particular night that might be helpful."

"Okay, but my primary responsibility is patrolling the towns I serve, not the interstate."

"I understand, but what I'm going to describe pertains to the Uniondale area."

Sam recounted witnessing a black BMW picking up a young teenager hitchhiking in Tolland and taking the Uniondale exit only a few miles up the road.

"It was the night the weather was misty with heavy fog developing in the area. Several days later, I realized that the student hitchhiking that evening was reported missing. The student is unlikely to be a runaway, and I suspect possible foul play. Although the car's owner resides in West Glasterbury, his family owns a summer home in Uniondale off of Old Hollow Brook Road. I'm inquiring if there was anything that seemed out of the ordinary on that road that evening."

There was silence for a moment.

"Are you still there, Curtis?" asked Sam.

"Yes, I was just thinking back. When you mentioned Old Hollow Brook Road, I remember an incident around that time. I wasn't on duty that night, but I learned later that there was a 911 distress call from that area. The 911 operator didn't get a response from the caller but heard what appeared to be an accident. The operator contacted our department, and it got referred to our Tolland barracks. The night sergeant assigned two troopers to search that whole area, but they found nothing unusual."

Simmons was interrupted as he took a message coming over his radio before continuing. "As I was saying, I wasn't working that night, but the next morning I was on my way to work when I saw a guy in a pickup truck parked on the side of that road. I stopped to question if the guy needed assistance. He told me he hit something that came out onto the road that night and searched the area but couldn't see anything because of the heavy fog. He figured it was a deer that ran back into the woods after being hit. When I inspected his pickup, his front fender was wiped clean, so I ran a DMV, and criminal record check on him with negative results other than a past DUI arrest. He said he worked near Hartford and was on his way home that evening. I searched the area the best I could, but it snowed that morning, covering the ground. When I got to the barracks, I found out about the 911 call of a possible accident and was surprised that it was in the same area where I stopped to question the guy in the pickup."

Hearing this, Sam thought it couldn't be a coincidence that someone made a 911 distress call in front of Harrington's property, where he suspected Harrington had taken the Richardson kid. "Curtis, could we meet so I can review your report regarding the 911 call and the information you have on the pickup driver? I'd also like to look at the area where this guy claimed to hit the deer. The snow is nearly gone now, and maybe we might see something that wasn't visible that morning."

"I could meet you tomorrow morning at ten o'clock at my Uniondale office."

"That works for me, Curtis. I'll have a Hartford Police detective with me. See you in the morning."

As Sam continued home, he called Detective Jenkins to inform her of the appointment with the trooper in Uniondale. They agreed on a place and time to meet so they could ride together.

*   *   *

The next morning, Sam and Detective Kalisha Jenkins arrived at the Uniondale town hall at nine-fifty-five. They saw a state police cruiser and an older Uniondale Police sedan parked adjacent to the basement entrance.

Inside, Sam rang the buzzer for the locked door of the resident trooper's office. A young officer buzzed them into the office. Sam identified himself and introduced Kalisha.

"Trooper Simmons is on the phone and will be right out. I'm Jerry Reed, a part-time constable. I help out around here whenever they schedule me."

Sam asked, "How long have you been on the job?"

"It's been almost a year now. I hope to get hired by the state police full-time once I graduate college this spring. As of now, I'm getting experience working with Trooper Simmons and waiting for the state to hire more troopers."

Moments later, Trooper Simmons appeared and invited Sam and Kalisha into his office, where they introduced themselves. "Officer Reed will participate in the day's activity as part of his on-the-job training," said Simmons.

Sam had no problem with Reed tagging along. They sat in the small office that housed two desks, file cabinets, a small mail basket, a document sorter shelf, and two visitor chairs in front of each desk. Simmons went over the notes he took from his interaction with Zake Barnes and provided them with the information he gathered from Barnes's license and registration and a printout of his record check.

"As I mentioned over the phone, as a result of a 911 distress call, our district barracks in Tolland was ordered to check out the area where Zake

Barnes claimed he hit a deer. When answering the 911 call, the operator didn't get a voice response but reported hearing a thump, a distressed yelp, and a vehicle driving off. They traced the call by geolocation to the general area of the 911 call. The sergeant dispatched two troopers to search the area for over a mile. They found nothing. The next morning, when I saw Barnes looking around the same area and later learning of the 911 call, I reported it to the barracks commander and made a formal report."

"That's important, Curtis. I'm glad you included the information on the 911 call. Does your report identify the phone number of the distress call to 911?" asked Sam.

Trooper Simmons looked through his file, found the cell phone number, and gave it to Sam. After reviewing the full report, Sam asked to head out to the accident scene. "The past few days were sunny, so most of the snow is gone. With another look, we might get lucky and find something that the other officers couldn't see that night."

Trooper Simmons said Officer Reed would ride with him and asked Sam and Kalisha to follow in their vehicle in case he got a call to respond elsewhere. Sam followed Simmons for about fifteen minutes before arriving at Old Hollow Brook Road. When the Trooper pulled over and stopped, Sam looked across from where they parked and knew his hunch was on the money. He turned to face Kalisha. "This is the front of Harrington's property. It can't be a coincidence."

Once out of their vehicles, they teamed up and searched the grass-covered shoulder about thirty yards from the mailbox, walking deliberately toward it. They did not find anything of significance until they were within fifteen feet of the mailbox. On the ground, covered partially by wet leaves, was a chrome headlight frame. Sam stopped Simmons from picking it up.

"Curtis, let me get latex gloves before we touch anything," urged Sam.

Sam fetched three evidence bags and four pairs of latex gloves to avoid placing fingerprints on anything they found that may prove to be evidence. He also retrieved a tape measure and a small notebook. As Simmons was slipping on his gloves, Sam and Kalisha took several photos of the frame with their phones.

While Sam slipped on his gloves, Trooper Simmons picked up the frame, and all four studied it. They noticed reddish-brown spots around the rim.

"This could be blood, so let's place it in the envelope, and each of us initial it," said Sam.

Sam took two measurements from the frame to the road's edge and the mailbox post. Then they decided to continue to search the area on the other side of the driveway when Sam's phone rang.

"This is Sam Caviello. Oh, hi, Lieutenant. Kalisha and I are in Uniondale meeting with Trooper Simmons."

Sam listened as Lieutenant Nelson informed him that a review of the Davis file revealed the unit's former detective had interviewed Davis's mother over the phone. "Mrs. Davis told the detective her son had left a message on her cell that he was offered a ride home from school by a professor. The professor claimed he was heading to Boston and was willing to drop Davis off on the way."

Nelson apologetically continued. "I don't know why this wasn't followed up on, only to say it took months before we had a replacement here. But I have to take some of the blame that we missed it."

"Missed what?" asked Sam.

"The kid's message said the professor drove a black BMW, like his dad's."

"What? That's big. That gives us a connection between two missing kids. So let's meet tomorrow at your office and discuss what we should do next."

When the call ended, Sam sighed in relief, knowing he was on the right path in this investigation. He was about to put his phone back in his pocket when an eerie feeling passed through his body. The sensation caused a tremor down his spine, followed by body shakes. He'd experienced such weird feelings many times before. While trying to shake it off, his cell phone, still in his hand, was quietly pulsating. Sam's body was still shivering as he looked at the phone's screen, thinking it was an incoming call, but the screen was black. Then, a moment later, the pulsating and his trembling stopped. He paused to consider why he'd gotten a sign at that very moment.

"Everything all right there, Sam?" asked Kalisha.

It took a few seconds for Sam to answer that he was fine. With his phone still in his hand, Sam sensed that his phone's vibration was a clue. He thought for a moment about what it could mean before it hit him. It was a long shot, but Sam decided to try it. He called Richardson's cell phone number.

After punching in the number, he could hear the rings on his phone, once, twice, then a third time. Thinking it was for naught, he was about to end the call when he heard a weak musical sound coming from the woods to his right.

Officer Reed shouted, "That's a popular ring tone on cell phones!"

They heard another weak chime before Sam, Kalisha, and Reed moved toward the sound where the brush and woods began. Pulling back branches while scanning the ground, Officer Reed spotted a flicker of light among the leaves and pointed to where he saw it as the ringing stopped.

Sam forced back some branches, shoving leaves aside like a child searching for an Easter egg. His heart raced, and his skin tingled in anticipation of finding Andy's phone. Swiping more leaves aside, he finally spotted a cell phone lying in a bed of leaves. He looked up to the sky like he just got a sign from the heavens finding Andy Richardson's cell phone in front of Harrington's property. He paused for a moment of peace and achievement regarding the significance of finding the kid's phone here.

He turned to Officer Reed. "Jerry, I saw a couple of stones on the side of the driveway. Can you find one about this size?" he said, spreading his hands about six inches apart.

Reed returned with a stone that fit the bill as Trooper Simmons joined the other three in their search. After cleaning off the rock, Sam took out a black marker and slowly initialed and dated it. He handed the marker to Kalisha and Reed, asking them to do the same. Sam then placed the stone next to the phone and took photos of the rock and phone together. Once done, Sam picked up the phone with his gloved hand, placed it in an evidence envelope, initialed and dated it, and asked Kalisha and Reed to do the same. He then brushed leaves back around the stone to hide it from being noticed.

As the four of them moved back a couple of feet, Reed commented, "I wouldn't have thought of marking the spot like that. I learned something new today."

Sam was dumbfounded, thinking about all that had happened over the past few minutes. His first reaction was that finding Richardson's phone was mind-boggling.

"That was unbelievable. I can't help but think the faint sound coming from the phone's dying battery was, uh—a cry for help from the Richardson kid."

CHAPTER
20

A
s they stood on the shoulder of the road, absorbing what Sam said, they heard the sound of a vehicle stopping along the side of the road. It was a Woodhaven Police cruiser.

Officer Fred Asckis stepped out of the vehicle and approached the four of them. "What's going on here? Can I help you guys?"

"No, we're all set here, but thanks," Sam sounded off immediately.

Asckis looked at Sam disparagingly, "Oh, you're that fed I saw snooping around here yesterday."

"I think your characterization that I was snooping around is way off base, Officer Asskiss."

The officer was incensed by Sam's mispronunciation of his name again. "My name's pronounced *Ache'is*. I corrected you when I pulled you over yesterday. As I recall, you were looking for a Michael Harrington and, as you know, he doesn't live here, but here you are back here again."

Toying with Asckis, Sam replied, "I apologize for the pronunciation of your name. I get it now. The pronunciation of your name is like an ache in the ass."

It visibly aggravated Asckis even more, but he only scowled while shaking his head and let it go unchallenged.

Trooper Simmons interrupted the juvenile debate saying, "We're investigating an accident that occurred here a while back. Do you know anything about that?"

"I never heard anything about any accident in this area," claimed Asckis.

Sam intervened, "Well, that's probably because you patrol in Woodhaven. Isn't that where you're supposed to patrol instead of here in Uniondale? Trooper Simmons and Officer Reed patrol this area. I can't help wondering why you continually patrol here outside your town."

Asckis, with a smirk on his face, said, "I'm just checking to make sure nobody is snooping around this property again."

Sam decided to stop playing word games with this neophyte and asked Asckis if he knew who owned the property.

"Yeah, I know who owns the property, but the owner wouldn't know anything about any accident."

"How do you know that?" asked Kalisha.

"This is just a summer home. The owner hasn't been here for months," answered Asckis.

When Sam asked for the owner's name, Asckis replied, "I'm surprised you don't already know. I thought you feds knew everything. But as you said, this is not my town, so I should leave and stay out of it. I'll let the owner know you were snooping around his property again. I'm sure he won't be too happy knowing you're here again."

Before Sam said another word, Asckis walked toward his cruiser, climbed in, and drove off, spinning his wheels like a teenage kid.

"What the hell was that all about?" asked Kalisha.

Sam looked disgusted. "I was checking out the area yesterday to get the lay of the land when that guy drove by as I was leaving the driveway. He made a quick turnaround and pulled me over. He gave me a hard time and questioned why I was in the area. Even after I identified myself, he scolded me for snooping around. I felt like clocking him."

Reed said, "He thinks he is some sort of super cop, and he's constantly patrolling outside his area. He's a part-time constable like me, only in

Woodhaven, and he shouldn't be patrolling here. He claims that a friend of his lives on this property and asked him to keep an eye on it."

"It's interesting that Officer Asckis knows the property owner. We may have to interview him at some point later," Sam said to Kalisha.

Trooper Simmons then spoke up. "It's now evident to me that Barnes hit that kid. The officers searched the area and didn't find him, so that kid may be alive, maybe injured, and wandered off seeking help. I'll have to call this into the commander and request a search of the whole area for the kid."

Jenkins agreed. "Curtis, I would suggest that a ranking commander from headquarters contact Forster Harrington to ask for his consent to search his property. Maybe coming from a high-level ranking officer, Harrington might be more receptive to giving his approval."

"You may be right. I'll recommend my boss have someone from headquarters contact Harrington directly. There's also a lake nearby, so I'll request a dive team to be available. I have to say, though, that when I tell my commander we found the phone and headlight frame, both evidence of a hit-and-run, he'll want to know why ATF has custody of the evidence."

Sam momentarily froze, thinking of how best to respond until Jenkins countered with a reply. "This is a Hartford Police missing person investigation, working jointly with ATF. The evidence found confirms our suspicion that Harrington kidnapped a student and brought him here. The violation falls under our and the federal government's jurisdiction."

"I understand, but I still will have to report this to my boss, and he may contact Hartford's chief of police to work out jurisdictional responsibility," cited Simmons.

"Well, you have to follow protocol, Curtis. Kalisha and I are done here for now. I want to thank you and Officer Reed for your help. I'm sure our superiors will be in touch with each other to work things out," added Sam.

Driving back to Hartford, Sam thought back to Kalisha's answer to the trooper's concern about the evidence. "Thanks for jumping in to tell Simmons we are working jointly on this investigation. I wouldn't have said it as perfectly as you did. I'll discuss this situation with the assistant US attorney and make the case that this investigation should stay with the HPD and ATF. The state could try to preempt Hartford's jurisdiction and take over the investigation. We need to retain investigative control to prevent any possible political influence in this investigation."

"I agree, but we still need additional evidence to confirm our suspicion without interference." Kalisha took a breath while trying not to get personal inquiring about Sam's health. "Not to change the subject, but while searching, you went into some sort of trance and got wobbly. I was a little concerned. Are you okay?"

Sam said he was fine and quickly changed the subject by theorizing possibilities in the case. Sam didn't want to try explaining the revelations he sometimes gets. It's a predicament he often has to face. All Sam knew was whatever revelations he experienced had to remain his secret.

When dropping Kalisha off, Sam waited for her to get in her car and drive off. He was impressed with her entire demeanor. She was an astute, talented detective with a pleasant personality but firm in her viewpoints. Although dressed down for fieldwork, Kalisha was always well-groomed and professional in all aspects. He liked her. She was an attractive woman who reminded him of his colleague, Jennifer Clarkson. Both were about the same height, around five feet, six inches tall, and slim, weighing about one hundred and twenty pounds. He didn't notice a wedding band and guessed her age between thirty-six and forty. He dispensed the thought of asking her out, and instead called AUSA Brian Murphy, hoping to initiate a joint ATF-Hartford Police investigation against Harrington. After finding the kid's phone, Sam believed he had enough information to rouse the prosecutor's interest in a compelling investigation.

Murphy answered Sam's call and agreed to meet with a caveat. "I'll be available as long as it doesn't take too long. I have another appointment later in the afternoon outside the office."

CHAPTER
21

S usan Michaels, the special assistant at the Harrington Construction Company, quietly knocked before opening the closed door marked "Forster T. Harrington, President-CEO."

"Sorry to disturb you, Mr. Harrington. Officer Asckis is on line 3 and said it was urgent."

"Okay, Sue, ask him to hold for a few minutes so I can finish this call."

A few minutes later, Harrington pressed line 3 on his phone. "What's so urgent, Fred?"

"That same federal agent, along with a state trooper and a Hartford detective, was on your property looking around."

Harrington responded, "When you say they were on my property, were they searching my house?"

"No, no, they were searching the shoulder in front by the road."

"That's not my property, Fred. That area is considered town property for water runoff and a place to plow snow off the road."

Harrington knew Asckis wasn't the brightest light on the tree, but helping Fred get hired as a constable provided him with someone who'd keep an eye on his property.

"Did they say why they were searching there?"

"The trooper said there was an accident there a week or so ago, and they were looking into it. The fed asked who owned the property."

"Well, did you give them my name?"

"I didn't because the fed is a wise guy and questioned why I was there since it wasn't my area to patrol. So, screw him. I told him to find out for himself."

Harrington asked, "Did you find out if there was a Michael Harrington in the area?"

"Yes, sir, but that's another reason why I'm suspicious about this whole thing. I went to the Uniondale town hall to find out if Michael Harrington was a resident in town. The clerk told me I was the second person asking about anyone named Harrington who owned property in town. She told me it was a federal agent who asked, and she gave the agent copies of the only two property listings, Michael Harrington's and yours."

"Okay, thanks, Fred, you did good. I appreciate you calling me about this. It's probably nothing, but I'll take it from here."

Forster thought about what Asckis had told him. *Why didn't the agent just ask if Michael Harrington owned property in town?* Curious, he contacted Ron Freedman, chief of staff for the governor. The call went to voicemail, so Harrington left a message for a call back as soon as possible.

Within the hour, Forster answered a call from Freedman. "Thanks for getting back to me, Ron. Do me a favor and find out why the state police and a federal agent searched near my summer home in Uniondale. In particular, ask if there was an accident that occurred nearby. It's probably nothing to be concerned about, but I like to be cautious and stay on top of anything that could potentially become a problem for me."

By the end of the business day, Freedman called Forster back and briefed him on what he had learned from the state police. The information Harrington received infuriated him so much he couldn't think straight. He paced back and forth in his office, considering his options.

He sat at his desk debating his next move. Forster could feel his blood pressure elevating and discomfort in his chest. So he slowly sat back in his chair, trying to calm down. Still agitated, Forster opened a desk drawer to take out a vial of pills. He dropped a tablet into his hand, took a full breath, and swallowed a Valium. After what Freedman told him, Forster knew he had to take steps to protect his good name and the company he operated.

He thought back to his father, William Forster Harrington, who started the construction company from scratch. His father taught him how to grow the business. First, don't allow anyone to tarnish the company's name. Second, pad the pockets of the right people. And finally, have an enforcer on the payroll to deal with people who got in the way, including union thugs. This philosophy led to fat contracts from the state, cities, and towns that helped build the company into a major construction powerhouse.

His father insisted he work at the company beginning when he turned fifteen. He taught his son how to make the hard choices for success. Work hard, do the best job for the money paid, and ensure the right people are taken care of, including politicians, union bosses, and police officials. After high school graduation, Forster started as a construction crew member and, with tutoring from his father, worked his way up to the top field foreman while attending night school and weekend classes. Forster took control of the company after his father had two heart attacks, the last being fatal. Forster didn't want to end his life that way.

Once Forster calmed down, he called his friend, Tony Dellagatti, but only got his voicemail, so he left a message to call back. Dellagatti and Harrington were high school teammates on the school's football team. Even though Forster was a senior when Tony was a sophomore, they clicked and became friends. Tony was popular among the fans because he was a physical force on the football team. When Tony tackled a runner or the quarterback, they often had to be carried off the field. Unfortunately, Tony had to drop out of school in his junior year to help out at home when his dad died. His mother had to stay home to take care of four children, and since Tony was the oldest at sixteen, he felt it was up to him to help his mother and siblings.

Tony had talent on the football field, but he wasn't a good student and had difficulty with academics. If Harrington hadn't helped him with his homework and how to cheat on exams, he never would have made it to his junior year. Tony's flair for playing football extended to dating girls and bullying kids who were smart-asses or avoided playing sports. A couple of years later, and with the insistence of Forster, Tony agreed to get his GED and join the army. Because of his physical size, he got assigned to a military police unit after initial training.

After Tony completed his army tour, Forster hired him to work at his construction company as both a crew member and a 'fixer' when brute strength was essential. Tony was six feet four inches tall and a muscular two hundred and forty pounds. Forster was always in awe of Tony's brutal tackles during high school football games. He felt he could use a guy like Tony when the situation called for 'physical persuasion' in the construction business.

His thoughts back to the old days helped calm Forster. He decided to leave his office when he received a call from Colonel Bennett of the state police. The colonel informed him of an accident in front of his Uniondale property where a young college student was hit by a truck but not found.

"The state police is establishing a neighborhood search party for tomorrow beginning at noon to search for the student. We're planning to search a large area near your Uniondale home, and we are requesting permission from all property owners to search their grounds for the student who may have wandered off looking for help. We are also asking for volunteers to help in the search."

Forster took his time to think of how best to answer. His mind worked wonders coming up with the perfect suggestion. "Colonel, sorry to hear that. Tell you what, give me some time, and I'll arrange for volunteers from my company to help in the search at my property, so your officers can concentrate on the larger areas nearby. I'll even volunteer and have a friend from the Woodhaven Police Department join me in the search. I'll get back to you in the morning with the particulars."

"That would be a great help to us, Mr. Harrington. Thank you. I'll talk to you in the morning." Forster made the connection between the call from the colonel and what Ron Freedman had told him earlier. He realized he needed to put a plan together. He knew what he had to do next, so he dialed his assistant. "Sue, call and tell my son and daughter to come for dinner at my house tomorrow afternoon around four. Then contact Gus Walker and tell him I need to speak to him now."

Walker called back within minutes. Forster gave him instructions to gather four men from the company to volunteer to work tomorrow morning at ten sharp at his summer home in Uniondale. Forster then called and asked Fred Asckis to join the search at his property and bring another constable. Before leaving his office, he called Tony Dellagatti again but only got his voicemail. He left a message for Tony to call him back. Later, when he arrived home, Forster answered an incoming call on his private cell phone.

"Hey, boss, it's Tony. You called. What's up?"

"Tony, I want you to come for dinner at the house tomorrow afternoon around four-thirty. After dinner, we'll sit and talk. I have a special job for you."

CHAPTER
22

L ess than an hour later, Sam was at the office door of Brian Murphy. Murphy was on a phone call and waved Sam in to take a seat. Brian, thirty-two years old, six feet tall, and one hundred and seventy pounds, was a handsome Irishman with light brown wavy hair and brown eyes. Murphy came from a more privileged home than the average Joe. His dad was an investment advisor earning millions, and his mom was a successful attorney. Both were heavy political donors, and that, in no small way, was why Brian, a Yale law school graduate, became a law clerk for one of the state's Supreme Court judges. Later, he worked at his mother's law firm for three years before being appointed an assistant US attorney in Hartford. After a year of being tutored by a seasoned attorney, he became one of two primary prosecutors handling ATF criminal cases.

Once off the phone, Brian greeted Sam. "Hello, stranger. It's been a while since we played golf. I can't wait until it warms up so we can go out and smack that little ball around, and hopefully not deep into the woods."

"I can't wait either, Brian. I remember the last time we played. I lost one in the woods and dropped two in the pond. That was pretty bad, but you topped that by losing four balls. Maybe, we should think about going on the pro circuit." They laughed at that idea.

"What brings you in this afternoon, Sam?"

Sam pulled out the missing person flyer on the Richardson kid and explained what he saw on that fog-filled night traveling to Boston. Murphy listened attentively to Sam's account of the BMW taking the exit for Uniondale only a few miles from where he picked up the kid.

"DMV lists the registration to Richard Harrington, the son of Forster Harrington, a major donor to the governor and legislators," explained Sam.

Murphy knew the name Harrington and his political influence in Connecticut.

Sam continued. "Well, Richard Harrington works at the statehouse, as does his sister, and his father has a summer home in Uniondale."

"So you think Harrington picked up this Richardson kid, brought him to the summer home, and did what?"

"Yes, I believe Harrington took the kid to the Uniondale home and did something unthinkable, resulting in the kid's death."

Murphy had a puzzled look on his face. "That's a huge assumption, going from giving a kid a ride to killing him. I assume you have more to tell me?"

"I met with the resident state trooper, who covers the area of Uniondale. The same night Harrington picked up the kid, the trooper said a guy named Zake Barnes hit something in front of Harrington's property while driving home from work. Barnes claimed he didn't see what he hit because of the thick fog that night and assumed it was a deer that ran back into the woods. The trooper added that Barnes hit something in the road the same night a 911 operator reported a distress call to the state police. That call came from what we now know to be Richardson's cell phone that we found buried among the leaves in front of Harrington's property. Richardson never responded to the 911 operator who answered his call, so the operator contacted the state police. The state police searched for nearly a mile in the vicinity of the distress call but didn't find anything,"

Sam continued, saying he and Hartford Detective Kalisha Jenkins met with the trooper to search the area again. "We found a headlight frame, likely from the guy's pickup truck, containing what could be blood splatter. I decided to call Richardson's cell phone on a hunch, and as luck would have it, we heard the phone ring. We found it among the leaves a couple of feet into the brush, close to where we found the headlight frame. The phone's battery must have had just enough juice left to ring a few times before the battery died."

Murphy sat back in his chair, looking through the notes he'd taken, while Sam continued to recap his investigative theory. When Sam finished, Murphy challenged his speculation.

"What you have is this guy, Barnes, who hit this kid with his truck. The kid was probably heading back to the highway to start hitchhiking again. That's what a good defense attorney might argue. Has Barnes been interviewed?"

Sam didn't hesitate to dispute Murphy's comment.

"Listen, Brian, does it make sense to you that a college kid, hitchhiking to Boston to meet up with his high school friends, would want to take a detour with a forty-two-year-old guy, and what, have dinner and a drink with him? Then start walking two or three miles, in an unfamiliar area, on a dark rural road in heavy fog, back to the interstate to start hitchhiking again?"

"No, of course not, but it's a possibility."

"Come on, Brian. The kid called 911 in front of Harrington's property before, and I emphasize *before*, Barnes hit him with his truck. Granted, Barnes probably didn't see the kid run out onto the road for help because of the fog. Maybe Barnes had been drinking, got scared, and drove off. What you are missing is the 911 operator reported the distress call to the state police, and they searched a large area from where the call was made and found nothing. So if the driver hit the kid and drove off, where's the body?"

Murphy agreed. "Maybe the kid got up and walked off seeking help."

"Based on the evidence we found, the resident trooper told me he's sure the state police will initiate a door-to-door search for the kid in the area to include Harrington's property. The trooper informed me that the state police would conduct a hit-and-run investigation and wanted the evidence I have in my custody. Is it possible the kid was only injured and wandered away searching for help? Yes, but my theory, and I'm confident I'm right on this, is the kid was probably running from Richard Harrington and called 911. Then, when he saw a vehicle approaching, he attempted to flag it down for help. He conceivably was hit by the truck just before the 911 operator answered his call. Right now, I need to get the headlight frame, and cell phone analyzed at a lab. I'm betting it's the kid's blood on the headlight frame, and with luck, we might gain additional leads from the calls made on the kid's cell phone that night. Once we confirm the blood is Richardson's, we'll interview Barnes."

Murphy listened intently, but it appeared he needed further convincing. He asked, "Where exactly did you find the cell phone, and where does the Harrington property line begin?"

"I have the property lot dimensions from the town hall, but I'm not a surveyor. When the phone rang, I certainly wasn't going to leave it behind. I would call it exigent circumstances after hearing the phone ring just before the battery died. It was miraculous that the battery still had just enough charge left to point us to where we found it."

"Okay, we can get around that. However, we may have to get the FBI involved since it's a possible kidnapping case, and we should use their lab instead of the states. I'm aware of Forster Harrington's political influence, but if his son is involved in anything heinous, we don't want his influence to cause the evidence to get lost or misplaced at the state lab."

Sam immediately took issue with involving the FBI. "I understand why you might think the FBI needs to be involved, but I'm already working with the Hartford detectives. I gave them the only lead in the case and followed it up with hours of background work. I certainly don't want this to become an FBI case and give them credit and the accolades for solving a major murder case when Hartford detectives and I did all the work. I'm sure the ATF lab could do as thorough a job as the FBI's lab. Besides, it's the Hartford Police who are heading up the disappearance of the Richardson kid. They have jurisdiction in kidnapping and murder cases as well. The lieutenant in charge of the missing person unit and his detectives are willing to work jointly on this case. Since getting back to Hartford, I haven't had a chance to talk to anyone in the unit, but I believe they planned on interviewing Harrington today or tomorrow."

Murphy was concerned that since Barnes most likely hit the kid, it would be difficult to convince a jury that Harrington was guilty of a crime without sufficient evidence.

"I obviously haven't convinced you that Harrington was criminally involved, but I think I will with what else I have to tell you. There were two missing person flyers I saw at the state police unit. The second college student missing is Josh Davis, who was heading home to Massachusetts from Connecticut at the end of his school year and never made it there. The mother reported she had received a phone message from her son the day he went missing, saying he had found a ride home with a professor at the school. The message mentioned the professor drove a black BMW. That's two college kids being offered a ride by a guy driving a black BMW. That's a connection we can't overlook."

Murphy was intrigued by this additional detail and admitted it changed things. "If all of what you say is true, we still need more than what you have so far. We need to connect Harrington directly to the disappearance and death of Richardson or the other kid."

"Brian, I'm convinced we'll find the proof. But, first, we have to find out what happened to Richardson's body. My hunch is that Harrington hid the kid's body."

"Really? Where do you presume Harrington hid his body and why?"

"Where else? Right on Harrington's property, a well-secluded wooded area. When I drove up the driveway to photograph Harrington's summer home, I noticed a backhoe in the back of the house."

"Hmm. I think it's worth pursuing. I'll run it by the US attorney, Debra Durrell. She'll have the final say about the investigation and FBI's involvement."

"Brian, when you discuss the case with Durrell, mention that the state police will conduct a neighborhood search for the kid's body tomorrow. I don't believe the kid wandered from the scene after being hit. I suppose anything is possible, but I don't think that's the case. We recommended to the resident trooper that a ranking commander from state police head-quarters should call Forster Harrington to get permission to search his property. It will be interesting to learn how Harrington responds to that request. I would also appreciate it if you explain to Durrell my position on not involving the FBI."

Murphy responded, "You make an interesting point about searching Forster Harrington's property. I'll let her know, but we'll have to wait for the outcome of the search before proceeding with a full-blown kidnapping and possible murder investigation. I'll get back to you after I talk to Durrell. Let me know if the state police search results in anything and what the detectives find out from their interview with Harrington."

"Don't forget the other issue. The state may want to take over the investigation from the local police, which could allow Forster Harrington to gain influence over the direction of the investigation. Instead, we should establish a joint investigation between ATF and the Hartford Police to maintain the integrity of the case."

"I'll mention that when I talk to Durrell."

As Sam left Murphy's office, he checked in with his own office, but his call went directly to the answering service. It was after five o'clock, so if anything urgent had come up, he would have gotten a call. He decided to make it a day and headed home.

CHAPTER
23

Late the next morning, Sam contacted Trooper Simmons to ask if the search had started and if Forster Harrington approved the search of his property.

"The search party is scheduled to start at noon. We've enlisted help from citizens in the neighborhood and help from Woodhaven. Colonel Bennett reached out to Harrington yesterday. Harrington volunteered employees from his company and arranged for two Woodhaven constables to help search his property. I heard Harrington volunteered to supervise the search himself, so I asked my boss if I could be a part of searching his property. My boss insisted I supervise one of the two neighborhood search parties."

"I guess that means Jenkins and I won't be a part of searching the Harrington property."

"Detective Jenkins and her partner will be part of the search party but not at the Harrington property. But, if you want to help, come on up."

"I have appointments for the afternoon. If I can break away later on, I'll join you. Detective Jenkins and I are a team, so she'll fill me in on how the search is going."

After ending the call, Sam immediately phoned Jenkins, who answered immediately.

"Hi, Sam. I was about to call you. I think I know why you are calling. Simmons called earlier this morning about joining the search. I discussed the situation with Lieutenant Nelson, and he agreed we should be a part of it. He figured you'd be busy meeting with the US attorney. Tom Griffen and I are at the site now. I'll keep you informed about how the search is progressing."

"Thanks, Kalisha. More importantly, let me know how the search at Harrington's property went down."

Although chances were slim that the police would find the kid's body, Sam preferred not to participate in the search. He wanted to avoid the awkwardness of having his theory proven wrong if they did find him. Besides, he was more interested in gathering more evidence connecting Harrington to what happened to Richardson. His first stop was to visit the public safety office at Bushnell College to follow up on Hartford PD's request for information the campus police may have gathered on Richardson's stop at the campus before hitchhiking. Sam entered the public safety office located on the lower level of a two-story campus building. No one was at the visitors' desk, but he could see the director's office door was open. His presence at the door drew the attention of the director, who appeared to be wrapping up a phone call.

Charlie Wharton, a retired Hartford Police lieutenant in the narcotics unit, now the director of public safety on campus, recognized Sam and motioned him to come into the office and take a seat. Wharton greeted Sam with a friendly smile and a handshake.

Wharton and Sam had met previously while Wharton commanded Hartford's narcotics unit. Anytime ATF executed an arrest or search warrant in Hartford, they always coordinated with and invited the narcotics officers to assist in serving the warrant. They rehashed times they'd worked together and discussed how Wharton enjoyed retirement and his new job on a college campus. When the small talk was out of the way, Wharton asked how he could help.

"I'm working with Lieutenant Nelson regarding the missing student, Andy Richardson. I wanted to know if any of your officers came up with any additional information that may be helpful."

"I had officers immediately canvass the campus. The officers interviewed students and staff with no initial luck. We posted the missing person information in every dorm, classroom building, administration office, and the athletics complex. After the word got out, we did hear from one student."

Wharton went to his file cabinet to pull out a file to review it.

"A student named Lucas Collins came into the office and advised us he gave Richardson a ride as far as Tolland. Collins mentioned Richardson was heading to Boston to meet friends, and since Collins lived in Tolland, he offered to drive him that far. Richardson accepted the ride and got dropped off on I-84 at the Tolland exit. I can give you a copy of the report if you want. I've already sent a copy over to Lieutenant Nelson."

Sam took a copy and thanked Wharton for his help. On the way back to his car, Sam received a call from Brian Murphy, who asked him to stop by his office to discuss the case further.

*   *   *

Back in Uniondale, the neighborhood search had begun. Forster Harrington started the search at his property early with the help of volunteers from his company and two Woodhaven constables. Forster instructed his company's foreman and Constable Fred Asckis to assist him in searching the woods in the back of his home. He asked the remaining volunteers to cover the area from the road to the house and immediately call him if they found anything out of the ordinary. While in the backyard of his home, Forster recognized backhoe tracks leading into the woods. Not wanting anyone to inspect that area, he assigned his foreman to cover the area left of the tracks and Asckis, the right-side section. Forster then followed the backhoe tracks and inspected the spot where it was evident that recent digging had occurred. He could see someone had raked leaves to cover the digging area. While faking an inspection of the site, Forster got a call from one of his employees who advised him they found a baseball cap in the front woods. Forster had his foreman fetch the hat and bring it to him.

When the foreman returned with the hat, he pointed out the initials AR inside the headliner.

"Oh, yeah, my neighbor's kids run through here a lot. One of the kids is named Adam. I'll make sure to return it to the family."

Other than the hat, they found nothing else during their search of nearly two hours. Forster made sure no one saw or inspected the area where digging had taken place. Not wanting to lie to the police, Forster asked Asckis and his partner to report that they found nothing on his property to the state police. Forster then instructed his foreman to drive the volunteers back to New Haven while he went inside to check on his house. Inside his home, he cut out the initials AR from the baseball cap, rubbed dirt all over it, and buried the hat among the half-full garbage container in the garage. Once the neighborhood search concluded, Forster planned to return to the house and burn the contents of the container in the backyard. It was nearly one o'clock and time for him to get home to have dinner with his family.

*   *   *

Sam showed up at Brian Murphy's office, who advised him that the US attorney agreed that the investigation of the missing kid was worthwhile and should continue with federal involvement pending the search results for the kid's body.

"Durrell understands your position about FBI involvement, but she feels kidnapping is the FBI's jurisdiction. She knows ATF has an excellent lab, but the investigation slants toward FBI expertise, so she prefers the FBI lab to analyze the evidence found. She also wants to ensure we have an interstate nexus; otherwise, the case primarily falls to the state for prosecution. We may need the expertise of the FBI in that regard."

"Brian, I've already researched the nexus issue. My research shows that in 2006 a federal statute was enacted that contains over one hundred different provisions for protecting children. The statute expanded the reach of federal jurisdiction by redefining the existence of interstate nexus. The law establishes a nexus when the offender uses the channels or instrumentalities of interstate commerce. It would include driving a victim along an interstate highway or using a backhoe not made in Connecticut to bury the body."

Murphy was impressed. "You've done your research. Maybe you should be working in this office. I'll discuss this with my colleague, Maggie McKinney, to get her thoughts since she has prosecuted kidnapping cases. But keep in mind that if we get to the point where we can charge kidnapping federally, we may have to bring in the FBI."

"Again, I disagree. Who will be the FBI's main witness to present evidence, an FBI agent who doesn't know anything about this case? No, it's going to be the Hartford detectives and me. I'm the witness who saw the BMW pick up the kid. Detective Jenkins and I are the ones who found the evidence to date, and the detectives and I will conduct most of the remaining interviews in the case. So, are you telling me that after the detectives and I do all the work and collect all the evidence needed for prosecution, you want us to turn it over to the FBI and let them take credit for it?"

"No, no, that's not what I mean. I'm just saying that the federal kidnapping statute falls under the FBI's jurisdiction. I know that there is competitiveness between law enforcement agencies and that the FBI often usurps authority over others. However, the experts should best handle certain aspects of kidnapping cases."

Sam came right back at him. "Firearm and explosive cases are ATF's jurisdiction and expertise, yet the FBI gets involved with firearm and explosive cases all the time. Does the FBI call in ATF to take over the case? No, that's never going to happen. Besides, the FBI does not prosecute cases, your office does, and if McKinney is good at what she does, she only needs the ATF agents and Hartford detectives to succeed in the prosecution. The only involvement needed now outside of us will be the FBI lab personnel, and that's only because Durrell wants it."

Murphy surrendered. "Okay, I hear you and don't want to argue the point. I'm sure Durrell will have the last say. I'll discuss prosecutorial issues with Maggie and get back to you later."

CHAPTER
24

S am sat in his G-ride in the Hartford PD parking lot, waiting to hear from Brian Murphy. Murphy said he would call him around two o'clock. It was two fifteen already. He waited another ten minutes before his phone finally rang.

"Sam, this is Brian. I just finished a conference call with Maggie and Durrell. Durrell wants the cell phone and headlight frame sent to the FBI lab. She agreed to only use their lab for now and an FBI agent to transport the evidence there. She promised to keep the use of other FBI personnel to a minimum unless it becomes necessary to get their expertise. I will personally contact the lab and have them prioritize the analysis. I need you here at my office today to transfer the property to the agent who will transport the evidence to the lab. We need to maintain the proper chain of custody."

"I'm at the PD now to meet with Lieutenant Nelson. I don't know how long I'll be here, but I assume it won't exceed an hour or two. I'll contact you as soon the meeting is over, and I'm on my way back to my office. Listen, Brian, I have no issues with the FBI. I'm only concerned that involving them will result in this case becoming an FBI public relations event and negate the work the detectives and I have done."

Sam ended the call, entered the PD, and got escorted to the lieutenant's office, where Marcus Nelson was alone. The lieutenant told

Sam he received a call from Colonel Bennett regarding the hit-and-run accident in front of Harrington's property. "The colonel questioned who should maintain custody of the evidence found at the scene. I told him we were maintaining the evidence since we suspect there may have been foul play before the kid got hit by the truck. If the state finds his body, we may consider a different strategy. Until then, we will maintain custody of the evidence until we complete our investigation. Then, we will turn the evidence over to the state. The colonel was adamant about taking custody of the evidence if they find the kid's body. That's where we stand on that issue. Let's consider interviewing Zake Barnes rather than waiting for the lab results."

Sam disagreed. He thought it was better to interview Barnes once the lab confirmed the headlight frame contained Richardson's blood. "If his blood is not on the headlight frame, the state could have it, but not the phone. We need to contact the Richardson family and, without revealing too much detail, let them know we found their son's cell phone and a headlight frame at the scene of a hit-and-run accident and that a search is underway for Andy. We should explain that we are running a trace on his cell number to determine any calls made by Andy that night. Let them know we need the passcode on Andy's cell phone. Maybe one of the family members knows the passcode. Also, we need Andy's blood type and a DNA sample from his mom. That's all we should mention other than we are making good progress and will keep them updated."

"I'll make the call," responded Nelson. "Regarding our interview with Richard Harrington, Detective Griffen and I met with him. He claimed he didn't pick up a hitchhiker on I-84 that night. He said he didn't feel well, went straight home after work, and spent the night in bed. Harrington confirmed his father has a summer home in Uniondale, but he hasn't been there since last fall. We asked about his car, and he conceded no one borrowed or stole it as far as he knew. He avoided answering additional questions and ended the interview by saying any further contact with him needs to go through his attorney."

"I'm not surprised. I figured he would lawyer up right away and not say a word, but you at least got Harrington to admit his car wasn't stolen or loaned to anyone. One thing's for sure; you got him worried. Anyway, can I review the investigative file on Josh Davis?"

After reviewing the Davis file, Sam had further recommendations. "We need to get as much information on Davis as possible, including his cell phone number and names of his closest friends at school. Maybe someone at the school saw the guy in the BMW and could identify him. We should also find out if there is a connection between other missing college-age students in Connecticut to a black BMW. More importantly, let's formalize a joint task force to go full throttle with additional manpower where it's needed. The US. Attorney's office is on board with working jointly on this case." Nelson agreed and said he would discuss a joint task force with his chief.

Sam left the PD and called Murphy to let him know he was on the way to meet him. Sam returned to his office to obtain the evidence from his office safe and met the FBI agent waiting with Murphy. Sam turned over the cell phone and headlight frame in separate sealed evidence envelopes to FBI Agent Tom Perkins. Both agents signed each other's chain of evidence documents.

"Lieutenant Nelson is reaching out to the Richardson family for their son's blood type and a DNA sample from his mother to confirm the biological relationship. Nelson will also find out if the family knows the passcode for Andy's cell phone. Hopefully, we'll know the passcode by the end of the day," said Sam, who provided Agent Perkins with the details on how to get in touch with the Richardson family. Once Perkins left the office, Sam requested Murphy to authorize an ATF-Hartford Police joint task force to coordinate the Harrington investigation.

"I had discussed a joint investigation with Durrell a few minutes ago. Her position is we must maintain control over the direction of the investigation. She agreed to meet with the Hartford Police Chief and the Lieutenant to discuss protocol. She agrees the investigation should remain with ATF and the Hartford Police for now with state police involvement on an as-needed basis only."

Sam's cell phone rang. Pulling the phone from his pocket, he took the call from Lieutenant Nelson. The lieutenant briefed Sam on what Detective Jenkins reported regarding the state's search for the missing kid. He then repeated the information to Murphy. "Nelson's detectives reported that Forster Harrington insisted he and several of his chosen volunteers from his construction company and two Woodhaven Police constables search his property. Unfortunately, the state police agreed to Harrington's request. To no one's surprise, Harrington's search of his own property found nothing, and neither did the state's search. Also, Mrs. Richardson agreed to provide a DNA sample and provide Richardson's blood type. She and her husband didn't know the passcode, but they spoke with their daughter, who did know it. I'll give you the passcode so you can relay it to Agent Perkins."

"Sounds like Harrington doesn't want anything damaging found on his property," said Murphy.

"I suspected he would try something like this to protect his son. Since I have your attention, Brian, I need to fill in my boss on what has transpired in this case. He might ask why I'm involved in an investigation outside our jurisdiction. I'd like you to support my involvement in this joint investigation. My boss might call you. I ask that you mention this could be a major, high-profile case and that I'm a key figure in the investigation."

Murphy agreed. "If he has any questions or concerns, tell him to call me direct."

That's what Sam wanted to hear. Sam answered an incoming call as he walked out of the US attorney's office. Trooper Simmons called to fill in Sam about Forster Harrington searching his own property with Constable Fred Asckis helping him. Simmons added their search turned up negative for finding Richardson's body. Also, the divers were still searching the lake and claimed they'd finish by the end of the day.

"I heard about the search of Harrington's property already from HPD, but thanks for calling to let me know about the search at the lake."

"No problem. You previously wanted me to ask Officer Reed if he had ever observed a truck and trailer going into or leaving the Harrington property within the last month or so. He did see a truck leaving the property during that time frame. He recognized the truck's logo, Atlas Excavation. It's a small one-man operation located just over the state line in Saundersville, Massachusetts. The guy's name is Randy Flemming. Reed said his father had used this guy once for a small job at his place. His father remembers Flemming mentioning he does contract work for Harrington's construction company. But, here's the interesting part. A record check on Flemming disclosed he did time for sexual contact with minors, so he's a registered sex offender."

"Interesting. The more we find out, the weirder this case gets, and the more it gives credence to my theory. Thanks for the callback, Curtis. The Hartford detectives plan on interviewing Zake Barnes, and I assume you'd like to be part of it."

Simmons responded, "Definitely."

"I expected that you would. The Hartford detectives and I want to keep the details of our investigation in-house to avoid any possible political influence that could hamper the investigation."

Simmons replied, "Well, I can tell you that the governor's chief of staff, I think his name is Freedman or something like that, contacted the barracks commander asking questions about why we were at the Harrington property."

"What did he tell him?" asked Sam.

"He told him we were investigating an accident near the property. The commander had pumped me for details. I wanted to be up-front with him since he's my boss, and he wanted me to keep him in the loop."

"Okay, was there any mention of Harrington picking up a hitchhiker and taking him to Uniondale?"

Simmons paused before answering. "Yeah, I told him you saw a black BMW stop and pick up a hitchhiker and then take the exit for Uniondale."

"Shit, I'm sure Freedman was asking questions at the request of Harrington's father."

Sam was pissed but didn't reflect his anger. Instead, he informed Simmons he'd be in touch regarding the interview of Barnes once the lab results came back. Sam then hung up before Simmons could ask what lab would examine the evidence.

When Sam got home, he called his boss, Steve Roberts. It was after normal business hours, but surprisingly, Roberts was still in the office and answered the phone. Sam spent the next half hour going over the preliminary investigation of Richard Harrington, including his coordination with the US Attorney's office and the Hartford Police.

As expected, Roberts questioned ATF's jurisdiction in such a case and why it took so long for him to report what he was doing. Sam answered his boss's questions the best he could, explaining his role in the investigation and having the US Attorney's backing for a joint effort with HPD. Roberts listened to Sam's explanation, which alleviated most of his concerns, but he didn't have the final say. "The SAC will most likely contact Murphy to get further details, and he'll probably want to know the extent of the FBI's role in the investigation."

CHAPTER
25

ate Saturday afternoon, Forster Harrington's daughter, Rachel, her husband, Mark Peterson, and their daughter, Olivia, arrived at the Harrington home. After greetings, hugs, and kisses, Forster asked to speak to his daughter alone.

"What's up, Dad? Anything wrong?" asked Rachel.

"No, no, I just wanted to make sure everything was good with you and the family. How are things going at the statehouse?" quizzed Harrington.

"Everything at work is fine. My boss praises my work and is prepping me for a promotion. Mark is also doing great at his job. He gets along well with his boss, who recently gave him a bump in pay. Olivia is a perfect kid, very happy and playful, and loves to read, but we do spoil her something awful."

Forster smiled and was pleased all was going so well and that he was very proud of her. He paused before asking, "How is Dickie doing? Do you two ever talk at work, and if so, how would you say he is doing there? Does he seem happy?"

Rachel looked puzzled by all the questions. "Dad, you still call him Dickie? He's a grown man now. He is not little Dickie anymore. Anyway, I don't see Richard that often."

Just then, Richard entered the room to say hi, and the three hugged each other. Forster asked Rachel to help her mother with dinner while he had a chat with Richard

"How are things at work, Dickie?" asked his dad.

"Everything is fine, I think. Why, did you hear otherwise?"

"No, of course not. We haven't talked or seen each other for a while, and I just wanted to make sure everything is good with you."

"Yeah, I guess everything is fine. No need to worry, Dad."

Forster sat back on the cushioned chair and stared at Richard trying to assess his son's pretense.

The look on his father's face concerned Richard. "Is everything okay, Dad?"

"I'm going to ask you a question, and I want you to be up-front with me. I want the truth no matter what. Understand?"

With his heart accelerating and anxiety spiking, Richard hesitated before answering. "Uh, yeah, Dad. What is it?"

"A couple of weeks ago, did you pick up a college student hitchhiking and drive him to our home in Uniondale? The truth, Son."

Richard averted his dad's gaze. "Where is this coming from? Why would I pick up a hitchhiker and bring him to our place in Uniondale?"

With anger written all over his face, Forster amplified his demand. "Dammit, Dickie, I want the truth!"

"I'm not lying, Dad."

"I asked you a question, and you answered with a question. Now answer my question. Did you or did you not pick up a hitchhiker on I-84 and take him to Uniondale? Tell me the truth!"

Richard's face flushed red while his forehead blossomed with specks of perspiration. He cupped his face in his hands, trying to hide his discomfort. Knowing the Hartford Police questioned him about the same issue, he wondered how his father could possibly know about it. His mind worked overtime, thinking about how he should answer his father. The first thought that came to mind was to have Randy remove the backhoe from the property.

"Dickie, the police and the feds are investigating the disappearance of a young college student hitchhiking, and someone saw you pick him up and drive to Uniondale. The state police called me asking permission to search my Uniondale property. They said there was a hit-and-run accident in front of my home, and they think the victim may have been injured and wandered off looking for help. Unfortunately, I can't put the wheels in motion to help you if you're going to lie to me."

While his right leg nervously bounced up and down, Richard realized the opening his father gave him and went with it. "It was an accident, Dad. The kid ran through the woods and out into the street, where he got hit by a truck. I saw it."

It was evident to Forster that his son was uneasy as he explained what had happened. "Dad, the truck driver might not have seen the kid because of the heavy fog that night. After he hit the kid, he just took off. I didn't know what to do. I was afraid. I thought the kid was dead, but I heard him moaning."

This confused Forster. "Why would you be afraid? The guy in the truck hit the kid, not you. He's the one at fault. Why didn't you call for an ambulance or the police?"

Richard said nothing. He just sat there on edge.

"Dickie, I'm your father, I love you, and I will help you. I'll do anything to protect you, but I don't know how to do that without knowing what happened. Why did you pick this kid up in the first place and take him to Uniondale? And why was he running through the woods? It doesn't make sense. Tell me why the police might be looking at you for something this truck driver did? I need to know everything. I can't fix what I don't know. Now tell me the whole story, and don't leave anything out."

Forster's wife, Patricia, came into the room with a concerned look as she stared at the two of them. "What's going on here? What's all this shouting about?"

"Just a difference of opinion. It's nothing. Give us a few minutes, and we'll be in for dinner," answered Forster.

His wife didn't look pleased with her husband's answer, shaking her head in exasperation as she left the room.

Forster waited for Richard's answer. Richard couldn't look at his father directly but reluctantly told his father why he couldn't call the police. When he got to the part about having sex with the kid, his father stopped him. Forster's face grew flushed with rage. He squirmed in the chair as his body tensed up, completely frustrated. He mumbled indistinguishable words to himself. He pushed himself back into the cushioned chair, looking up at the ceiling with closed eyes. He appeared to be counting back numbers to reach a more relaxed state. Finally, he leaned forward and was more composed to ask a question he felt his son had no acceptable answer to. "Was the sex consensual?"

With his eyes glued to the floor, Dickie knew he had to downplay what really happened. "It started consensual, but when it was over, the kid got nervous and just ran out the door into the woods."

Forster was sure his son wasn't telling him the truth, but he had heard enough for now. He felt pain in his chest as his heart raced rapidly. He wanted to avoid repeating what had happened to his father. Feeling lightheaded and trying to reduce his stress, Forster looked at his son with pity and concern. He then sat back in his chair and spoke calmly.

"Dickie, a friend of mine, who was a cop, will be joining us for dinner. Afterward, I want you to tell me and my friend everything that happened, from the beginning, without leaving out a single detail. Then after we know everything, my friend and I will decide on how to fix this and hopefully make it go away. But you have to give us every frigging little detail without leaving out a single thread of truth. Do you understand, Dickie?"

Richard grudgingly nodded in agreement while wiping away tear-filled eyes. Forster made it very clear to his son to be on his best behavior while the investigation continued. At that point, Forster stood up, patted his son on the back, and left the room to join the rest of the family.

That afternoon everyone seated at the dining room table was upbeat in their conversation. Now joined by Tony Dellagatti and his girlfriend, Angie, the Harrington family reminisced about the old days, telling stories and occasional jokes that filled the room with laughter and compliments to the cook for the delicious food and wine.

Richard, however, was detached from the pleasant conversation. Uneasy, with the feeling of butterflies in his stomach and a pounding headache, Richard was virtually absent from the talk around the table. Occasionally, he'd crack a fake smile while others laughed and enjoyed themselves. He stared out into open space, agonizing about his father's demand to know everything that happened that night.

When it was time to clean the table and help with the dishes, Forster asked for a private moment with his son and Tony. They moved to Forster's office, where he asked his son to describe every detail of what happened that night and not leave anything out.

Hesitant to tell such a sordid story, especially to someone outside the family, Richard hoped that his dad, and the former police officer, could keep him out of trouble.

Tony listened to Richard tell his story about what happened when he picked up the hitchhiker. Of course, he wasn't shocked to hear such a sleazy account of what Richard had done since he always felt Richard was a little odd and it wasn't like Tony hadn't committed similar or, even worse, scandalous acts. However, not mentioned was the part about what became of the kid. Having seen recent digging in the backwoods of his property, Forster refused to accept what might have happened to the kid. He wanted to believe the injured kid was alive and could walk away and seek help somehow.

Tony was indebted to Forster for all that he had done for him. After serving in the army and working at Forster's construction company, Tony asked him for help to become a cop. Since Forster was a principal donor to the New Haven mayor's campaign, he used his influence to get Tony hired as a New Haven police officer. With Harrington's help, Tony managed to graduate from the police academy by the thinnest of margins. However, it didn't take long for Tony to mess things up as a police officer, and he ultimately was terminated by the police department.

Too often, Tony used excessive force, foul language, and bullying when dealing with the suspects and the general public. In addition, he didn't get along with his sergeant because he reminded Tony of the know-it-all kids he bullied in high school. Tony's boss gave him multiple written warnings to improve his behavior and performance, but he didn't heed them. As a result, his boss suspended him without pay for a month. During the suspension, Tony took a side job with a known loan shark. His responsibility was to convince those who borrowed money to pay up or endure severe pain. When his suspension ended, and he was back on the job as a police officer, he continued with his lucrative side occupation as an enforcer for the loan shark. However, not long afterward, he was arrested during a police loan sharking sting and charged with aiding and abetting an illegal enterprise and assault and battery. The arrest resulted in the police department terminating him.

Forster Harrington hired a top-notch attorney to represent him on the pending charges. The attorney arranged for the charges to get reduced through a plea bargain deal. Tony ended up serving no time, only probation and community service. Money talks, and Tony walks. Forster put Tony back on the company payroll as a trusted confidant and fixer. Tony had a persuasive temperament to convince adversaries that it was better to do it Forster's way or else.

After Richard's confession, Forster asked his son to leave the room. Forster needed privacy so Tony and he could work on a plan. During the next several minutes, Tony suggested ways a scheme might work and described three different scenarios to his mentor, who liked certain parts of all three.

"Tony, do you still get together with Rocco Marcello?"

"Yeah, boss. We get together now and then for drinks, talking about the ole days on the team."

"Good. We'll need Rocco's help. I'll think about your suggestions and come up with a workable plan. Meet me tomorrow morning at our usual café around nine. Call Rocco and see if he can join us. We'll agree on a plan together and put it into practice."

Tony grinned in acceptance. "Sounds good, boss. I'll call him, and I'll be there in the morning."

Forster gave Tony a stern look. "I want it to happen soon with no screw-ups."

CHAPTER
26

On Monday morning, Sam received a call from Detective Jenkins informing him she and Griffen monitored the search of the lake for Richardson Sunday midafternoon. "The search continued after we left, but I got a call minutes ago that they finished there and found nothing. I'm with you on this one, Sam. I believe Richard Harrington is responsible for the kid's disappearance. We have to move forward with our investigation."

"Thanks for the heads-up, Kalisha. Now that the search has ended, I'll push for the US attorney's office to put this investigation into high gear."

It was close to two in the afternoon when Sam wiped his desk clean and secured his office. He planned to go to the gym near home and then later meet his son, Drew, for dinner. Sam informed his assistant he wouldn't be returning for the rest of the day. The phone rang as he was heading for the door.

"Oh no. Peg, tell them I'm out on the road if it's for me."

Peg, holding her hand over the receiver, whispered, "It's Ziggy."

Sam took the call. "Ziggy, I hope you are not calling for anything that requires my presence. I'm about to head to the gym."

"I thought we could meet at the café I mentioned Saturday on the way home. You know, the place where those lovely gals were staring at me the whole time we were there."

"All I know was the sexy blonde was looking at me, not you."

"Ha, in your dreams. Anyway, we're both out of luck because I'm just kidding. I'm calling to let you know that Terry Baker called to say they're all set for the UC buy-bust tomorrow night. He asked me to call you in case you wanted to help out with the arrest. We could go out for a cocktail afterward with Jennifer and Pete. They volunteered to help out with the arrest too."

"That sounds okay with me. I'll be there."

"We're supposed to be at the task force office for a four o'clock briefing. The buy goes down at seven."

"Let's work an adjusted day. I'm sure we'll be working late into the evening. I can meet you for lunch at the bakery café again down the road near you. Let's meet at two tomorrow afternoon."

"See you then at the café."

Sam left the office in a hurry to squeeze in a good workout at the gym. He worked out for nearly two hours, first running three miles on the treadmill and then ending his routine using fourteen different pieces of weight-stacked equipment to tone and strengthen his muscles. Then, back at his apartment, he showered, dressed, and headed out to meet his son for dinner.

Twenty minutes later, he was seated at the restaurant and ordered a glass of Chardonnay while waiting for Drew. Drew arrived fifteen minutes late, blaming heavy traffic for his delay.

"So, how are you doing in school, Drew?"

"I'm doing good. So far, I'm averaging a B with the studies. I'm happy with how it's going so far."

"Are you dating the same girl you introduced me to a few weeks back? She seemed nice, attractive, and smart."

"Uh, nope. Too many issues got in the way, so we're not dating anymore. I had a date with another girl a few nights ago, and so far, so good."

The two of them ordered dinner. Sam and Drew were close, and their conversation was more like two friends conversing than the typical father-to-son talk. While they enjoyed dessert, Drew asked about the kid from Bushnell College that was missing.

"What's the story about that kid? I'm thinking about attending school there, but I wonder if there are safety problems at an inner-city school. Do you know anything about it?"

"All I can say is it's only in the preliminary stage, and since it's an ongoing investigation, I can't say much. However, I don't think you would have to worry about safety at that school. Whatever happened to that kid, it didn't happen on or near campus."

Sam couldn't tell his son that a suspect was under investigation for abduction and murder of the kid.

CHAPTER
27

S am and Ziggy met for lunch at a local bakery café as planned on Tuesday afternoon. It was a lovely sunny day but a little cooler at forty-eight degrees. Sam enjoyed their chatter, as he could always depend on Ziggy to lighten the mood with a hilarious story. After lunch, they headed out to the task force office.

Upon arrival, Baker thanked them for helping out. "We need all the bodies we can get on this one. These guys are always armed."

Sam enjoyed getting out of the office and working in the field with his team. "There's nothing like a buy-bust to get the juices flowing, Terry. There's no excitement reviewing reports behind a desk. I'm sure I don't have to tell you that. So, no thanks necessary. We're here to help."

Sam and Agents Ziglar, Macheski, and Clarkson attended the briefing. Sam considered these three his top three performing agents who always volunteered to help others in the office. Statistically, Pete led the office with the most cases sent for prosecution, with Ziggy and Jennifer right behind him. All three did most of the undercover assignments. However, Jennifer was the most successful, especially in the inner cities. Being an attractive woman of color with fluency in Spanish, she was good at blending in and getting accepted by the street gangs and drug dealers. Sam had an excellent collegial relationship with the three of them and considered them friends.

Baker's briefing identified where the buy was going down and summed up the overall operational plan and assignments. "I don't want all the cover vehicles to arrive at the same time. Try alternating your arrivals about five minutes apart and blend in with all the other cars there. Ensure you're in position by six forty."

Eight unmarked police sedans would surround the area of the drug buy, with two officers in each vehicle. In addition, two marked state police cruisers hid away from where the deal would occur. Baker would signal them in at the time of the arrest. Once the briefing was over, Sam contacted his boss regarding their participation in the undercover operation.

A short time later, the units began arriving at the designated location. Sam was assigned to ride with Agent Clarkson, and Ziggy rode with Macheski. While in position, the covering officers waited in anticipation of the arrest following the drug buy. There was always a tad of uneasiness before an arrest, especially when the suspects were armed. Using the undercover name Ace, the UC Agent Acevedo was alone, awaiting the suspect, Tato, and his associates to arrive. The UC officer was most vulnerable during a drug buy, especially when alone and surrounded by three armed drug dealers. Not all officers seek to work undercover. It requires self-confidence, complete composure, and fortitude. The UC agent depends on competent backup officers to respond in seconds if an operation goes wrong.

It was several minutes after seven, and Tato was a no-show. Many planned operations, such as drug buys, often went by the wayside because the dealer didn't show up.

"Let's be alert if this bust goes down," Sam said to Jennifer.

"Will do, boss. I have a young daughter, so I always want to go home to her at the end of the day."

"I've never met your daughter. I plan to take everyone at the office out for dinner to show my appreciation for doing such a great job. I hope you can bring her along. Her name is Jalissa, right?"

"Yes. She's the love of my life. She's going to be seven years old next month. But, wait—hang on, I think that's the Mercedes circling the parking lot, boss."

"Yeah, that's him. By the way, my name is Sam, not boss, okay, Jen?"

"Got it, boss. I mean Sam."

Twenty minutes after seven, Tato, driving his black Mercedes, circled the Walmart parking lot, checking for a police presence. He slowly circled twice before approaching Ace's position, where he parked away from most cars in the lot. Tato parked adjacent to Ace's silver Mustang. He and two of his associates exited their vehicle. Ace wore a transmitter as part of his cell phone attached to his belt. All the covering officers would hear the conversation between Ace and Tato.

"Ace, my man, I'm in a rush tonight. I got the product. Now let's see the cash," said Tato.

"I'll show you the money when I see the product, bro," replied Ace.

Tato turned to his associates with a smile on his face. "Ya believe this shit? The man don't wanna trust me, eh?"

When Tato turned to his associates, his unzipped jacket revealed a gun tucked in his waist. He nodded to one of his associates, carrying a brown paper bag. The associate stepped forward, opened the bag, and pulled out a clear plastic-wrapped white brick.

"I need to test a sample, bro," said Ace.

Tato nodded again to his associate, who brought the brick close to Ace. Ace made a small cut using a sharp blade and lifted a bit of white powder from the brick onto the blade's tip. He emptied it into a small vial to mix with a testing agent inside while Tato's associate stepped back with the brick toward Tato.

"Looks good," said Ace while nodding his head in the affirmative, letting the covering officers know it was cocaine, including the officers in the van video recording the transaction. Ace walked back to the trunk of his car, took out a black canvas bag, and stepped back toward Tato with the bag open to show Tato the cash inside. Tato had a broad smile seeing all that money. "Dat looks mighty fine, Ace. Whatcha think, boys?" Tato faced his associates and nodded his signal. All three pulled out guns while Tato shouted, "Drop da bag, Ace, and back away, or I'll put you down, man!"

With his hands high in the air, Ace stepped back. "Okay, bro, don't do anythin' stupid. I'm walkin' back. There are a lot of people shopping here. You don't want any witnesses."

Seeing the suspects pull out their guns, Sergeant Baker instantly ordered, "All officers move in now!"

One of Tato's associates grabbed the money and moved backed toward the Mercedes. As Tato turned toward his car to leave, all eight police sedans moved from their discrete positions toward Tato's Mercedes with their police emergency lights flashing.

Seeing the police, Tato's associates dropped the cash and brick and ran toward a fence instead of getting trapped in Tato's car. Tato, caught completely by surprise, was about to slide into his car but saw the police cars surrounding his vehicle. Boxed in with no place to move, Tato thought about running, but it was too late as police quickly surrounded him with guns pointed at him. He dropped his weapon and raised his hands as officers ordered him to his knees.

Five officers, including Sam, Jennifer, Macheski, and two task force members, chased after the two suspects on the run. The suspects ran around the end of a fence and into an open field.

As Sam ran into the field to join the officers, he heard a shot fired and immediately felt a stinging sensation in his left arm. He got hit by the bullet but continued to run after the suspects. His arm felt like it was on fire.

With his running shoes on, Sam made up ground on one of the suspects, shouting, "Stop, police."

The ground was soft and a bit soggy from previous rainfall. Sam was a lightweight compared to the guy he was chasing. As he closed in on the guy, he figured the guy at just shy of six feet tall but the better part of, if not more than, two hundred and fifty pounds.

Knowing he was at a considerable disadvantage size-wise, Sam lunged and tackled the big guy at his ankles. He then quickly moved on top of the suspect's back just as the guy, with a gun in his hand, swung his left arm around, hitting Sam in his head, causing a two-inch gash. Sam instinctively grabbed a tight hold on the pistol's barrel to prevent it from sliding along the frame, effectively hindering the gun from firing a round.

With his superior size, the suspect tried to overpower Sam. With his grip tightening around the barrel and frame, Sam yelled for help. Pete Macheski was there in seconds and shoved his gun in the suspect's face screaming, "Let go of the gun, asshole, or I'm going to blow your brains out."

The suspect submitted and released his grip on the pistol. Sam quickly pulled it away from him and swiped the gun across the guy's face saying, "That's for shooting at us, asshole!"

The suspect yelled, "Fuck! That hurt, man! I neva shot at ya. It was'n me!"

Pete rolled the guy onto his stomach and cuffed him while keeping his knee on his back. "Jen, check the gun!" commanded Sam.

Jennifer received the gun from Sam, removed the magazine, and ejected the round in the chamber. She took a sniff at the open chamber. "Sam, this gun hasn't been fired."

"I tol' ya, man, I neva shot at yooz."

Macheski needed help from Sam to pull the heavy suspect up off the ground. As Sam trailed behind them, Jen and Macheski slowly escorted the suspect back to the parking lot. The culprit who had fired the round escaped, but thankfully the task force members had previously identified him from photos they had taken during the first undercover drug buy. They'll find him. The police knew where he lived and hung out.

When they returned to the parking lot, Sam, Jennifer, and Pete learned the round that winged Sam also hit the driver-side window of a task force vehicle, just missing an officer standing close by. The scene at the Walmart parking lot became chaotic, with store patrons gathering around to see what was going on. Police were all over the scene, and once the press got word, news vans started to arrive.

Sergeant Baler asked Agent Clarkson to take Sam to the local hospital, where it was learned the bullet only grazed his arm. A doctor cleaned and bandaged the wound and the gash on Sam's head. A nurse finished cleaning the scratches on his hand.

It wasn't long before Baker arrived at the hospital to check on Sam. Once he saw Sam was okay, he thanked him and the agents for their support and asked Jennifer to take Sam back to his car so he could head home rather than report back to the task force office. Baker announced, "We put out an all-points bulletin on the suspect that got away. If he tries shooting at us again, we'll take him to the morgue instead of the lockup."

Agent Jennifer Clarkson drove Sam back to his car. "How are you feeling, Sam? I know you might feel okay now, but you'll feel it more tomorrow."

"Yeah, I'm okay. The doc gave me some painkillers if needed. Do me a favor. When you get to the task force office, let everyone know from me they did great out there. That goes for you too, Jen. I'm glad everyone's going home safe tonight."

Sam wanted to stay with the group, but it was late; he was tired and still coming down from the adrenaline high. His arm felt sore, and the gash on his forehead throbbed and ached.

He decided to stop at the drive-up window at a restaurant on his drive home and pick up a sandwich. He was famished since he hadn't eaten since two. Once at his apartment, he relaxed while eating but couldn't help thinking back to the scene chasing down the suspect. He thought he was nuts for tackling that guy who was twice his size. However, although it was nerve-wracking, he felt it was part of the job.

Sam was aware of the hazards on the job, but it was more dangerous now than in years past. He gave considerable thought to his responsibilities, not only supervising the agents in Hartford but also supervising and participating in high-risk operations as a member of the Special Response Team. He needed to reassess how much one guy could do. It was enough anxiety just ensuring his agents got home safely to their families.

After eating, he called his boss and gave him a detailed report on the buy-bust operation, including his injury. His boss recommended he take the rest of the week off.

"We're too busy here for me to take time off right now. I'm fine. I'll be in the office tomorrow to send a report on this arrest. I also need to coordinate with the Hartford PD and the US attorney's office on the case we're jointly working on."

"Incidentally, I briefed the SAC on that kidnapping case, and he approved you working it with Hartford. It certainly sounds like a high-profile investigation. Good luck with it, and great job tonight."

Sam appreciated the compliment from his boss and started to prepare his report on the night's arrest. It took a while to finish the report since he lost concentration at times, thinking back to the night's episode. When he finally finished the report, Sam was ready for bed as it was already eleven o'clock. While undressing, he noticed his wallet was missing from his back pocket. Thinking back to when he stopped for takeout, Sam remembered leaving it on the front seat. So, he zipped up his trousers and went outside to retrieve his wallet from the G-ride, parked next to his personal car in the outdoor carport.

Once in bed, the soreness from Sam's arm wound intensified. It was the first time on the job someone had shot at him, never mind wounding him. He tried not to dwell on it any further, but the anxiety hadn't yet totally dissipated. Sam tossed and turned for a while until finally fading into sleep.

CHAPTER
28

Shortly after eleven o'clock, a woman exited the Manchester Value Inn adjacent to the Manchester Mall not far from Sam's apartment. The woman, carrying a large shoulder bag leisurely walked toward the parking lot.

A black four-door sedan appeared and followed slowly behind her. She was oblivious to the car until it abruptly stopped beside her. The driver's door swung open, and a man dressed in dark clothes rushed toward the woman. The driver confronted her, resulting in a struggle. The woman's arms flailed at her attacker's head. The assailant appeared to punch or stab the woman in the midsection until her body slumped over. The sedan's trunk lifted open. The assailant dragged the woman toward the rear of the car and lifted her body into the trunk. The attacker had his face covered with a black neck gaiter. While closing the trunk, the assaulter looked around the parking lot to ensure no one saw what happened and then quickly slid back into the car and drove off as the car door slammed shut. The black sedan circled the lot and exited it. It all happened in a matter of minutes, and then it was all quiet.

*   *   *

The next evening, two men, one tall and rugged-looking and the other slender and much shorter, walked into the Manchester Value Inn, flashed their police badges at the check-in clerk, and asked to speak to the manager. When the manager arrived a few minutes later, the rugged-looking of the two men showed his badge identifying them as police officers and said he had received information that a murder had occurred in the hotel parking lot the night before. He said they were there to check if the hotel CCTV security system had captured the incident.

The manager noticed the badges were not those of the Manchester Police Department and asked to see photo identification. The shorter guy pulled out a photo identification for the manager to examine. "Shouldn't the Manchester or state police be investigating?" asked the manager.

The shorter guy stood dumbfounded, glancing at his partner for an answer.

"We are part of a statewide task force made up of officers from the state police and five other local departments where similar murders have occurred. We suspect this guy may be a serial killer. We need to identify this guy before he kills another woman. After seeing if your security camera system captured anything, we would notify the Manchester Police to assist the task force in identifying the killer. Your cooperation will go a long way in helping law enforcement stop this guy before he kills again."

The manager was upset that a murder had occurred in the hotel's parking lot. However, he understood it was necessary to cooperate with law enforcement and thought his assistance might be instrumental in the police arresting a serial killer. Furthermore, if his cooperation helped get the killer, he could earn recognition from management and the police, so he asked the two officers to follow him to the security room.

The security room had four monitors, two digital video recorders, and high-resolution LED monitors atop a long desk. The monitors were split into six screens for viewing different areas of the hotel. Three monitors covered the exterior areas, including the front parking, and a fourth monitor covered interior zones, including the main lobby and check-in desk. The manager searched the previous night's recording for the time the detectives requested, just after 11:00 p.m. He selected play on the DVR, and a moment later, the sequence of the incident began.

The three of them watched a woman walk out to the parking lot as a dark-colored car came into the picture, slowly following behind her. The car pulled alongside the woman and stopped. The driver exited and began to assault her. It appeared he stabbed the woman multiple times before throwing her lifeless body into the car's trunk and speeding away. The Connecticut license plate on the car was visible.

"We're going to need a copy of the video since it is evidence of an apparent murder. Don't record over the original. Maintain it in a secure location until called to produce the original in court. Understand?" said the rugged officer.

The manager took a sheet of paper with the hotel letterhead and logo and prepared a receipt for the officers to sign. "You will have to sign a receipt. I'll need you to legibly sign and print your name, department, and badge numbers. I'll need to see your badges and identification again to ensure the accuracy of your signatures."

The two officers scribbled their signatures and badge numbers on the receipt. The manager saw they were indistinguishable, so he asked, "You'll have to print your names so I can read them. I can't make out your signatures."

Once satisfied, the manager viewed their badges, copied the sequence of the incident onto a flash drive, and turned it over to the officers. "I would like a contact number from one of you, so I could call you if there are any questions."

The shorter officer gave him his cell number, which the manager wrote on the receipt. The manager shook hands with the officers and handed them his business card. "My name is Mitchell Brooks, and my direct number is on the card. If you need any additional assistance from the hotel, please call me."

The officers thanked him and left the hotel with grins on their faces.

About thirty minutes later, the tall, rugged officer called his boss that all had gone well, and he secured the video. His boss provided instructions regarding where to turn over the video to the appropriate prosecutor. More importantly, he reminded the officer to complete the rest of the assignment immediately as planned. After the call ended, the officer's boss called the prosecutor with a message. "Based on information from a confidential source, the police obtained a copy of a security camera video that captured a potential murder. I've arranged for the officer to turn the video over to you. This video evidence will get headlines for not only solving a homicide but, more significantly, because of who committed the murder. You'll be on local and national news, as a result."

CHAPTER
29

On Thursday afternoon, after completing the review of investigative reports, Sam decided to surveil the statehouse garage with the hope of catching Harrington leaving work early. Fifteen minutes later, he positioned his G-ride across the statehouse exit artery.

As luck would have it, he only had to wait thirty minutes before observing the black beamer take a right onto Capitol Hill Drive and then turn onto the entrance ramp for I-84 East toward Boston.

Sam quickly moved into traffic and took the entrance ramp. He managed to maintain sufficient distance from the BMW. Sam was uniquely aware of all the surveillance techniques used to avoid detection. Stationary surveillance can be monotonous, but moving surveillance was more of an art. Nevertheless, he maintained the proper distance to avoid detection.

He followed the beamer over the Connecticut River Bridge into East Hartford and through the various turns and streets until he saw the BMW turn into the Main Street Tavern parking lot.

Sam drove slowly into the parking lot and remained away from where Harrington parked. Sam observed Harrington walk into the tavern's rear entrance from his vantage point. Sam then found a parking space hidden but closer to Harrington's car. He opened the passenger-side window and snapped a picture of the car's rear, capturing the license plate number, DICKH 1.

Sam exited his car, entered the tavern's front entrance, and seated himself at the bar. He asked the barmaid for a menu and a cup of coffee and scanned the bar and the dining area tables for Harrington but didn't see him. When the barmaid returned with a menu and the coffee, he noticed her name tag on her sweater. "Kim, I'm meeting a friend who called me a few minutes ago and said he was already here, but I don't see him anywhere."

"Maybe your friend is in the restroom."

"Ah, why didn't I think of that? Where are the restrooms?"

Sam waited a few more minutes for Harrington to appear, but he didn't. Then, finally, the bartender returned and told him the specials and said she'd be back in a few minutes to take his order. Sam sipped his coffee and decided to check the men's room.

At the end of the bar, he followed the sign for the restrooms. The ladies' room was on the left and the men's room on the right down the hall. Straight ahead were two swinging doors he figured were the entrance to the kitchen. He entered the men's room, but it was empty. He washed his hands and returned to the bar.

Sam had seen Harrington come into the restaurant but wondered if he'd left right afterward. *Did he notice me following him and ducked back out when I entered the front?*

He signaled the barmaid over. "I checked the men's room for my friend, but no one was in there."

The bartender looked at him and smiled. He smiled back with a puzzled look.

"Did your friend mention that he would meet you in the back room?" she asked.

"No, he just said to meet him here at the tavern. Is the back room part of the tavern?"

"Yes, hon, it's a separate room to meet people your friend probably knows or hopes to meet."

"I'm not sure I know what that means," said Sam.

"Oh, you will. Follow me, hon. I'll take you to the back room."

Sam left a five-dollar bill for the coffee and tip, followed the barmaid past the restrooms, and turned right past the kitchen doors. She led him down a short hall to another set of swinging doors. She stopped and said with a smile, "Right through here, hon. Have fun."

Sam stepped through the doors into another room with a bar and dining booths. He looked around and saw only men, some holding hands. Finally, it dawned on him it was a separate room for gay men. He looked around with more focus and saw Harrington seated at the bar drinking a martini.

Sam decided not to stay too long, but he wanted to study the guy's habits and modus operandi. He didn't want to sit at the bar because Harrington might start a conversation and remember him if he saw him again. So he found an empty booth and sat on the side that faced Harrington. Sam noticed a sign on the wall that said happy hour, four to six every afternoon. He was surprised the place was not that busy during happy hour on a Thursday.

"What can I get you, hon?" asked a male waiter who had slick gelled hair, half blond and half green, rouged cheeks, heavy eye makeup, and purplish lipstick.

Sam respectfully answered. "Well, aren't you all dolled up."

"Oh, thank you, sweetheart. Which part do you like the best?"

"I like all of it. It all blends in nicely," Sam said with a smile. "I'll have a cheeseburger, medium, with ketchup on the side and a coffee, cream only."

"Thanks, handsome. I'll bring your coffee first."

Sam took out his phone to check for messages. When Harrington wasn't paying attention, Sam snapped a couple of photos of him.

As he was looking at the pictures he took, a guy approached Sam. "Hi, there. Want some company?"

"Uh, sorry. I'm waiting for a friend," responded Sam

"Lucky guy," said the patron as he walked to the bar.

This place is making me nervous. I've only been here for a couple of minutes, and I'm already getting hit on. Sam placed his phone on the table as the waiter returned with coffee. Sam noticed Harrington wasn't conversing with any of the men at the bar, most of whom were between thirty and fifty-something years old. Instead, Harrington periodically turned to stare at the area behind where Sam was sitting. When he no longer was staring in that direction, Sam took a quick peek behind him and saw one young guy that looked not close to twenty-one years old in the booth two behind him, teasing and having fun with someone sitting across from him.

Sam slowly sipped his coffee while sizing up Harrington. He concluded Harrington wasn't interested in men but only targeting young kids to terrorize them and then somehow get rid of their bodies. Sam had friends who were gay, and he knew they would be appalled by Harrington's perverse criminal proclivity.

It wasn't long before Sam's burger arrived, and to his surprise, it was delicious and cooked just right. In addition, it came with unique spicy fries that he enjoyed. He ate his meal leisurely, hoping he would gain something he could use against Harrington. He didn't know how long Harrington would remain at the tavern, but he wanted to leave soon since Harrington kept staring in his direction. When he finished his burger, he waved to the waiter for a coffee refill and the check. Sam decided to wait out in the parking lot rather than sitting alone watching Harrington. He finished his coffee, left cash for the bill, and exited through the back door.

Waiting for Harrington to exit, Sam deliberated on what steps he could take if Harrington left with some young kid. It took another half hour before Sam spotted Harrington leaving alone from the back entrance. He snapped a few photos of Harrington getting into the BMW. Harrington then drove out of the parking lot and turned right in the direction of Route 2 and West Glasterbury. Sam followed him at a distance into West Glasterbury and to the address listed on Harrington's driver's license. Sam couldn't tell if it was an apartment or condominium complex, but he figured Harrington was in for the night and decided to head home.

CHAPTER
30

Back at the office on Friday morning, Sam radioed Ziggy to meet him at the Hartford PD. Later, Ziggy met Sam at the PD and were escorted to Lieutenant Nelson's office. Sam introduced Ziggy to the lieutenant and Detective Jenkins. Nelson immediately reported what his detectives had done since their last meeting.

"We talked to Josh Davis's mother, Donna, by phone and confirmed she still had her son's message that he left on her cell phone. Mrs. Davis gave me the names of roommates and friends at his school, and I made arrangements to interview her at her home in Southbrook," reported Jenkins.

"That's not all," Detective Griffen said. "I contacted the school's campus police department and requested that a detective contact Davis's friends, classmates, and dormitory roommates to determine if they saw or heard anything the day Davis got a ride home. Later, the detective called back and said he interviewed Josh's dormitory friend who, on the day in question, walked with Josh from their dormitory to the student union, where Josh pointed to a black BMW, saying that was his ride home."

All five officers looked at each other while the lieutenant said, "I think we got our man."

It was Sam's turn to add what he had learned. "I spoke with Trooper Simmons. I was disappointed when he told me his boss received an inquiry from the governor's chief of staff, Ron Freedman, asking about the accident investigation in front of the Harrington property. I'm sure the Woodhaven constable was the one who alerted Forster Harrington about the trooper, Kalisha, and me investigating the accident there. Unfortunately, Simmons told his boss about Richard Harrington picking up the hitchhiker and taking him to Uniondale. I'm certain Freedman's inquiry was on behalf of Forster Harrington."

The five of them brainstormed for an additional couple of hours on what interviews were needed and then scheduled further discussions following the upcoming holiday weekend. Being a Friday before the MLK holiday, Sam decided to head home early and finish reviewing and preparing reports at home. He and Ziggy left the PD in different directions. Sam took longer than usual to get home since the traffic was especially heavy. He felt relieved as he finally made the turn into his apartment building parking lot.

As he made his way to his carport parking space, he noticed a dark-colored four-door Ford sedan with four occupants and, further up, a state police cruiser with two troopers sitting in the front seat. He turned into his parking space next to his personal vehicle. Sam exited his G-ride and started walking toward the apartment entrance door.

Two state police detectives and two uniformed troopers approached him halfway to the front door. One of the detectives spoke out. "Sam Caviello, stop where you are! We have a warrant for your arrest."

"What? You're kidding, right? I'm a federal agent. This has to be a mistake."

"We know who you are, Caviello. There's no mistake."

As the detective put handcuffs on him, Sam had only one thought. *This has to be Harrington calling in political favors to stop the investigation.*

A trooper started patting Sam down for weapons and emptied his pockets. "Where is your gun?"

"My gun and ammo are in the tactical bag. Why are you guys doing this? Why am I under arrest?" No one answered him. "It would have been nice if you showed professional courtesy and had me voluntarily appear at your office," Sam said with resentment.

"We're just following orders. We have search warrants for your apartment and your personal and work cars," said a detective.

"What are you searching for, Detective? What's this all about?"

Again, there was no response other than the detective taking Sam's government car keys and his tactical bag, saying, "We'll need the keys to your personal car as well."

Sam didn't answer, thinking, *they don't answer my questions, why should I answer theirs?*

The detective asked again, "We'll need the keys to your personal car. Where are they?"

"You didn't answer a single question I asked. So why should I answer yours? You have a warrant, go search for them, but you're not going to find anything of a criminal nature anywhere in the cars or the apartment."

"As I said, I'm only doing what I'm ordered to do."

"Yeah, right. But, I see you're doing it with great enthusiasm," Sam said sarcastically. "You're treating me like a common criminal. At least tell me why you're arresting me."

The detective finally answered a question from Sam. "Murder."

"Murder! Now I know you're making a huge mistake. This is insane. I didn't murder anyone."

Sam's thoughts went haywire. *Murder! Jesus, can Harrington have that much influence, or is the political system that corrupt?*

The detective looked at Sam's face and then his hands and said, "No, huh? Why do you have cuts and bruises on your forehead and your hand? You got into a tussle with someone?"

Sam looked squarely into the detective's eyes. "You evidently did a poor-ass job investigating, Detective. Either that or you are just as corrupt as the person setting me up. What's your name?"

The detective didn't answer.

"This is a huge blunder on your part, Detective, and when you finally realize it, your reputation will be rubbish for what you are doing here."

Again, there was no response from the detective.

"Are you the affiant for this arrest, Detective? If you are, I am going to sue you for false arrest. I didn't murder anyone."

"That's what they all say," responded the detective.

"I ask again, what's your name?"

"Lieutenant Detective Roger Mastin, and yes, I am the affiant for the warrants. I answered your questions. Now answer mine. Where are the keys to your personal car?"

Sam hesitated before answering. "Read me my right to remain silent first. Then allow me to call my attorney, and then I'll answer your questions. As a law enforcement colleague, can you at least extend that courtesy to me, Detective Mastin?"

After Mastin read Sam his rights, he said, "I'll allow you to call your attorney once we complete the search."

It took about two hours for the police to finish the search. Other than Sam's personal computer, cell phone, and tactical bag, Sam didn't notice any other property taken from the search. Two of the four men in the detective's unmarked vehicle were forensic technicians who took the longest time going through the trunk of Sam's personal car and interior and the government car.

Sam overheard them tell Detective Mastin both vehicles were clean. Mastin advised the team that a tow truck was on its way to impound the his personal car for further forensic examination.

"Why are they searching my car?" asked Sam.

"It was used in the assault," he answered.

"My car? No freaking way. How do you know it was my car, and when did this so-called assault occur?"

"We know it was your car because it was video recorded in the parking lot of a hotel three nights ago. The hotel security camera recorded your license plate."

"You mean Tuesday night? What time?"

Mastin answered, "Around eleven."

While Mastin told his crew to pack up, Sam thought back to where he was that Tuesday evening.

"It's getting late. Let's move out of here. We still have to transport this guy to lockup," Mastin yelled out to his crew.

"What about the call you promised me?" asked Sam.

Mastin handed him his state police cell, but Sam said he needed his cell phone for the contact number for his attorney. So Mastin obtained Sam's phone from another detective and asked for Sam's passcode and the attorney's name. Once found, Mastin pressed the call button and listened for a man's voice to answer before handing the phone to Sam.

Sam turned his back on the detective and whispered, "Ziggy, it's Sam. The state police have just arrested me at my apartment. Contact Brian Murphy and let him know somebody set me up for a murder charge. Have him get a copy of a video recording of an incident on Tuesday night around eleven. The video shows an assault by someone driving a car similar to mine with my license plate on it. Also, find out where the state police will impound my car. Arrange to go there and take pictures of it from every angle. Once you have the video of the car used on the night of the incident, bring a copy to me along with the photos of my car so I can compare the two cars side by side. Also, contact Lieutenant Nelson at the PD, my boss, and my son, and let them know."

Sam paused, turned to face the detective, and spoke louder. "The arresting detective is Lieutenant Roger Mastin. Find out all you can about him and any possible connection he has to Harrington."

"Okay, Caviello. You've had enough time. End the call," ordered Mastin.

"Where are you taking me, Lieutenant?"

"To the Hartford jail."

Sam handed his phone back to Mastin. "You have my tactical bag, which contains ATF property, not mine. It's the property of the US government. The bag is never in the my car, only the government vehicle."

"We'll hold it for now until we check it out. That wasn't a call to your attorney, was it? Why were you asking to have someone check on me and any connection I have with someone named Harrington?"

Sam repeated, "If any of that ATF property goes missing, it will be your head that rolls."

Again, Mastin asked, "Who is this Harrington guy you mentioned?"

Sam responded, "He most likely is the guy you are helping to set me up for something I didn't do. If you had done a thorough investigation, you would already know who he is and why you should have done a better job investigating."

Mastin grabbed Sam's arm and started walking him toward the detective's cruiser before Sam shouted out to the technician still looking over his personal car. "Hey! Check to see if there is a front license plate on the car!"

Mastin yelled back. "No need! They'll do it at the impound facility!"

Sam saw the forensic technician looking at the front of his car. "There's no plate," shouted the technician.

"Did you check that before arresting me, Lieutenant?"

"It's not an issue in this case. Let's go."

Once in the cruiser's back seat, Sam indignantly said, "I see you planned this arrest to happen after court hours on a Friday night before a long holiday weekend. That ensures no court hearing or possible bail for me until next week. Just following your master's orders, right, Lieutenant?"

"Right now, that's the least of your worries," replied Mastin.

They transported Sam to the Hartford Correctional Facility. As the police sedan pulled up in front of the jail, Sam saw a crowd of news journalists waiting and knew it was a preplanned photo opportunity for the press.

Sam was pissed. *They arrest me on a Friday night, so I spend the long weekend in jail, and my arrest is the top news story for the whole weekend. Just great.*

"Wow, Lieutenant, the place is surrounded by reporters shortly after you finished your search of my apartment. The reporters must be able to read your mind, or is this just part of the setup plan you're following?"

The lieutenant said nothing.

"Well, guess what? When the truth comes out, whoever gave you your orders will pretend he doesn't even know you, and these same reporters will be writing derogatory things about you. Then, it'll be you embarrassed because you didn't do a thorough investigation instead of taking orders from the scumbag trying to set me up."

Lieutenant Mastin, peeved about dealing with reporters, got out of the vehicle and made a brief statement citing the arrestee's name, title, age, address, the charges, and the time and place of arrest. He did not answer questions.

He took Sam out of the vehicle while the press took a slew of photos of the handcuffed federal agent while escorted into a jail facility.

While escorted through the maze of reporters, questions were flying at Sam, which he paid no attention to, except when one reporter yelled, "You're a disgrace, Caviello. You're going to spend the rest of your days in prison. Your days harassing upstanding citizens are over!"

Sam looked back at the heavyset reporter yelling out insinuating remarks. Sam was distraught, and his mind had disturbing thoughts. *This is not good. Too many people believe what they read in the papers.*

CHAPTER
31

Brian Murphy's cell phone rang as he helped his wife clean the dinner table and place the dishes and glasses into the dishwasher. He asked his two girls, ages seven and nine, fighting to help clear the table, to be quiet as he answered the phone.

"Brian, it's Rick Ziglar. Sorry to bother you at home. Bad news. The state police just arrested Sam Caviello. He called me and said it was a setup for a murder charge. He wanted me to notify you."

Murphy was dumbfounded. "Shit. That's not good, Zig."

Ziggy continued outlining what Sam had requested and added a warning. "If word gets out in jail that Sam is a fed, his life will be in danger. He needs our help to get him out of there fast. Can we do that?"

"I'll contact Durrell and discuss our options. Most likely, one of us will contact the state's attorney and request particulars on the arrest. If you could, I'd like you to be on standby in case the state's attorney agrees to that request tonight. I'll need you to obtain a copy of the video and to take photos of Sam's personal car as he requested. We'll find out where his car is stored and get you access to take the photos. I'll call you back later."

Ziggy then made calls to Sam's boss, Lieutenant Nelson, and Sam's son, Drew, notifying them of the arrest and filling them in on his conversation with Murphy. Ziggy also contacted the rest of the Hartford agents to bring them up to speed and told them to get ready to work the weekend.

Ziggy knew Sam would never assault anyone and certainly wouldn't commit murder. It was obviously a setup. He was angry and swearing under his breath that this could happen. After finishing all the calls he had to make, he felt sure it would be another working holiday weekend.

*　　*　　*

After Lieutenant Mastin completed processing Sam at the jail, he returned to his office in Meriden to secure the evidence they seized during the search warrant. He then called the state's attorney, Frank Reynolds, asking whose idea was it to have the press ambush them at the jail.

Reynolds said, "In such heinous cases, it is important for my office to be transparent and inform the public of good police work and getting a violent person off the street."

"When am I going to get the chain of custody report? It's a critical piece of evidence in the investigation. I want to know who obtained the security video and from what hotel so I can conduct the necessary interviews."

"Lieutenant, you'll get the chain of custody document in good time. My staff is assigned to interview those at the hotel."

Mastin wasn't pleased with what Reynolds told him. He thought back to Caviello accusing him of following orders instead of conducting a thorough investigation. Even though his orders came from the top cop in the state, Mastin felt uneasy about how the state's attorney handled the case.

After ending the call with Mastin, Reynolds called Ron Freedman, the governor's chief of staff, who provided the initial information on the assault. Freedman was pleased to hear everything went down without a hitch. After the call ended, Freedman called his contact, who was ecstatic with the news and couldn't wait to turn on the television to watch the story's coverage. The contact sat back in his chair, relaxing for a few minutes to absorb the details he had just learned. One specific point discussed got him thinking, though. Not wanting to leave anything to chance, he made a call to get assurance from his associate that the backup person completed the remaining task timely. His call rang several times before it went to voicemail. He knew it was late, so he left a message to call back first thing in the morning.

CHAPTER
32

After conferring with US Attorney Debra Durrell, Brian Murphy placed a call to State's Attorney Frank Reynolds's cell phone. Reynolds answered the call.

"Frank, this is Brian Murphy. Why didn't you inform our office you were arresting a federal agent? Durrell and I are not pleased and would like the particulars on the arrest of Agent Caviello."

"Brian, this is an apparent stabbing of a woman outside a Manchester hotel with evidence pointing directly at the agent. A hotel security camera captured the incident on video, including the license plate on the agent's car. We have no doubt it was Caviello."

Murphy listened to Reynolds describe the incident as evidence "pointing" to Sam. "So are you telling me that the video positively identifies Caviello as the assailant, or did you say the evidence only points to Caviello because of the license plate captured?"

Reynolds, equivocating, finally replied, "We have additional information that definitively puts the agent at the scene."

"What is this ironclad information you're referring to?"

Reynolds ducked the question and said the information must remain confidential for the time being.

"We want a copy of the video to judge for ourselves," insisted Murphy.

"It's a holiday weekend for chrissake, Brian. People have the weekend off."

"Frank, employees work seven days a week in the criminal justice system, and priority cases require people to work weekends and overtime as justice dictates. As the state's attorney, I know you only have to make one phone call and order someone to make a copy. I'll have an agent pick it up tonight, or at the latest, first thing in the morning."

"What's your interest in a murder case? It's our jurisdiction, not the feds. Are you representing the agent as his personal attorney?"

"C'mon, Frank, seriously? You arrested a federal agent, and that's of interest to us. For starters, I'm coordinating a joint ATF-Hartford Police kidnapping investigation in which the agent is the lead investigator, and the state employs the prime suspect. I've known Agent Caviello as a trustworthy and hard-charging investigator, so it's difficult to believe he was involved in an assault, let alone a homicide. I would appreciate your cooperation in helping our office decide if you are right about him or if there has been a terrible mistake. I doubt that providing me with a copy of the video will affect your case, but it will certainly help us judge the strength of the case against him. We are also very concerned with the timing of his arrest after the courts close for business at the start of a long holiday weekend. That seems intentional to prevent him from having a bail hearing and ensuring he will spend several days in lockup. If the word gets out at the jail that he is a law enforcement officer, his life will be in danger. If precautions have not been put in place to protect him from other prisoners, this will lead to a lengthy federal investigation into handling his arrest and incarceration."

There was a long silence from Reynolds before he spoke again. "I'll see what I can do. I'll make a few phone calls and get back to you on Tuesday or Wednesday."

"That's unacceptable, Frank. I have an agent on standby to pick up a copy of the video now. I didn't think I would have to mention this, but US Attorney Durrell insisted I mention this is an official government request with the utmost urgency. In addition to a clean copy of the security video, we request its chain of custody to identify who obtained it and from whom.

We also want our agent to take photos of Caviello's impounded vehicle. We need your authorization and the location of the vehicle. It's essential to get this done immediately."

Again, there was silence from Reynolds.

"Are you still there, Frank?" Murphy asked.

"Yes, I'm still here. You're throwing a lot at me, and I'm just trying to absorb it all. I'm thinking about who I can call to get the ball rolling by tomorrow morning if it's at all possible. So let me make some calls, and I'll get back to you within the hour."

"I'll be waiting for your call, Frank. Don't disappoint us."

Murphy was not happy with Reynolds's cooperation. He immediately placed a call to Durrell summarizing his conversation with Reynolds. "He seemed hesitant to provide a copy of the video and the chain of custody. Also, I'm concerned about how Reynolds described the video. It's doubtful the video unmistakably identifies Caviello as the assailant."

Durrell calmly replied, "Let's wait for his callback and see what he delivers. I've known Frank for a few years, and I'd like to believe he would cooperate one-hundred percent."

"What if Reynolds claims he can't deliver the video until next week? That could result in Caviello spending days in jail. So there had better be protective custody measures in place. Otherwise, it could be a big problem if the word gets out he's an agent."

"Well, if he's uncooperative, I'll request that a federal judge sign an order exercising pendent jurisdiction and take over the state's case. It may be a stretch, but it's a way to force cooperation from Reynolds. Let's hope it doesn't come to that. I'm concerned that the video may not positively identify Caviello as the assailant. We need to view that video. We can decide from there." Durrell ended the call.

Murphy didn't like the idea of Sam being in jeopardy in the jail. He couldn't imagine what Sam must be going through. We can't abandon him. We have to get him out of there as soon as possible. He kept looking at his watch, anxiously waiting for Reynolds's callback. After an hour passed, he grew concerned that Reynolds wouldn't call. Another twenty minutes passed when he decided he would call him back. Murphy looked at the clock again and reached for his phone just as his phone rang. He saw it was from Reynolds and answered it.

"Okay, Brian, a copy of the video will be available tomorrow morning at ten. Your agent can meet up with Lieutenant Mastin at his office in Meriden. Mastin will provide the copy and accompany your agent to the impound lot so he can take photos of Caviello's car. As far as the chain of custody, we will hold off on that for now," insisted Reynolds.

"Why is that, Frank?"

"I feel that after you view the video for yourself, you'll be satisfied that our case against the agent is solid, and there will be no further need for your involvement in the case."

Murphy was annoyed by Reynolds's statement. "That's yet to be determined. We'll review the video and go from there. In the meantime, thanks for the copy and for allowing us to take photos of Caviello's car."

After they ended the call, Murphy called Agent Ziglar. "Ziggy, pick up a copy of the video from Lieutenant Mastin tomorrow morning at ten at his office in Meriden. Mastin will accompany you to Sam's car to take the photos. Then meet me here at my office so we can review the video."

Murphy thought that if the state's case against Sam relied only on a video that doesn't undisputedly identify the assailant, it would help Sam get released from jail. Otherwise, he may be in there much longer than anticipated.

CHAPTER
33

Dickie drove down the long driveway to Randy's so-called funhouse deep in the woods. He was uneasy joining Randy in sharing his fantasies with a young girl. Girls always made Dickie nervous when he was in school. Girls talked about him behind his back and made fun of him. However, Randy didn't mind switching to a girl now and then.

Dickie sounded his horn as he parked near the small cottage's front door. Exiting his beamer, he saw Randy at the front door. Inside the place, Dickie heard moaning and sobbing coming from the bedroom.

"Did you start without me?" asked Dickie.

"No, man. She's a screamer. I neva expected her to have this much fight in her. She can't weigh more than ninety-five pounds, for Pete's sake. While tryin' to tie her to the bedpost, she slapped and kicked at me. I still need to tie her feet. I'm just waitin' for the drug to kick in."

Dickie followed Randy into the bedroom and saw a naked girl with her hands tied to the bedposts. She was gagged with a hand towel in her mouth, squirming and kicking while whining as loud as the gag allowed.

"Uh, you think you're going to have fun with that? I don't want any part of her," said Dickie.

"I'm not done with her yet, Dickie. When I tie her ankles to the bedpost, we do our thing and enjoy it while it lasts. She might squirm around a bit, but pretend you're ridin' one of those electronic bulls in a bar."

"I don't know, Randy. This is crazy."

"Well, she downed more Coke before you arrived. She's a freaking terror now, but she'll calm down once that mix kicks in."

Randy reached for the twine he kept near the bed and, with Dickie's help, managed to tie each ankle to opposite sides of the foot rail. Dickie stared at her as she continued to moan. It felt strange for him to see a naked girl, so natural and up close. He was fixated on her beauty and wondered how it would feel with a girl. The more he stared, the more he sensed the craving to experience an unfamiliar kind of satisfaction.

"You go first, Randy," said Dickie. He was concerned the girl was still squirming like crazy.

A cell phone in silent mode vibrated. Randy reached in his pocket and looked at his phone.

"I have to take this, Dickie. It's a possible job for me, and I need the work. The reception isn't good inside, so I'll have to take it out front. You go first. She won't bite you!"

Dickie noticed she was simmering down as the drug finally was working. Like a kid, he was nervous but mesmerized by the young girl, wondering if there was a difference in how it would feel. Dickie dropped his pants and underwear while keeping his eyes glued to her movements just in case. Then, watching the girl closely, he cautiously put his knee on the corner of the bed and noticed her eyes were now closed.

Feeling she was now harmless, he gingerly placed his knees on both sides of her legs. He wasn't fully ready like he usually was with young boys as he noticed her legs moved farther apart. He considered it an invitation, and that got him more excited. Then, he shifted to a position where he was at the pinnacle of entering her. He moved his body inches from her when, unexpectedly, the young girl swung a free arm as hard as she could and hit him close to his eye with a closed fist. He fell off the side of the bed and screamed like a child.

Randy had left the young girl alone while he unlocked the front door after hearing Dickie arrive. He was unaware the young girl struggled to get her left hand free from the loosely tied knot around the bedpost during that time. She untied her other hand before reaching down to free both ankles with Dickie on the floor moaning and Randy outside on a call. She faltered as she climbed off the opposite side of the bed and nearly fell. Still shaky, she reached for her clothes on the floor and struggled to put them on. Disoriented from the drug as she dressed, she managed to stagger to the front door. Not knowing where Randy was, she peeked out the door and saw him standing outside, facing away from her, talking on his phone. She tiptoed out onto the steps, hoping he wouldn't notice her. As she did, Dickie yelled out. "Randy! The girl's gone!"

Randy quickly turned and saw the girl stumbling off the front steps. Ending his call, he grabbed her arm and pulled her toward him. She greeted him with an angry punch in the side of the face. Grabbing hold of her arms, he yanked her closer, trying to put both arms around her to gain control. Unfortunately, he left himself open for her knee to strike him hard in the groin.

"Ow, you bitch. I've had enough of that!" He pushed her hard, forcing her to fall backward. He dropped to his knees, holding his groin area in pain, not realizing the girl fell backward, hitting her head on the stone steps. She went out like a light.

"Randy, what did you do?" yelled Dickie as he came to the open door.

Randy straightened up and stared at the young girl as blood seeped from her head onto the stone step.

"She kneed me in the balls. The bitch deserved it."

*   *   *

Thirty minutes later, Randy finished excavating a hole in the woods behind the cottage. While Dickie watched, he gave Randy a bewildered look.

"What? Why are you lookin' at me like that?"

"You promised me this would be a fun night, and I would enjoy it. It wasn't, and I didn't. All I got was a black eye and watching you dig a grave. I should've stayed home."

"She sucker-punched me and kneed me in the balls! What was I supposed to do, just let her run for help? No freakin' way. So now, I bury her ass."

As Dickie started to walk toward his car, he stopped, turned, and responded. "She was going in the ground anyway after we had our fun. But instead, we got zip, man. I neva should have come here."

CHAPTER
34

The following morning, the arrest of a federal agent for an alleged assault and the murder of an unnamed woman filled the local television networks. Moreover, since it was an arrest of a government agent, several national news networks picked up reports of the incident.

An ATF public affairs representative in Washington, DC, made a brief statement, advising that the agency would not comment on an ongoing investigation but that the agency's Office of Professional Responsibility would be conducting an internal investigation in cooperation with the Connecticut State Police.

The most damaging story in the local newspaper was by Buzzy Dunnledd, the reporter who shouted negative comments toward Caviello outside the jail on the night of his arrest. His column reported events that were not factual and contained volumes of hearsay and fabricated accusations. It did, however, mention the name of the hotel where the assault occurred.

*   *   *

That same morning, Forster Harrington received a call from Tony Dellagatti. "Yeah, boss, what's up?"

"Make me happy, Tony, and tell me your friend dropped off the borrowed item and the samples as instructed."

Tony assured his boss his friend got it done.

That didn't convince Forster. "I'm glad you trust him, but I don't know him, so tell me you already talked to him, and he gave you his assurance that he finished the job."

Tony sensed the anger in his boss's tone, so he said he would call his friend for confirmation and call him right back.

"Are you telling me you don't know for sure that he got the job done?"

"Sorry, boss, he probably called to let me know, but I was busy all day yesterday and probably missed his call. I'm sure he got the job done, but I'll check with him and get right back to you to put your mind at ease. Give me a few minutes."

"You better be right, Tony. You know I hate it when somebody doesn't do the job he got paid to do. Now get back to me within minutes, and it better be good news."

It took nearly an hour before Tony called back. Forster answered the phone with a forceful tone. "Make me happy, Tony."

Tony cleared his throat and responded with a guarded answer. "I'm sorry, boss. He didn't finish the job, but it wasn't his fault. The state police were waiting there when he arrived, so he got the hell out of there. He waited around until the police left, but the guy's car was gone."

"Damnit, Tony, that doesn't make me happy one bit. When did he go there?"

"He said yesterday afternoon after dark, around five or so."

Forster, now really pissed, lashed out at Tony. "Those weren't his fucking instructions! He was supposed to do it the next fucking night on Wednesday! Doesn't this guy understand English? Is he some kind of fucking idiot? Friday is when the cops impounded the car, which is now under lock and key by the state police!"

Tony, uptight from Forster's anger, tried assuring him he could still fix it. "Boss, this guy can still do the job. He is the best at what he does. I swear. He'll get it done if you can tell me exactly where they have the car. Even if it's in a locked warehouse, this guy can easily break in and get it done. Member boss, the cops, ain't the experts. They took the car where the lab guys will examine it, and they're not doing it over the holiday weekend. So we can still do the job. We'll do it tonight."

Forster was infuriated. "It may be too fucking late!"

Tony didn't respond and waited for Harrington to calm down.

Forster took a deep breath to calm down a bit but remained upset. "I'll make a call and find out where they have the car. When I find out, tell your fucking idiot of a friend he better get it done, or he may become the newest resident at the city morgue. You understand, Tony? I'm holding you responsible. He's your guy."

Tony promised everything would work out. "Boss, he'll get it done because I'll be with him with my gun to his head."

Forster replied, "I'm trusting you on this, Tony. Don't disappoint me." He then slammed the phone down on his desk, ending the call.

CHAPTER
35

While in jail the next day, Sam was sitting on his metal bunk, considering his situation. He speculated that Forster Harrington had to be behind this. Still, he could not understand why the state's attorney and a ranking detective didn't conduct a thorough investigation that would have cleared him of any wrongdoing.

He laid back in his bunk, thinking about his predicament. He never expected this could happen with today's checks and balances. He's out there trying to stop a killer, and he's the one who ends up in jail. The arrest could put the whole investigation on hold now. Sam worried about how this would affect his reputation as a law enforcement officer. It troubled him how his son, friends, and colleagues would take his arrest. The situation was like a bad dream, and he wanted it to end.

He began to think back to when he was a kid lying in bed near death, or was it an awakening after death as his brother Jim kept telling him? He wondered how his mom and dad would think about his arrest.

His dad was a typical Italian blue-collar worker who had a calm demeanor but was not happy with his life. He worked at a local textile mill earning low pay that, in some way, was responsible for him starting to gamble on horse racing, believing he could win money to help make life better for him. In time, his dad got a better-paying job at a submarine building company in Groton that the family hoped would help improve his perspective on life and curtail his casual gambling. Although he enjoyed the higher pay, he didn't like the new job any better than the textile mill. He gambled more often, causing more losses and less money for groceries and paying bills. Like many gamblers, Sam's dad waited for a miraculous windfall from a big win to improve his life, but it never happened. Sam's family became functionally poor. Sam had to wear his older brother's hand-me-down clothes and forego medical and dental checkups as money became scarce, even for the essentials.

Sam's brooding thoughts ended when the jailhouse guard called his name. "You have a visitor. You'll have fifteen minutes."

It was close to noon on Saturday. The guard escorted Sam to a private room where Drew waited at a small round table. It was the first time Drew had ever entered a correctional facility. When Drew proceeded through the visiting process, his stomach tightened in knots. Goose pimples gathered on Drew's skin causing nervous trembling knowing his dad was jailed among criminals. The only jail facilities he had seen were in the movies and TV shows. While waiting for his dad to enter the room, Drew's only thoughts were how this tragedy could happen to his dad. Drew considered his dad a dedicated, trusted public servant and an exceptional loving father. He knew there was no way his dad would ever commit murder, and he certainly didn't belong in a hellhole with common criminals.

When Sam entered the room, Sam put his arms around Drew and squeezed him like he never wanted to let him go.

"There's no touching allowed," shouted the guard.

As they both took a seat, Sam spoke to his son quietly. "Don't believe a single thing you read in the paper or heard on the news. None of it is true. The arrest is a complete scam to set me up, most likely to obstruct the case I'm working on with the Hartford PD. We're getting close to solving a kidnapping and possible murder, and someone is trying to stop us."

"Dad, I don't believe anything the news has reported. I know it's all bullshit. But they claim they have a video of your car outside a Manchester hotel near your apartment. According to the state's attorney, the video shows the driver, who supposedly matches your description, stabbing and then throwing a woman into the trunk of your car."

"Drew, the main suspect in the case I'm investigating, works at the statehouse, and his father is an influential political donor to the governor and other politicians. I don't know for sure he's behind this scam, but I bet none of the news reports say they positively identified me as the assailant. Am I right?"

"The paper only reported that you match the physical characteristics of the assailant in the video."

"That's a novel way of identifying a suspect, but it shows they can't say for certain that it's me."

"Dad, I hear what you are saying, but I'm worried. Powerful people in the state are working on getting you convicted. Who's to say they won't succeed. I only wish I could help somehow. I feel helpless. I overheard some guys at school and my part-time job talking trash about you. I've come close to bashing one of them in the face."

"Don't do anything stupid. I don't want you ending up in here too. Think before you act. Don't let jerks influence the person you are."

Sam paused as he noticed Drew's eyes water. "Drew, listen to me. They claim to have a video of the assailant who physically matches me. That can only mean they don't have proof it was me. Once I get to see this video, I'm convinced I'll be able to prove it was not my car that was there that night. I did a lot of thinking back to the night they said this happened. I remember I was home typing a report until late. It was around eleven o'clock when I finished. I remember going out to get something out of the government car. When I did, I saw my car parked there in the carport. It couldn't have been at this hotel at the same time. Do the newspapers identify the woman or report any motive?"

"No, they only say the state police are investigating."

The guard spoke again, saying time was nearly up.

"Drew, stay strong and ignore rumors or what you read in the papers. I love you."

Against the rules, Drew hugged his dad again, whispering, "I believe you, but I'm still worried. I hope you can prove what you told me. I love you too. I only wish you could get out of this place. It sucks knowing you are in here."

"I don't like it here either. Have faith."

As the guard took Sam from the room, a second guard waited to escort Sam back to his cell. When the two guards exchanged words about a retirement party, Sam noticed the name R. Marcello on the second guard's shirt. As Marcello escorted Sam back to his cell, the first guard yelled, "See you tonight, Rocco."

Drew's visit affected Sam emotionally. His eyes welled with tears as he walked down the corridor to his cell. He loved Drew, and it bothered him that his son had to hear trash talk at school and work about his dad. Sam worried about how this would affect Drew's studies at school and his relations at work.

As Marcello and Sam approached his cell, Sam noticed a heavyset inmate with tattoos covering both arms, his face, and neck, mopping the floor near his cell. When Sam stopped at his cell door, Marcello mentioned it was time for Sam to get something to eat in the mess hall.

"I'm not hungry. I'm tired, and I need to get some sleep. Open up so I can get back to my bunk."

Marcello shook his head no, saying he had to eat, but Sam insisted on sleeping. *I'm not going anywhere near other inmates,* thought Sam.

Knowing there was another option, Marcello opened the cell door and then started to back away. The jailhouse was an old, outdated facility. The cell doors were unlike new facilities where they opened and closed electronically. Since Sam didn't hear the jail door clang shut behind him, he turned to find out why the door was still open. That's when he spotted the colossal inmate approaching his cell while Marcello backed several feet away. He immediately shouted to the guard. "What going on, Marcello? What's this guy up to?"

"That's Schitzo. He's washing the floor, that's all."

"Bullshit. This is all on video, man. You're in trouble for what you are allowing here."

"I'm not sure about that, Mr. Smith in cell 29, if that's even your real name. For some reason, the camera here is not working. I understand someone will fix it this afternoon."

Sam knew what was about to happen. He also knew there was no way to escape. He would have to fight for his life. The Schitzo guy was massive and mean-looking. Sam saw the big guy drop the mop and reach behind his back for a shiv. Sam's whole body felt like a wet blanket saturated with nervous sweat. His anxiety peaked as his heart hammered in panic against his chest. His eyes roamed the entire area, trying to detect any means to defend himself against this beast coming to slice him apart.

CHAPTER
36

After acquiring a copy of the hotel surveillance video and photographing Sam's impounded car, Ziggy arrived at Brian Murphy's office on Saturday. Brian placed the drive into his laptop, and they stared at the monitor.

"What's this shit?" snapped Ziggy.

The already poor-resolution picture fluttered with horizontal lines as they continued watching, making it impossible to make out any discernable picture.

After letting it run for a few more minutes, Murphy hit the stop button and expressed disappointment. "The video is essentially worthless. I'm sure this wouldn't pass muster for an arrest. Did you get a chance to review their copy before Mastin gave this to you?"

"No. Mastin already had the envelope marked 'For ATF' written on it. What if they gave us this piece of crap on purpose?"

"That would be a big mistake on their part."

Murphy picked up his cell phone and called Frank Reynolds. Unfortunately, Reynolds's phone went immediately to voicemail, stating that he was out of the office and wouldn't return calls until Tuesday.

"Crap," cried out Murphy. "No answer, and his message said he's out until Tuesday. I'm going to call Durrell and let her know. The newspapers reported that the assault occurred at the Manchester Value Inn. I want you to head over there and interview whoever's in charge and find out who they released the video to. Get all the details and review the original if they still have it. If they do, get a clean copy for us, and ask if they got a receipt when they released a copy to the police. Take a Manchester detective with you. Private companies are generally more receptive to their local police requests than requests from the federal government."

Ziggy called ahead to the Manchester Police Department. When he arrived at the PD, Detective Dania Gardner met Ziggy in the lobby and introduced herself. She said she would get her car, and he could ride with her. While traveling to the hotel, Ziggy provided some background to the detective but was careful not to divulge too much. Gardner mentioned that she had heard about the alleged incident on the news.

"Our captain had sent another detective to the hotel to investigate, but he's on leave today. Otherwise, I'm sure he'd be accompanying you, not me."

Once at the hotel, they approached the reception desk clerk, displayed their official identification, and asked to speak to the manager. A moment later, Mitchell Brooks came out to the front desk. Ziggy and Gardner identified themselves and informed Brooks why they were there. The manager led Ziggy and Gardner to the security room.

When questioned about who requested the video, Brooks described the encounter with the two officers. "I was surprised the two were not from the Manchester or the state police. They told me of the incident in the parking lot and requested to view our security camera footage. I asked to see photo identification before playing the video as I was a bit suspicious that one of the officers was from New Haven and the other from Woodhaven. I didn't even know there was a Woodhaven in the state. I asked why the Manchester Police were not involved. They said they were part of a state police task force investigating a serial killer. After they showed ID, we viewed the video that showed a man assaulting a woman."

Brooks said he felt he had to cooperate because of the seriousness of the incident outside his hotel. "I told the officers I would provide them the clip of the incident since the video contained twelve hours of recording. Once I copied the segment of the incident, I asked them to sign a receipt and made sure they signed and printed their names, their department, and their badge numbers."

Brooks showed Ziggy the original receipt while he corrected himself. "I might have only seen the Woodhaven officer's photo identification, but both displayed badges."

"Mr. Brooks, would you be able to identify the two men who came into the hotel for the video?" asked Ziggy.

"Yes, I'm sure I'd be able to identify them."

"Great. Soon, agents will contact you. They'll visit and show you a group of photos and ask if you can pick out the two men who obtained a copy of the video. While we are here, Detective Gardner and I would like to view the video."

Brooks inserted the video and fast-forwarded it to the start of the incident. Ziggy noted the video was clear and unobstructed, unlike the copy the lieutenant had provided. He asked Brooks for a copy and the original receipt. Brooks initialed and dated the original receipt and made a copy for his records. Before leaving the hotel, Ziggy had Brooks sign a sworn statement describing the night the two men requested a copy of the video.

The two officers left the hotel. While driving back to the police station, Gardner expressed interest in helping with the federal investigation.

"I'll keep that in mind, Dania. I have a question for you. After watching the video, would you arrest someone based on what you viewed?"

She thought about the question before replying. "The video clearly shows the license plate on the car used. Even though a DMV check would identify the owner, I would need to investigate further, including interviewing the car's owner, before deciding I had enough to make an arrest. Someone other than the owner could have been driving that night."

"Exactly. No seasoned investigator worth a damn would make an arrest based solely on this video." Back at the station, Ziggy thanked Gardner for tagging along and then rushed back to the federal building to update Murphy.

*   *   *

Knowing the gruesome-looking hulk the guard called Schitzo was about to end his life, Sam positioned himself inside his cell with his hands on the unlocked iron cell door. The hideous Schitzo smirked at his prey while approaching the door. When Schitzo reached just outside the door, Sam shoved the door hard into Schitzo's head, knocking him several feet back with a gash on his forehead. It allowed Sam to race out of the cell to retrieve the mop left on the floor to use as the only possible weapon available. He snapped the wooden mop handle across his knee, creating a pointed edge on one end to use as his weapon. Schitzo laughed at the paltry stick in Sam's hands. Infuriated by the pain from the bruise on his forehead, he wobbled a bit as he advanced toward Sam with rage.

*   *   *

Meanwhile, Arthur Dempsey, the deputy warden at the jail, met with his lieutenant for a random inspection of the facility. The first area inspected was the security room, where Dempsey could get a quick view of the activity within the facility via the internal camera monitors. As he studied the monitors, he saw one monitor was black. "What's the situation with this monitor?" he asked the guard overseeing the monitors.

"I'm not sure why it's not working, sir, but we scheduled someone to come here and repair it."

"Exactly what area is that camera covering?"

"It's in C block where we put the new inmate that came in last night, sir."

Agitated, Dempsey turned to the lieutenant and, with a scowl, said, "Grab a couple of men and follow me to section C immediately!"

*   *   *

The beastly inmate, carrying a handmade shiv, marched toward Sam like the giant in "Jack and the Beanstalk," ready to cut down Jack and his stalk. Sam moved back, but not quick enough, as the inmate's sudden arm swing slashed across Sam's prison shirt, penetrating deep enough, cutting a four-inch slice across Sam's belly. The cut was a close call. Rather than panic, Sam's adrenaline and anger intensified. He was now pissed off and went on the offensive, thinking this guy was serious about killing him.

Training set in as Sam faked moving left but quickly went right, bringing the mop handle up high and ready to strike at Schitzo's head. As Sam's arms were about to come down to attack, Schitzo raised his left arm to deflect the hit. Quick to see Schitzo's arm movement, Sam made a sudden change in the angle of his strike and smashed a hard blow to Schitzo's right wrist, causing him to drop the shiv. Then, swinging the mop handle up again, Sam gave an explosive slam into the side of the guy's right thigh, causing Schitzo's knee to buckle. Sam quickly raised the handle and swiped the pointed end across the inmate's face, opening a five-inch tear across his left cheek. It caused Schitzo to turn his head to the right, taking his eyes off Sam. Taking a step back, Sam lowered the handle and took a power swing up, whacking Schitzo squarely in the groin. That caused the inmate to drop to his knees, giving Sam his next target, a mighty swing down and across the back of the inmate's head. That massive hit caused Schitzo to fold over and hit the floor hard and unconscious.

When Schitzo hit the floor, the lieutenant entered C block, followed by two guards screaming, "What the fuck is going on here?"

Marcello raised his arms in a surrender manner and answered. "Schitzo was mopping the floor when I brought the prisoner back to his cell. The prisoner surprised me, trying to grab my baton. I tried fighting him off, but he pushed me back. That's when Schitzo came to help me, but this fucker grabbed the mop, broke it in half, and started swinging it at us."

"That's a damn lie, and you know it, Marcello. You had this beast waiting here to stick me with a shiv." Sam pointed at the shiv on the floor. "That's the shiv that this shithead had, and he cut me. See for yourself." Sam raised his shirt, revealing the cut across his midsection. "If you check that shiv for prints, you'll find that Schitzo, or whatever his name is, has his prints on it." Sam spoke directly to the lieutenant while pointing at the guard. "That sucker, Marcello, was part of this setup. He wouldn't lock me in the cell and said no one would see what happened here because the security camera was not working. He's just as guilty as this Schitzo guy for trying to kill me. I need to speak to the warden."

Just then, the deputy warden, Arthur Dempsey, entered the room. He'd heard Sam's account of the incident from just outside the open door. Repulsed by the incident, the warden ordered the lieutenant to have one of his men bring Marcello to the security room and hold him there.

"Retrieve the shiv with latex gloves and secure it for evidence, and bring Schitzo, as you all call him, for medical treatment and then confine him in solitary."

Dempsey was troubled that someone brought an unaccompanied inmate to C block, where they housed a law enforcement agent. Dempsey took custody of Sam and would personally bring him to the hospital for treatment. He would have to report the assault to the U.S. Attorney's Office and have the Hartford police investigate the incident. He also will order an internal investigation that he promised would lead to the termination of one or more personnel at the jail.

CHAPTER
37

Ziggy walked into Murphy's office just after two o'clock. Before Murphy could say a word, Ziggy spoke with anger.

"Those bastards are fucking with us, Brian! Get this! The hotel manager said two guys came into the hotel asking to see the security footage. They identified themselves as members of a state police task force investigating a serial killer. One of the guys identified himself as a Woodhaven Police officer, and the other as a New Haven cop. Do you know where Woodhaven is? It's a small rural town near where Harrington has a summer home."

Ziggy described what he saw in the video. "It wasn't more than three or four minutes long, and you can't identify the woman or the assailant. If that's all they have, I don't see how they justified an arrest. I had the manager freeze the video several times while I snapped photos of the car used in the assault. We need to have Sam look at the photos at the jail. He knows cars better than I do and certainly knows his own car."

Ziggy rambled through his words with excitement in his voice. He took a breath before continuing. "The manager required the two guys to sign a receipt and print their names and badge numbers. It looks like a Woodhaven cop named F. Asckis and a New Haven cop named T. Delovate were the two so-called cops. Both scribbled their names, but the manager was smart enough to have them spell and print their name so he could read them."

Ziggy handed the document to Murphy, who appeared in a trance staring at Ziggy. Ziggy waved his hand by Murphy's eyes. "Oh, sorry, Zig. I was in deep thought. A few minutes ago, the assistant warden called to say an inmate stabbed Sam at the jail, and they're transporting him to Hartford Hospital. We'll meet them there."

"What? Didn't they keep him separate from the other inmates? Is Sam okay?"

"He's okay. We'll find out what happened when we get to the hospital. Let's finish up here. Call the New Haven and Woodhaven Police Departments to verify that they are current officers. I'll call the state police about this supposed serial killer task force. We need to get this done quickly."

After waiting for the transfer of Murphy's call to the state police colonel, Nathan Bennett finally answered. "Colonel, this is Assistant US Attorney Brian Murphy in Hartford. I'm trying to verify if two men, who claimed to be local police officers, are part of a state police task force investigating a serial killer. I suspect they are not, but need to confirm that."

"First of all, we do not currently have a task force investigating a serial killer. Give me their names and departments, and I'll check if we have them assigned to any of our task forces."

Murphy guessed as much. "One of them gave the name F. Asckis, first initial F-Foxtrot, last name Asckis, spelled Alpha, Sierra, Charlie, Kilo, India, Sierra. He represented himself as a Woodhaven Police officer. The second guy has a first initial T-Tango, last name Delovate, spelled Delta, Echo, Lima, Oscar, Victor, Alpha, Tango, Echo, and represented himself as a New Haven Police officer."

Bennett took Murphy's number and said he'd get back to him within the hour.

Ziggy came back into Murphy's office with his report. "The Woodhaven Police Department is made up of six part-time officers, of which Asckis is one of them. He works under the supervision of the resident state trooper. Asckis is employed as a constable and would not get assigned to any state police task force. The New Haven PD desk officer said he would have a supervisor return my call, so it might be better for you to take the call."

Murphy and Ziggy went back and forth speculating on how many people could be involved with a scheme to have Sam arrested. They agreed that the most plausible scenario would include Forster Harrington using his political influence to discredit and embarrass Sam, hoping it would end the investigation of his son.

Ziggy's cell phone rang. He quickly answered it, seeing that the number was a New Haven exchange. The assistant chief of police was on the line asking who inquired about an officer named Delovate. Ziggy responded that he would turn the call over to Assistant US Attorney Brian Murphy and handed the phone over to Brian.

"Good afternoon, Chief. This is Brian Murphy, Assistant US attorney in Hartford. Two individuals claiming to be police officers and members of a statewide task force recently obtained a security video recording from a local business in Manchester. One of the two showed a New Haven Police Department badge with badge number 8024. He identified himself using the first initial T-Tango and last name Delovate. I'll spell it for you."

"No need. Give me a moment. I need to check something on the computer."

A few minutes later, the chief spoke. "As I expected, the guy didn't give his correct name. Some years ago, we had a police officer named Anthony Dellagatti, better known as Tony, whose badge number was 8024, but we forced him to resign. He had a few run-ins with the law since but managed to escape serving any significant time, thanks to his high-priced attorney."

Murphy asked, "How could Dellagatti afford to pay for such an expensive attorney?"

The chief answered, "As far as I know, his high school friend, who now operates a successful business, hired him. The scuttlebutt is that Dellagatti's well-to-do buddy paid for the attorney whenever he got into trouble."

"Chief, would you happen to know the name of his kind benefactor?"

"I do. His name is Harrington, and he owns the biggest construction business around here. They do a high-volume business within the state. So there's no doubt in my mind that Harrington had something to do with the department hiring Dellagatti as a police officer."

Murphy was ecstatic by what the chief told him. "Chief, Dellagatti impersonated an active New Haven Police officer and a state police task force member in his attempt to set up a federal agent for murder. Could your department fax or email me a photo of Dellagatti?"

The chief said he'd get one sent to him shortly. Murphy thanked him and advised that if there was anything he could ever do for him to contact him directly. He gave the chief his direct number.

"Brian, there is something you can do for me. I'd like to assign one of my detectives to meet with you and obtain the particulars on Dellagatti. Nothing would please me more than to arrest him for impersonating a New Haven Police officer. Maybe he'll serve some time in jail for once."

"I'd be more than happy to do that, Chief. Have your detective give me a call, and we'll make the arrangements." When the call ended, Murphy informed Ziggy what he had learned from the chief while placing the thumb drive copy of the video into his laptop.

After a quick review of the video, Murphy was just as surprised as Ziggy that the state police would arrest a federal agent based on just the video since it was impossible to identify the assailant.

"Ziggy, get two agents to head up to Woodhaven immediately and find out how and why they hired Officer Asckis. Have them obtain his photo and ask if Forster Harrington had any influence on his hiring. I need that information by close of business today."

Just then, the receptionist's voice came over Murphy's intercom line. "Colonel Bennett is on line two."

Murphy answered. Bennett informed him that Asckis and Delovate were not associated with any state police task force. With that information. Murphy and Ziggy headed to the hospital a few blocks away. On the drive there, Brian called and filled in the US attorney. When he ended the call,

Brian asked Ziggy to make sure he received the information on Asckis as soon as possible.

"So you know, Zig, the US attorney requested a judge stay available for an emergency call to get Sam transferred to federal custody. At the hospital, we'll have Sam view the video. Hopefully, he can tell us something we don't already know that will get him released from jail today."

CHAPTER
38

Agents Jennifer Clarkson and Luis Sanchez called ahead to the Woodhaven first selectman and the resident state trooper to schedule an urgent interview. While they rushed to Woodhaven, Ziggy updated them on the case and what information AUSA Murphy needed.

They first met and interviewed the first selectman at the Woodhaven town hall, who, after reviewing Asckis' personnel file, briefed them on his hiring.

"We hired Fred Asckis only after the state police conducted a thorough background check and he passed a physical and psychological exam. Asckis had three excellent references for the job. The first was Forster Harrington, a highly respected Connecticut businessman who owns several acres of property in Woodhaven and has been a generous donor to our town. The second reference was State Representative Clark Edwards, who represents this district, and the third reference was me. I've known the Asckis family for many years, and they are an upstanding family."

The selectman claimed to have only one photo of Asckis in his file, so agent Clarkson took a picture of it on her cell phone. They interviewed Resident State Trooper Brett Rozier next regarding the hiring of Asckis. The trooper said he had little say in the process since Asckis made the best-qualified list, passed all the requirements, and had excellent references.

Asked to provide an objective performance rating on Asckis, Rozier reflected for a moment before giving a short assessment. "Asckis is still learning the procedures and policies of the job and is showing improvement. He is enthusiastic and wants to be a full-time state officer but needs to slow down and learn the basics of the job before trying to do too much, too fast. When on patrol, he sometimes forgets where the town line is and needs reminding that his area of responsibility is only in Woodhaven."

The agents asked if there were any complaints made against Asckis.

"There were a couple of minor complaints regarding him pulling over drivers outside the town limits of Woodhaven. As I mentioned, I counseled him on working only within the town's limits."

Once Clarkson and Sanchez completed the interviews, agent Clarkson called AUSA Murphy to provide him with the details of their interviews and emailed him the photo of Asckis.

*   *   *

Brian Murphy and Ziggy drove the short distance to the hospital emergency entrance. They identified themselves and were given directions to where the doctor was treating Sam. Murphy noticed Warden Dempsey with two corrections officers up the hall. Dempsey greeted Murphy and Ziggy and briefed them on the assault on Sam by an inmate aided by a guard at the facility. The warden advised that he had reported the assault to the Hartford Police.

"Thanks, Art. I'll contact the PD as well. The state's attorney assured me that security measures were in place to protect Caviello. Any idea how the inmate got close to where you assigned Sam? I assume only you and the warden knew Sam was a federal agent."

"Yes, we were the only ones. Rest assured, the warden, and I will investigate how the inmate got to your agent and what guards were involved. You will know what we learn before anyone else, Brian."

"I appreciate that, Art. We may consider charging the inmate and the guard. Charging them might help get their cooperation in finding out who masterminded the assault."

Murphy and Ziglar pushed open the curtain in the small treatment room where a doctor had just finished stitching Sam's belly wound.

Sam was overjoyed seeing them as they entered the room. "It's great seeing both of you. I hope you guys have good news on getting me out of that shithole before someone succeeds in killing me there."

Murphy shook Sam's hand. "I'm sorry this happened to you, Sam. Somebody screwed up, and when we find out who, they will be held accountable. We're working hard to get you released. We brought a copy of the hotel security video that I want you to watch and give us your thoughts after seeing it."

It took Sam about fifteen seconds to react. He chuckled. "I can't believe how stupid those assholes are. Look, the Honda in the video has only one exhaust pipe, meaning it has a four-cylinder engine. My Honda has a V6 engine with dual exhausts. You can easily see the two chrome pipe extensions on my Honda. Also, look closely at the steel wheels on the Honda in the video. They are different than the wheels on mine. The Honda they used is a newer model, most likely a 2015 or 16. Mine is a 2014 model."

Ziglar put up his knuckles to bump with Sam's. "Wow. That was easy. I'm sorry I overlooked that. I guess I figured you'd examine the cars with finer detail."

Murphy gave an approving nod. "Sam, do you recognize the names Asckis and Dellagatti?"

"I recognize the name, Asckis, better known to me as Fred Asskiss. He's a constable in Woodhaven but likes to patrol Uniondale to keep an eye on Harrington's property. He pulled me over when he saw me coming out of Harrington's driveway and gave me a hard time."

"It's all coming together. As we expected, that scumbag's father is behind this setup," said Ziggy, who then brought Sam up to speed on what he and Murphy had learned in the past several hours.

"I think we have enough to get you out, Sam, and hopefully very soon," added Murphy as he and Ziggy stood up to leave.

"Thanks, guys. I appreciate everything you're doing, and I can't express how happy I am to hear you say that, Brian. I haven't gotten any sleep worrying that someone would eventually stick a shiv in my back. I thought my last day had come when that huge psycho cut me. When I get out, I'm going to get even with those bastards who set me up!"

When Murphy and Ziggy left the room, Sam got off the bed and gave an ecstatic two-step dance. "Yeah, I'm getting out of that rat hole! I knew Brian and Ziggy wouldn't let me down."

Dempsey and the correction officers interrupted Sam's celebration and ushered him outside to the waiting transport van. Outside, Sam took in a deep breath of fresh air and admired the sun shining down on him. Then, exhilarated, he clenched his fist and raised his arm in a victorious gesture before entering the van.

As soon as Murphy and Ziggy got back to the federal building, Murphy called Durrell and described what they learned from Sam and the information on the connection between Asckis and Harrington.

"An inmate attacked Sam with the help of one of the guards. The inmate cut Sam with a shiv that needed several stitches. We need to find out who was behind the attempt on his life. We should begin by charging the inmate and the guard. Maybe that will convince them to cooperate. More importantly, we need to get Sam the hell out of jail now," urged Brian.

Durrell replied, "I agree. I will call the federal judge now to set that in motion."

Two hours later, Durrell called Murphy and told him he would soon receive a copy of the judge's habeas corpus to turn Sam over to the custody of ATF and brought before a US Magistrate in Hartford.

CHAPTER
39

L ater that Saturday afternoon, off-duty State Trooper Dan O'Connell drove to his office in Meriden to pick up files needed for his scheduled Tuesday-morning appointments. As he approached his office building located just before the vehicle impound lot, he noticed an older-model blue Hyundai Elantra parked on the side of the road, with two men sitting in the front seat. O'Connell didn't recognize the Hispanic driver. Moreover, he didn't think either man was a trooper or staff member.

The Hyundai seemed out of place where most vehicles were police cruisers. The parking lot was practically absent of staff vehicles, especially late Saturday afternoon during a long holiday weekend. O'Connell took a left turn into the parking lot and circled to the far exit, taking him beyond the Elantra to make another pass by the suspicious car. He slowly drove by the Elantra again and saw it did not bear an employee vehicle sticker. He noted the plate number and contacted the dispatcher for a vehicle registration check.

While parked in front of his office building, the dispatcher responded. "It's registered to a Luciana Almaraz, 1418 Franklin Drive, East Haven, CT, on a 2012 blue Hyundai Elantra. There are no wants or warrants, but the system shows a recent check on the vehicle was made just yesterday afternoon at 1645 hours by Trooper Luke Morris."

"Can you give me a number to reach Trooper Morris?" asked O'Connell.

After receiving the number, O'Connell called the trooper, who answered on the fifth ring.

"Luke, this is Trooper Dan O'Connell. I'm at the Meriden office and just drove by a blue Hyundai with two men in the front seat that looked suspicious. I ran the plate number, and dispatch said you did the same check yesterday afternoon at 1645 hours."

"Uh-huh, yeah, I remember that car. I was on surveillance, waiting to assist in the arrest of an ATF agent outside his apartment. We kept an eye on the agent's car to search it for evidence. That's when the Hyundai drove right up near it. It appeared the driver reached for something in his car before getting out and walking to the trunk of the agent's car. He turned to look around and must have spotted our cruiser because he quickly jumped back into his car, backed out to the exit, and drove off. I did a registration check, and it came back to a female in East Haven with no wants, so I took no further action."

O'Connell asked, "Did you see what he was carrying?"

"No, it was too dark."

"Okay, thanks for the input. I'm going to keep an eye on these two. Oh, did the agent's car get impounded for forensic inspection?"

"Yes. It should be in the lot where you are."

O'Connell quickly put two and two together and decided it wasn't a coincidence that this Elantra was near the impound lot. So he called his office for backup.

Shortly after that, six state troopers began foot surveillance on the Elantra. The sun was setting as daylight subsided. The troopers saw the two men exit their vehicle. The two men looked around to ensure no one was watching, then moved away from the road along the east side of the impound lot's fence. As the two men moved, so did the six troopers, three on the east side and three on the west side of the lot; the trooper with the eye on the two men communicated with the others.

Three of the troopers on the west side quietly made their way to the gate entrance. They kept their bodies low and hidden. They unlocked the gate and glided into the lot using the impounded vehicles in the lot as cover. They moved in unison, tracking the direction of the two intruders toward the small tech building used for forensic examinations. When the two suspects stopped, the trooper with an eye on them radioed to the others.

"The suspects put on ski masks and are using wire cutters to prop open a section of the fence." There was a pause in his communication. "They're now entering the lot and heading toward the tech building."

The tech building, a former garage used for vehicle maintenance, was now a forensic facility for impounded vehicles. It was a one-story brick building with two metal garage doors, a steel entrance door on the left, and a window facing east.

As the two suspects approached the building, the ranking trooper whispered in his mic, "Standby until they enter the building." Then all six officers advanced toward the building, maintaining their cover.

Once the two men were at the building door, the shorter suspect appeared to work the door lock mechanism while the other held a flashlight. It took about two minutes before the door opened. Before entering, the shorter guy paused to look around.

"Come on, let's go!" snapped the bigger guy while pushing the other into the building.

"I thought I saw a flash of light behin' us," whispered the shorter guy.

"You're seein' things. I don't see anythin'."

"Whata we gonna do if sumbody sees us?"

"Don't worry about it. No one's around, but if anyone does see us, run like hell."

After entering the building, all six troopers silently advanced and met at the door. All had their guns drawn and flashlights in hand while the ranking officer peeked in and saw the two men near the rear of a black Honda. As soon as the trunk opened, he motioned for all to enter. Then, with their flashlights illuminated on the two men, a chorus of voices echoed inside the shop.

"State police, place your hands in the air and don't move."

The ranking trooper flicked the interior lights switch on and saw both men standing motionless and terror-stricken, seeing a half dozen state troopers closing in with guns drawn. Both of them raised their hands high.

"Slowly turn around, keeping your hands high, and drop to your knees," was the following command.

Two troopers advanced to the kneeling suspects and handcuffed them. The ranking officer checked the open trunk and saw a small vial containing a dark red substance, a torn piece of fabric with spots on it that appeared to be blood. Also inside the trunk was a Connecticut license plate matching the rear plate on the Honda. Both men were arrested, searched, and read their rights.

The troopers found a wallet containing a driver's license, credit cards, and over twelve hundred dollars while searching the big guy. The driver's license identified him as Anthony Dellagatti. On him, they also found a Glock 42, .380-caliber semiautomatic pistol, fully loaded with one in the chamber, and a cell phone, both seized as evidence.

The shorter Hispanic suspect carried a wallet with eight dollars and a driver's license identifying him as Benjamin Garcia. Unlike Dellagatti, he was unarmed. While two officers collected the evidence, the other four brought the two suspects back to their office for processing.

While at their office, the troopers discussed the situation. All agreed they should contact Lieutenant Roger Mastin before interviewing the suspects since he was in charge of the investigation leading to the federal agent's arrest. It was nearing six o'clock when the ranking trooper called Mastin's cell and left an urgent message for a callback.

An hour passed before Mastin returned the call. "This is Mastin. What's so urgent?"

The sergeant in charge gave Mastin the details of the arrest.

"I should be there in less than an hour. Don't anyone interview them until I get there." While driving to Meriden, Mastin was troubled by what the sergeant told him. *Why are two men attempting to plant evidence in the agent's Honda?* Mastin couldn't stop dwelling on Caviello's words of a setup and the lack of a thorough investigation before arresting him. *Shit, maybe he was set up.*

Mastin arrived at the Meriden facility just before eight o'clock. When he entered the office, he listened to Trooper O'Connell describe seeing the suspicious vehicle and running his wants and warrants check on the Hyundai, which ultimately led him to call Trooper Morris, who was part of the Caviello arrest team.

"I remember that car showing up," stated Mastin.

The trooper in charge then described how the two men broke into the garage, at which point they arrested the pair trying to plant evidence in the agent's Honda. The suspects had the vehicle's front license plate with them.

Mastin listened while developing a sick feeling in his gut. Uneasiness set in, knowing this could become a nightmare for him. He knew he had cut some investigative corners to satisfy the state's attorney's zeal to arrest the agent and reap headlines. He began planning how he would justify his actions before the arrest of Caviello. He then asked to see the record checks on both Dellagatti and Garcia.

Reviewing Dellagatti's record jogged his memory. "I remember this guy Dellagatti. He was a New Haven cop that the department forced to resign. If my memory serves me right, he was suspended and later arrested as part of a loan shark operation."

Mastin became further tormented after seeing the arrest record reporting that the Harrington Construction Company employed Dellagatti. *Dammit,* he was thinking to himself. *I remember the agent asking whoever he called to check if I had a connection to Harrington. Shit. I was used as a pawn to set him up.*

"Has either of these two birds said anything yet?" asked Mastin.

"Negative. You asked us not to interview them until you arrived," responded the sergeant.

Mastin looked at his watch to check the time since it was getting late. "Okay, you and O'Connell come with me. We'll start with Garcia first."

As Mastin walked to the interview room, his cell phone rang. He was surprised to see the call was from Colonel Nathan Bennett at this late hour and answered the call.

"Lieutenant, this is Colonel Bennett. I just got off the phone with the US attorney informing me that a federal judge signed a habeas corpus order to have agent Caviello brought to the federal courthouse in Hartford, where it will be determined if his detention was lawful. The judge also ordered the feds to take over the state's case and for the state to release all evidence collected. I faxed a copy of the order to the commissioner through legal. The US attorney is not happy we arrested a federal agent with what appeared to be scant and insufficient evidence. She added that the federal government has gathered, in just hours, evidence that the vehicle in the security video is not the agent's car and the persons obtaining the video were impersonating police officers. What kind of fucking evidence did you have to arrest the agent, Lieutenant? Didn't you follow protocol to ensure the evidence was solid and properly obtained?"

Before answering, Mastin moved to another office for privacy.

With an embarrassing tone, he tried explaining the best he could. "State's Attorney Reynolds believed the security video was sufficient evidence to make the arrest and obtain a search warrant for the agent's car. He assured me that they had sufficient evidence for the arrest, and it was approved and signed by a judge."

"Where are you now, Lieutenant?"

"I'm currently at the Meriden facility responding to the arrest of two suspects who were breaking into the impound lot trying to plant evidence in the agent's car. The suspects had the front license plate from the agent's car that was missing when we impounded it. As things stand now, it appears the agent was set up, and I fear Reynolds may have played me on this one."

There was a long pause while Bennett thought about Mastin's response. "What are you planning to do now?"

"I was about to interview the two suspects. After I get the facts, I'll call Reynolds to see what he has to say about this mess."

"Well, Lieutenant, I strongly urge you to do just that, but it may not do any good. I hope the department doesn't end up on the front-page news for doing a shit-ass job."

"Trust me, sir, I'm going to find out who's behind this, and if Reynolds is involved, I'm going to nail the bastard."

Bennett interrupted. "Hang on. Don't hang up. I have to put you on hold. The US attorney is calling again."

Mastin was on hold for nearly ten minutes before Bennett returned. "Durrell initially requested that you report to the federal courthouse in Hartford tomorrow at nine sharp to turn over your investigative file and all the evidence. To demonstrate that we're fully cooperating in this matter, I advised her of the arrest of the two trying to plant evidence in the agent's car. She was pissed off and told me she wanted to send her assistant and a team of ATF agents to meet you in Meriden before conducting any interviews. I suggest you wait for their arrival. The assistant US attorney wants to be a part of any interviews since they are now taking over the case."

"Colonel, I think it's important that I get the first crack at these guys."

"I'm sure you do, but it's their case now and for the sake of cooperation and full transparency, do the interview together to avoid any suspicion. Understood?"

"Yes, sir," Mastin said disappointedly. "Should I turn over the file and evidence when they arrive here or wait until reporting to Hartford tomorrow?"

"Let them make the decision, but it may save you a trip to Hartford if you could turn everything over to them tonight."

While waiting for the AUSA and the team of agents to arrive, Mastin sat alone preparing his story to justify his actions in arresting Caviello, but his justifications now seemed baseless.

CHAPTER
40

Forty minutes later, AUSA Murphy, agents Rick Ziglar and Jennifer Clarkson, and Hartford Police Detectives Kalisha Jenkins and Tom Griffen arrived at the Meriden State Police facility. Lieutenant Mastin met them at his office and escorted them into a private room.

Murphy served Mastin the judge's order. "This is a court order for you to turn over all files and evidence in possession of the state police regarding the investigation and arrest of Agent Caviello."

Mastin turned over everything he already packaged for them without even studying the document.

After that, Mastin tried to absolve himself of any investigative shortcomings. "Listen, I was just following orders from State's Attorney Reynolds, who prepared the affidavits for Caviello's arrest and the search of his apartment and cars. Reynolds is the top law enforcement officer in the state, and a state judge issued the warrants."

"Lieutenant, how did Reynolds acquire the video?" asked Murphy.

"Reynolds said he received the video from a police officer who got a tip on an assault at the hotel in Manchester. I asked Reynolds for the chain of custody document, which would have identified who obtained the video, but I never received it."

Ziglar chimed in. "How did you verify that the person in the video was Caviello?"

Before Mastin could answer, Murphy also asked, "Not only that, did you verify that the Honda in the video was unquestionably Caviello's?"

"Reynolds told me that the suspect's physical characteristics in the video matched Caviello, and a DMV registration check confirmed it was his Honda."

"Under the circumstances, particularly as Caviello is an active law enforcement officer, you didn't consider interviewing him before the arrest?"

"The state's attorney informed me the case was solid, and he wanted a quick arrest to pressure Caviello to reveal the victim's identity and whereabouts. However, when I arrested Caviello, he had cuts and bruises on his face and hands, which are prima facie evidence that he was involved in some sort of struggle. He was allowed to explain, but he refused."

"That was after you arrested him, not before you gave him the chance to explain the cuts and bruises. He's smart enough to know anything he says will be used against him. I'm sure he didn't trust anyone at that point," replied Murphy.

Mastin was about to speak, but Murphy held up his hand to interrupt him and placed two sets of photos in front of him. "Take a look at these two photos and tell me if you see any difference between the two Hondas. Take your time. You are a trained police officer. Are those two vehicles identical?"

Mastin took his time to compare the two cars. "Well, I see one has two exhaust pipes, the other only one."

"What about the wheels?" asked Ziglar.

Again, Mastin studied the two photos and replied, "They're different."

Murphy confirmed, "Yes, they are different. The Honda with two exhaust pipes belongs to Caviello. The other Honda with only one exhaust pipe belonged to someone trying to frame him. The video does not support that the assailant was Caviello or that it was even his car."

Mastin shook his head in disgust, thinking, *Reynolds really fucked me on this case.*

Murphy continued. "A good investigator would have carefully studied the evidence. Instead, you relied on an unsubstantiated video obtained by unknown persons and what Reynolds told you. You should have taken the time to conduct your own interviews. If you had interviewed Caviello, he would have told you he received those cuts and bruises from a suspect during a recent state police arrest of a drug dealer. I'm disappointed that a seasoned detective like you skipped so many investigative steps before arresting a highly respected federal agent and paraded him before a crowd of tipped-off reporters."

Mastin could not rebut Murphy's statement, so he remained silent.

Murphy continued, "Colonel Bennett informed us that the state police arrested Anthony Dellagatti. He is a former New Haven Police officer who was fired and had numerous arrests. He also works for the father of our suspect in a kidnapping case. Dellagatti and a part-time constable from the town of Woodhaven, who also has connections to the suspect's father, are the two men who obtained the security video while impersonating members of a state police task force. Did you bother to interview the hotel manager to determine who he turned the video over to?"

Mastin mumbled, "Reynolds never told me what hotel the video was obtained from before the arrest and said his staff was handling that end of it. He assured me they had probable cause, and the warrants were issued, so who am I to argue with the state's attorney and a judge? I simply followed the judge's lawful orders. I'm not happy with how this turned out and would do anything to make it right. Maybe I should get an attorney because I feel like you're questioning me like I committed a crime. I only followed legal orders."

Ziglar spoke up loud and clear. "Well, now you know how Caviello felt."

Sitting back in his chair, Murphy paused to give Mastin a chance to gather himself before continuing. "Agent Ziglar, Detective Jenkins, and I will interview Garcia first since we believe he is the weaker of the two suspects. I suspect Dellagatti won't talk to us. He always lawyered up in the past and got off with a slap on the wrist with the help of high-priced attorneys paid by the suspect's father, Forster Harrington. So we'll work on Garcia to get what we need against Dellagatti and anyone else involved."

Mastin asked that he participate in the interview, but Murphy declined. Murphy, Ziglar, and Jenkins entered the room where Garcia sat at a round table still cuffed. A state trooper was in the room the entire time, keeping a watchful eye on him. Agent Clarkson, Mastin, and Detective Griffen observed through a one-way viewing window from an adjoining room.

Murphy introduced himself and investigators Ziglar and Jenkins to Garcia. Before questioning, Ziglar read Garcia his right to remain silent.

"Benni, you are faced with numerous charges, including breaking and entering into a state facility, burglary of a motor vehicle with the intent to plant evidence, theft of property from a motor vehicle, conspiracy, and aiding and abetting in an assault and possible murder," explained Murphy.

"What? What murder? I neva killed nobody," argued Garcia.

"Not only will there be state and local charges, but also a slew of federal charges."

Garcia shook his head again. "I didn't do no murder. I just helped Tony put that stuff in the car."

"We know all about the scheme at the Manchester hotel where you staged an assault on a woman. But before you say anything else, let me explain a few things to you. I'm the prosecutor, and I can help you if you fully cooperate by answering my questions truthfully. Cooperating could go much easier on you since I decide the final charges against you. We'll be talking to Tony later. What we have on him is more serious than what we have on you. But if you don't cooperate and he does, he'll be the one who gets to make a deal, and you'll be holding the bag. I'm only offering a deal to the one who cooperates first. We're giving you the first chance to tell us what we want to know. You understand what I'm telling you, Benni?"

Garcia nodded his head that he understood. "My girlfriend is havin' our baby. I can't go to jail. I'll tell ya what ya wanna know."

Garcia grudgingly answered all the officers' questions, admitting that he worked with Dellagatti for many years and had committed minor crimes with him. "Tony works for a big construction company and is friends with the owner. I only knew Tony's boss as Mr. Harrington but never met him. Mr. Harrington axed Tony to do him a favor, and Tony axed me to help him. Tony got me part-time work at the company when they needed extras. He took good care of me, so when he axed me for help, I helped him if I could."

"Tell us from the beginning how things went down at the hotel. Start with stealing the license plate from the agent's car, where you found another Honda, then describe what happened at the hotel," asked Murphy.

"Tony toll me to take the front license plate off a black Honda at an apartment place in Manchester. When I got it, I drove him to pick up a Honda he borrowed from a Honda place in New Haven. Mr. Harrington got the dealer to let us use the car. Tony axed me to put the plate on that Honda, and we drove to Manchester with Jenny, Tony's friend. I don't know her. Tony said she was a hooker. She's Asian. We park in the lot at the mall near the hotel, and Tony toll Jenny and me what to do three times, so we don't make mistakes. Jenny walked to the hotel, and when Tony called her, she came out to the parking lot. Tony gets out of the car, and I drive into the parkin' lot to get at Jenny."

"So, Jenny didn't check into the hotel?" said Murphy.

"No. She goes in, waits for Tony's call, and goes out."

"Okay, what happened next, Benni?"

"After I drove up alongside her, I stop, jump out, and make-believe we argue and fight. Then I put her in the trunk. I drive back to where Tony is waitin' near the mall. I got Jen out of the trunk, and we then drove back to New Haven and dropped off the Honda at the dealer. We get in my car that I left there, and we go get something to eat at a café."

"Where does Jenny live?" asked Detective Jenkins.

"I dunno. I dropped her off on the corner. I think it was Parker and Franklin in New Haven and then drive Tony home. Tony paid Jenny and me five hundred for helpin' him."

"What did you do with the license plate?" asked Jenkins.

"Tony wanted me to go back the next night to put it back on the car. He wanted me to put blood drops on a piece of cloth and put it in the trunk. I woulda went back the next night, but my mom wanted me to help my sister move into uh apartment in East Haven. It took a couple of days before I could go back with the plate. When I went back, the cops were there, so I left and waited for them to leave. When I saw them go, I go back to the car, but it's gone. I member seein' a tow truck, but neva saw what it towed. Tony called me this mornin' saying Mr. Harrington was pissed that I neva put the plate back. He said we had to do the job tonight."

The agents recorded Garcia's story, and he signed his sworn statement. It took well over an hour to complete the interview. Then, AUSA Murphy left the room while Ziglar arrested Garcia on federal charges.

Murphy planned his following interview of Dellagatti with Agent Clarkson and Detective Griffen. As the three of them entered the room, Dellagatti abrasively said, "Don't bother askin' me any questions. I want my attorney, and I'm not sayin' a fucking word until he gets here."

Murphy sat opposite Dellagatti. "We know you directed Benni and Jenny to fake an assault at the Manchester hotel. We also know that you and Fred Asckis impersonated police officers to obtain a security video of a staged assault that you orchestrated. Today, the state police arrested you for breaking and entering a state impound facility while armed. That's a serious offense, especially since the state revoked your license to carry. Between the federal, state, and local police charges, I estimate you are looking at a minimum of fifteen years in prison, maybe more. With your cooperation, I can get that reduced."

Dellagatti just smirked. "As I said, I have nuttin to say. I want my attorney here now. He'll have me out before the night is ova, and I won't spend a fuckin' night in jail."

"That's where you are wrong. You'll be spending the next two nights in jail, and I promise it will be a lot longer than that when we are through with you."

Dellagatti responded, "We'll see about that."

Murphy directed Agent Clarkson to arrest and process Dellagatti federally. ATF agents then transported Dellagatti and Garcia to the Hartford Correctional Center until a scheduled court hearing.

The state police had Dellagatti's cell phone and his firearm. Murphy requested Mastin to turn both items over to ATF, stipulating that both would get returned to the state police when needed for their case. Mastin argued that both were seized during a state crime by the state police. They negotiated until Mastin ultimately compromised by temporarily turning over the cell phone so that the feds could analyze it for additional evidence. In addition, Agent Ziglar took a photo and description of the gun for tracing.

Murphy asked Mastin a few additional questions.

"When did you ask Reynolds about the chain of custody?"

"As soon as I saw the video. I told Reynolds I needed it to identify the officer who got the tip about the assault and took custody of the video. Reynolds told me he'd take care of it, only that he wanted me to expedite the execution of the warrants, hoping that we could determine if the woman was still alive."

"What about the slew of reporters waiting outside the jail after you arrested Caviello?"

Mastin claimed he had nothing to do with that. "Once I had Caviello in custody, I contacted Reynolds to report the arrest as he instructed. I can only assume that it was his doing."

Murphy informed Mastin that Caviello was released to the custody of ATF by order of a federal judge. "He was released on personal recognizance by a magistrate and ordered to appear before a judge on Tuesday morning at eleven. I would like you to be there to give supporting testimony, as you described to us this evening."

Mastin asked, "Is it necessary for me to be there? You have the information needed to convince the magistrate that someone set up Caviello."

"It's important that you inform the court that you only acted on orders from the state's attorney."

"I would need to get permission from my supervisor and Reynolds."

"I strongly recommend not contacting Reynolds. The US attorney will contact the state police commissioner for approval to have you testify. If you do not show up, I'm afraid we'll have to subpoena you. I'd prefer you show up voluntarily. I recommend getting there at nine-thirty for a quick prep session before heading into the courtroom."

That same evening, AUSA Margaret "Maggie" McKinney and Agents Pete Macheski and Luis Sanchez met with the warden at the Hartford Correctional Center to provide the habeas corpus order for Sam's release.

CHAPTER
41

The following morning, Lieutenant Mastin received a call from Colonel Nathan Bennett. "The commissioner called and informed me that the US attorney wants you to testify in federal court on Tuesday. I understand why the feds want your testimony. Now I want to hear what you think about testifying."

"They want me to testify because they believe Frank Reynolds could be involved with the setup. Reynolds was the one who received the video from Dellagatti, a known flunky for Forster Harrington. It appears Harrington wanted Caviello discredited because the agent was investigating his son for kidnapping and possible murder. Reynolds wouldn't tell me where the video came from, only that he would take care of it. He pushed me hard to get the agent arrested."

"Did you talk to Reynolds about testifying?"

"No, the feds told me not to call Reynolds."

"Well, you work for the state, not the feds. You might want to give Reynolds a heads-up and see what he advises, just to protect yourself. That's not an order. I'll leave that decision up to you. If Reynolds is okay with you testifying, so am I."

Bennett ended the call, leaving Mastin in a quandary.

*   *   *

ATF Agents Pete Macheski and Jennifer Clarkson visited Benni Garcia, incarcerated at the Hartford Correctional Center. Clarkson showed Garcia a photo spread of Asian females known to be escorts in the New Haven area and internet photos of Honda car dealerships in the greater New Haven area.

Garcia picked out the photo of Jenny, who the agents later identified as Jenny Chen, better known by her escort name, Kandi. A criminal record check on her only reported she was a victim of an assault and robbery in Stamford while working as an escort.

Garcia also identified Honda of West Haven as the dealership where Dellagatti and Garcia borrowed the black Honda they used for the staged assault at the Manchester hotel. Garcia only remembered Tony saying the manager's first name was Earl.

The two agents left the jail and drove to the Honda dealership to meet with the manager, Earl Howard. Howard escorted them to his private office, where Macheski questioned him about the loaned Honda.

Howard didn't hesitate to cooperate. "Forster Harrington called me and asked if I had a used black four-door Honda Accord. My inventory showed I had only two, a 2018 and a 2015. Harrington asked if the 2015 looked like a 2014 model, and I told him they were almost identical. He requested the 2015 model for the day and promised to return it either that night or the next morning. I didn't question Harrington's need for the car. I had the car cleaned and ready for Harrington's employee to pick it up the following morning. I had his employee sign for the vehicle after showing a valid driver's license."

Agent Macheski asked for the signed receipt. Howard turned over the document reporting the one-day rental of a 2015 black Honda Accord to the Harrington Construction Company, identifying the car's VIN, the dealer's license plate number, and its mileage. Anthony Dellagatti signed the document with an attached copy of his driver's license.

Clarkson asked Howard the amount of the rental fee. "There was no fee. Harrington Construction is a prized customer who purchased several trucks and vans from the dealership along with continual maintenance of those vehicles."

"Do you still have the black Honda?" asked Clarkson.

Howard searched his computer and advised, "Yes, I still have it in inventory."

Clarkson asked to see the car. She followed Howard to the used car lot and verified the VIN to ensure it was the same car.

Agent Clarkson took photos of the car from all angles and had Howard unlock it so she could check the trunk and interior of the vehicle. Macheski asked Howard to secure the car for seventy-two hours so that a state police forensic team could inspect it. Howard voluntarily turned over the rental documents to the agents and signed a brief statement.

Macheski and Clarkson then drove to the New Haven address for Jenny Chen. They agreed that Clarkson would take the lead in the interview. The agents entered the outside apartment complex door and rang the buzzer for apartment 14A, listed to J. Chen. A woman's voice asked through the speaker above the mailboxes, "Who is it?"

"Hi, I am Special Agent Jennifer Clarkson. I would like to ask you a few questions about an investigation I'm working on."

"What's this about, and how do I know you are an agent?"

"I have a badge and identification. You can come down to the inner door and see for yourself."

Chen agreed but needed a couple of minutes to get dressed. Several minutes later, Chen came to the locked glass inner door and examined the agents' credentials. Then, she opened the door and led the investigators to her apartment. Chen stood about five feet, one inch tall and couldn't weigh more than one hundred pounds. She was an attractive twenty-eight-year-old Asian woman with a charming smile who spoke good English.

Clarkson asked, "Do you know Forster Harrington?"

Chen replied, "I know the name but never met him."

Clarkson followed up, "What about Tony Dellagatti and Benni Garcia?" Chen's pleasant expression immediately turned to a look of concern and worry.

Clarkson advised Chen, "You are not in trouble yet, but lying to us is a federal crime. We know that Dellagatti paid you to put on an act of being assaulted in a hotel parking lot. We could arrest you for conspiracy to set up a federal agent. Now do yourself a favor and tell us how this all happened."

Chen's eyes swelled with tears, and her lips quivered as she spoke. "It was just fun. Tony is a good client—I mean a friend. He say his boss asked him for a favor, and he want my help. Tony want me to be a woman who get beat up at hotel. He promise me no trouble. I just want to help him because he was always nice to me." Chen explained that she and Garcia staged the assault outside a hotel and then drove back to New Haven, laughing that it was just a fun game.

Clarkson asked, "How much did Dellagatti pay you?"

She replied, "Uh, Tony give me five hundred dollar."

Based on Chen's responses, Clarkson prepared a written statement for her signature. Clarkson recommended that she avoid Dellagatti and not discuss their visit with anyone.

Clarkson and Macheski drove back to the Hartford US attorney's office and gave Brian Murphy the statements and documents they obtained from Chen and the Honda dealership manager.

"I have an additional assignment for you two. We subpoenaed the carrier of Dellagatti's cell phone for the record of all his calls. We came up with a phone number we suspect is Forster Harrington's private cell phone from the records. The listing for the cell comes back to a small construction company located in North Haven. A check with the Secretary of State disclosed that it's a limited liability company with a recent amendment to its ownership. Previously, the company listed Thomas Donavon as the sole proprietor, but Gus Walker's name got added as a partner within the past year. I want you two to interview both Donavon and Walker to determine if there is a connection to Harrington and find out who's the primary user of this cell phone. I suspect it is Harrington, but we need confirmation. Once confirmed, Durrell wants the FBI to analyze all the calls to connect the dots between Harrington, Dellagatti, Reynolds, and any others involved in the scheme to have Sam arrested."

The following morning, Agents Macheski and Clarkson interviewed Thomas Donavon at his company's office in North Haven regarding his amended Connecticut registration to operate in the state.

"Can you tell us how the change came about, Mr. Donavon?" asked Clarkson.

"My company was close to filing for bankruptcy when an investor proposed a partnership that would settle a fair amount of my company's debt and a guarantee to keep the company in business as a subcontractor."

"Who made the generous offer to pay your outstanding debt and keep you in business?" asked Macheski.

"Forster Harrington, who operates the largest construction company in Connecticut. I agreed to a partnership with his company with the understanding that I could continue to operate as the manager under my current business name. However, Harrington wanted his business manager, Gus Walker, as a full partner with Harrington serving as the silent chief executive of the business."

"Can we assume you have direct access to Mr. Harrington? If so, do you have to go through Walker, or has Harrington provided you with his private direct line?" asked Macheski.

"Yeah, I have access to call him direct at the company and his private number after hours."

Donavon gave the agents the two direct numbers he had, one of which was the cell number in question, verifying it belonged to Harrington.

Donavon was curious about the inquiry. "I maintain supervisory control of company employees, and Walker simply oversees expenses and quality control of our work. Can I ask if there was a problem with the partnership? Did we violate some state regulation or law?"

"No, no, Mr. Donavon. We are simply working with state authorities to verify and confirm LLC ownership and the payment of fees and taxes. We see no irregularities here, and you are good to go. We appreciate your cooperation. Thank you."

On the drive back to Hartford, Clarkson called Murphy. "Brian, Thomas Donavon confirmed the cell phone belongs to Harrington. As an added confirmation, Pete called the number to inquire about a small excavation job, and Forster Harrington answered the call."

CHAPTER
42

On Tuesday morning, before the court hearing began, Murphy received a call from FBI Agent Tom Perkins with the lab analysis report. "The specks on the headlight frame were confirmed as human blood, type A positive, same as Andy Richardson's blood type. Also, the DNA analysis of the blood compared to the sample provided by Marci Richardson identified her as a biological parent. The analysis of the recorded 911 call from Richardson's phone reported the sound of a vehicle coming to a quick stop, an impact noise, what appears to be a male yelling out, and then fifty-two seconds of silence before the sound of the vehicle driving away. As the vehicle drove off, there was the sound of another passing vehicle heard. Next, a moaning sound was detected, followed by sounds that could be the movement of leaves and brush. While the 911 operator continued to hold, they tracked it to its estimated location. With the location identified, the operator reported the distress call to the Connecticut State Police."

Murphy thanked Agent Perkins and asked that he expedite the official report. He glanced at his watch to see how much time remained before the court hearing. He noted one witness had yet to appear. Disappointed that Mastin was a no-show, Murphy called him just in case he was delayed.

When Mastin answered, Murphy was polite. "Good morning, Lieutenant. I was hoping you would be here at the courthouse by now."

"Well, I didn't get the authorization to testify. I work for the State of Connecticut and have to stay in good graces within the state system. So I felt compelled to inform the state's attorney, who recommended that I not testify."

Murphy asked, "Did he give a reason why?"

"Reynolds said that any action taken in the investigation was in good faith, and he didn't need his office portrayed unfavorably."

"I'm surprised that after Reynolds used you to set up Agent Caviello, you continue to follow his instructions. But, irrespective, we will get to the truth and hold those involved accountable, regardless of the position they hold."

Murphy expected Mastin to continue defending himself, but there was only silence.

"I only hope those who unknowingly aided in the cover-up don't become entangled in a conspiracy simply because they wanted to be a team player. But, one way or another, we will get your testimony, Lieutenant." Murphy ended the call.

Before the hearing, US Attorney Durrell and Murphy conferred with Magistrate Dominic Rubino in his chambers. They informed him of the state's attorney's assistance to Forster Harrington by coordinating the issuance of Caviello's arrest warrant based on evidence that was flimsy at best and later determined to be completely fraudulent. Also, the state's attorney had barred the arresting detective from testifying at that day's hearing.

At eleven o'clock, US Magistrate Rubino began the closed hearing session. Durrell sat at the prosecutor's table with Murphy, McKinney, and Sam Caviello.

Sam was apprehensive about the outcome of today's session. He usually sat there assisting the prosecutor, but now he was sitting there before a judge who would determine his fate.

Hearing voices behind him, Sam turned around to see Ziggy and Jennifer Clarkson enter the courtroom with Sam's son, Drew. Sam and Drew nodded to each other with a smile.

The bailiff called the court to order as the judge entered the room. First, Durrell called Sam to the witness stand to give testimony, followed by Hartford Police Lieutenant Nelson, ATF Agents Ziglar and Clarkson, Trooper Dan O'Connell, Benni Garcia, and the Manchester hotel manager, Mitchell Brooks. During the hearing, Murphy introduced into evidence the video and photos of the two Hondas, comparing the Honda used in the orchestrated assault to Sam's Honda.

Following all the testimonies and the presentation of evidence, Magistrate Rubino expressed exasperation over the overwhelming evidence that someone had framed Caviello, resulting in his imprisonment and humiliation. He directed the US attorney's office to vigorously investigate those responsible and ensure they were held accountable to the fullest extent of the law. Accordingly, he dismissed the charges against Sam with prejudice.

Upon hearing the judge's order, there were sounds of congratulatory applause. Drew rushed from the gallery to his dad's side as they embraced each other. Drew was relieved by the ruling as he nervously struggled with his words. "I'm so glad this is over, and you are out of jail. I heard about the assault on you. I was worried and glad you are okay."

Both had watery eyes as Sam said, "I'm sorry you had to go through this, son. Now it's time to hold those responsible for putting me in this awful situation."

When the handshakes subsided, Murphy singled out Trooper Dan O'Connell for his instincts in suspecting Dellagatti and Garcia, leading to their arrest while trying to plant evidence in Sam's Honda.

News reporters, informed earlier that the US attorney would make a short statement following a court hearing, were waiting in the hall outside the courtroom. Buzzy Dunnledd was among them and slowly inched his way next to reporter Allison Gaynor. "Have you heard anything about this hearing? I don't understand why we were not allowed in the courtroom. It must be something big, seeing all the agents and police officers enter the courtroom."

Gaynor, who despised Dunnledd's reporting style, did her best to snub him. "I wouldn't tell you even if I knew." She then quickly moved away from him, leaving Dunnledd with a puzzled look on his face.

When Durrell exited the courtroom accompanied by Sam, cameras began flashing, and reporters yelled out questions one after another. When seeing Sam with Durrell, Buzzy Dunnledd shouted, "It's about time the feds are charging you, Caviello! You're a murderer and an embarrassment to the government. Where did you hide that woman's body?"

US Attorney Durrell gave Dunnledd a disgusted look while holding her hand up for quiet. "I will make a short statement without taking questions. US Magistrate Dominic Rubino held a hearing to determine the facts surrounding a staged assault at a Manchester hotel parking lot last week. Based on volumes of evidence collected during an ongoing federal investigation, the judge determined unnamed persons orchestrated an incident to set up agent Caviello to obstruct his efforts to investigate a kidnapping and possible murder. Our office developed undeniable proof there was no assault at the hotel. We have arrested two suspects who staged the incident while the investigation continues to identify those who aided in the scheme. As a result of the testimony and evidence provided today, Magistrate Rubino exonerated Special Agent Sam Caviello of any wrongdoing and ordered others shown to be involved in the scheme be held accountable."

She then pushed her way through the crowd of reporters as the agents and police followed behind her. Dunnledd continued to grab attention with his outburst. "This is absurd! Is this a government cover-up?"

In the US attorney's conference room, US Attorney Durrell convened a multi-agency session to discuss investigative strategy regarding the missing students, Richardson and Davis. Her assistants, Murphy and McKinney, Sam, the FBI and ATF agents in charge, and Hartford Police Department members were present. Durrell knew it would require additional manpower resources to determine what happened to the young students. While settling on a strategy, Durrell got paged that a reporter wanted to speak to her privately.

Durrell met with the reporter in another office. Allison Gaynor introduced herself as a reporter with the *Hartford Post*. Durrell, already familiar with the reporter, told Gaynor she had already made her statement and had nothing further to add.

"I'm not here to ask questions or obtain additional information. Instead, I wanted to provide information that might be of interest to you. When all the reporters left the building, I saw a black Lincoln stop in front where Buzzy Dunnledd was waiting. When the rear window came down, a long conversation ensued with Dunnledd."

"So, why is that of interest to me?" asked Durrell.

"The person in the back seat of the Lincoln speaking with Dunnledd was Forster Harrington. After a lengthy conversation, Dunnledd got into the back seat with Harrington, and the car drove off. I'm not a big fan of how Dunnledd reported on agent Caviello's arrest, and his callous questions outside the courtroom today were demeaning and downright unprofessional. I'm for reporting facts, not malicious accusations and rumors."

"Thank you for that information, Allison. It's good to know. Is there anything else, or is there something you expect in return?"

"You can call me Alli. I've talked to ATF agents, police officers, and others who said Sam Caviello has a solid reputation and work ethic and is well-liked. I also know a little about your background as a former Naval JAG officer and a no-nonsense but fair attorney. Obviously, there's a bigger story here, that being Sam's kidnapping and murder investigation. I would certainly like to be on the inside when it breaks. An exclusive interview with you, maybe with Agent Caviello too, when it's over."

Impressed, Durrell responded, "I've read your columns. You gave an objective account of the events of Caviello's arrest without making baseless accusations. Give me your card, and I'll consider your request, although there's no guarantee."

With a smile, Gaynor said, "I'll take it. Thank you."

CHAPTER
43

The next morning at nine sharp, Trooper Curtis Simmons pulled into the dirt driveway at Zake Barnes's small cottage and parked his police cruiser directly behind his pickup truck. Since Simmons first had contact with Zake Barnes, Sam asked him to arrange a follow-up interview with him.

Sam was sitting in the front passenger seat of Trooper Simmons's cruiser, and Constable Jerry Reed sat in the back. Detectives Tom Griffen and Kalisha Jenkins parked behind Simmons in an unmarked tan Hartford Police sedan. Behind them was a state police cruiser driven by Trooper Ethan Shaw with his cadaver-sniffing German shepherd, Nacho, the nickname given by Shaw's colleagues. Nachos were Shaw's favorite snack, and his colleagues couldn't help but laugh when they saw his dog with nacho chips falling from his mouth. Shaw thought the name was fitting and decided to keep it. He and Nacho waited in the car until they received the signal to search the property for a buried body.

Barnes waited at the front door after seeing Simmons and the others arriving from his window. As Simmons approached the open door, Barnes, looking puzzled, asked, "Why so many? I thought only you were comin' to ask a few questions."

"You'll understand why the others are here once we are inside. With me are Hartford Police detectives trying to find out what happened to a young college student who disappeared, and we believe he was near the area of your accident that night. Could we come in, Zake? We think you can help us better understand what happened that night. You are not the only one we will interview. There are others nearby we'll be talking to as well."

Barnes, visibly shaken by the number of officers, decided to cooperate by answering a few questions. Then as the officers entered his home, Barnes asked, "Do I need an attorney?"

Sam spoke before Simmons responded. "We already have a good idea of what transpired that night, and we don't believe you acted with criminal intent. However, someone was hurt that evening, and we are hoping you could help us establish a timeline and fill in some blanks. If you want to call an attorney, you are free to do so, but we need your cooperation, and it could prove favorable for you."

Barnes was noticeably jittery and nervously stuttered when he spoke. "Are ya guys gonna arrest me? Are ya sure I don't need to call—?"

Sam interrupted, "Listen, Zake, you did not hit a deer that night. We know there was a dense fog and it wasn't easy to see around the S-curve. Help us put the pieces together to find out who else might have seen it and what they did after you left the scene."

"Ya think someone saw what happen'? I didn' see nobody else. I wanna help ya, but you're all scarin' the crap out of me."

Sam stopped Barnes from continuing. "Zake, sit down, take a deep breath, relax, and answer Trooper Simmons's questions as best you can."

Sam and the Hartford detectives had prepared a list of questions for Simmons to ask. Simmons started with questions to get Barnes in a trusting mode, such as where he worked, what time he left work, whether he stopped anywhere on his way home, and what time he hit what he thought was a deer.

"I got outta work at, uh, four o'clock. I spent time in the men's room doin' my business and washing up. Then, I stop at a burger joint for sumthin' to eat on my way home. When I got to the area where I went around the curve, the fog was so thick I couldn' see nothin' in front of me. That's when sumthin' ran out in front of me. I hit the brake hard and stopped. I got outta my truck and looked aroun' the area there for a few minutes but saw nothin'. I think it was about six or six-thirty."

"Were you under the influence of alcohol or drugs when driving home?" asked Simmons.

"Hell, no," uttered Barnes.

Simmons asked, "Is it possible you hit a person instead of a deer?"

Barnes paused to think about how to respond. He then gave a clever answer. "I'm not sure what I hit. The fog was too heavy to see what came outta nowhere. My eyes were on the road, not what was cumin outta the woods. I stop to look to see what it was, but I saw nothin' there, so I just figga it was a deer because they come out on the road a lot around here."

Sam decided to tell Barnes the facts. He pulled a chair up next to him. "Zake, we found the headlight frame missing from your truck on the shoulder of the road. It contained what the lab found to be human blood, the blood of a young college student. That student was on his cell phone calling 911 when he got hit by your truck. We found his cell phone near your headlight frame. You should know they record all calls made to the 911 operators."

Sam paused for Barnes's reaction. Barnes could feel the tension in his stomach as it tightened and felt like it was tumbling like a clothes dryer. Concerned about the trouble he faced, Zake felt his heart throbbing hard against his chest. Although Sam kept talking, Zake was utterly zoned out, not hearing a word he said.

"Zake, you need to listen to this. Are you okay?" asked Sam.

"Uh, yeah. You're scarin' me, man. I, uh, I didn' know it was a kid."

Sam played a recording of the 911 call while Zake listened. Sam described what was happening as he played the recording. "That's your truck's tires skidding when you saw something in the road. That thud you just heard was the sound of your truck hitting the kid, followed by his yell. There was silence lasting only fifty-two seconds, and that's the sound of you driving away. There was no sound of you exiting the vehicle and getting back into it. Searching for only fifty-two seconds is not much of a search. I understand it was difficult to avoid hitting him because of the fog. Perhaps you were frightened at the thought of hitting a person. We understand that. What we don't know is what happened to the boy's body because it was never found."

"What? Uh, whoa! I didn' do nothin' with no kid. I neva saw a kid. I thought it was a deer."

"Well, Zake. That's what we need to figure out. We need to know what happened to the kid after the accident. Now, tell us truthfully about everything that happened that night."

Sam intentionally paused again to let Barnes absorb what he said. "Zake, before you answer, you should know we will confirm what time you left work. We'll find out exactly where you stopped for dinner and how long you were there because we know from the 911 call that the kid was hit by your truck much later than six-thirty. So please, be honest with us because it's a crime to lie to a law enforcement officer. If we find out that you are not telling us the truth, we will prosecute and send you to jail. If we do charge you, you will need an attorney, which will cost you plenty."

Barnes fidgeted in his chair. He remained silent while contemplating whether he should ask for an attorney or just be more truthful. He didn't have money for an attorney since his wife took most of what he had when they divorced.

"Okay, okay. I got spooked that night. I didn' wanna get in no trouble, you know. When I left work, I went to Nick's Bar and Grille, just down the road from work. I had to eat. I had a few beers, but I wasn' drunk. I was okay drivin'. Because of the weather, I went very slow that night. I didn' wanna get in any accident because my truck is the only way to get to work. When I went aroun' that curve, I couldn' see nothin' in front of me. I was lookin' more to the right, makin' sure I wasn' gonna go off the road, when all of a sudden, I felt this bump on the side of my truck. I didn' know what the frig it was because I didn' see nothin'. I stopped, man. I was lookin' with my flashlight. I saw nothin', so I figga it was a deer. Maybe it was only a minute, but it seemed a lot longa to me."

Barnes stopped talking and took a deep breath, His forehead was dripping sweat, and his hands were shaking. "I saw lights from another car comin' at me from around the next curve. I didn' wanna get hit, so I drove back to my lane. It was too dangerous out there in the fog. I figga it be betta for me to go home, rest up, and come back in the mornin' and look again in the daylight. I was so nervous my mind wasn' thinkin' straight. When I got home, I was still shakin' and had to lay down. I thought of callin' the police, but I just dozed off and didn' wake up till hours after. I honestly figga it was a deer. Everybody knows deer always runnin' out from the woods to the road." Zake squirmed in his chair again, breathing heavy. "Shit, man, I didn' know it was no kid."

Sam figured there was nothing more they could get from Barnes, so he informed him they had a search warrant for his home, truck, and property. Barnes appeared to be less concerned about a search. He knew they wouldn't find anything on his property. Sam asked Barnes if he owned any other property. He answered he did not. Trooper Simmons signaled Trooper Shaw to start the property search with his dog, Nacho, while the other officers searched Barnes's home and truck.

After two hours of searching, the only possible evidence recovered was an old white T-shirt with reddish-brown stains found under the truck's seat.

Sam showed the shirt to Zake. "Did you use this shirt to clean the front headlight area after the accident?"

"I dunno, but I might've."

"Okay, Zake, we're done here. We're taking the shirt to the lab to determine if the red spots are blood. Here's my business card. Call me if you remember anything important about the accident that night."

They seized the shirt for forensic examination to determine if the stains were Richardson's blood. The team of officers waited an additional ten minutes for Nacho and Shaw to finish the search of the grounds. Finally, finding nothing else pertinent to the case, the team wrapped up their search and left the property.

Sam thanked Simmons and Reed for their support and then left with Detectives Griffen and Jenkins to interview Constable Asckis at the Woodhaven Town Hall.

CHAPTER
44

S am had already made arrangements with the Woodhaven resident
state trooper to have Constable Asckis available for an interview.
Once at the town hall, the interview team entered the room where
Asckis was seated.

Asckis had a confused look on his face when he saw Sam. He thought
the interview might be regarding a full-time job with the state police that
Forster Harrington promised. However, Detective Jenkins identified
herself and read Asckis his Miranda rights, putting him on notice that this
was a criminal investigation, not a job interview. Jenkins took the lead in
questioning the constable due to Sam's past confrontations with him. She
told Asckis they knew he and Tony Dellagatti impersonated police officers
at the Manchester hotel.

"I wasn't impersonating a police officer. I am a police officer."

"You are a town constable, not a full-time police officer. Nevertheless,
you and Tony Dellagatti identified yourself as state police task force
members to obtain a fake video to set up a federal law enforcement agent.
Impersonating a member of a state police task force is a serious offense. If
convicted, it would end your chances of becoming a police officer, not to
mention spending time in jail."

Jenkins let that sink in before continuing. She could see Asckis squirm in his chair with squinting eyes and a troubled look. "If you have any smarts and consider yourself an honorable police officer, you should help us in this investigation. Your cooperation could mitigate your foolish actions in helping a criminal. We arrested Dellagatti already. He's in jail awaiting arraignment as we speak. Or, you could decide not to help and be charged with conspiracy and obstruction and join Dellagatti in jail."

"I was told Anthony was a New Haven Police officer, and my assistance to him would go a long way in getting me on with the state police," answered Asckis.

Sam spoke out. "Who told you it would go a long way in getting a job with the state police?"

Asckis remained silent.

The resident state trooper piped in. "It certainly wasn't any member of the state police who told you that. So I suggest you be truthful and answer the question."

Jenkins pulled no punches. "The agent asked you a question. It would be best if you stood with your law enforcement colleagues. No bullshit, no covering up for friends, no lies. If you do lie, it is another criminal offense that will likely result in jail time. You have a choice. Help us so that we can help you. Tell us how this scam at the Manchester hotel came about. Tell me everything and name names. No covering up for anyone."

Asckis just sat there thinking. He figured he was in trouble if he lied, and it wouldn't serve him well now to protect Harrington.

"So, will you help us solve a murder and help yourself too, or are you just going to sit there and protect criminal associates?" pressed Jenkins.

His voice was shaky and hoarse from nervousness, causing Asckis to clear his throat before he spoke. "I got a call from Forster Harrington asking for a favor. He wanted me to meet with Tony, who Harrington said was a New Haven Police officer, to obtain evidence in a murder case. Harrington said my help would go a long way in getting me to become a state trooper. All I had to do was meet with Tony and follow his instructions. That was the extent of it. Once we got the video, my part ended."

Asckis identified Dellagatti from a photo spread and agreed to sign a sworn statement about the events leading up to helping Dellagatti secure the video.

Detective Griffin whispered something into Detective Jenkins's ear. Jenkins nodded and advised Asckis, "It's important that you do not contact Forster Harrington, or anyone else, regarding our talk today. Do you understand?"

Asckis nodded yes as Jenkins gave him a warning. "If we find out you tipped off Harrington or anyone else about this matter, we will come down hard on you."

After obtaining Asckis' sworn statement, the team met alone to discuss whether to interview Richard Harrington's associate, Randy Flemming.

Sam suggested, "Let's wait a few days to see if the surveillance teams turn up anything of value before we do any further interviews."

As they left the town hall, Sam called AUSA Murphy. "Brian, what's the status of the surveillance teams? We need them in position now."

*   *   *

Randy Flemming used his backhoe to help Dickie Harrington plant a few large spruce trees along the backyard tree line at the Harrington summer home. Dickie wanted a wall of Canadian pine trees to separate the backyard from the woods.

While digging, Flemming noticed Harrington was troubled. "Dickie, you look a little pale. Are you still worried about the feds snooping around?"

"Yeah, Randy. I'm a nervous wreck, not only about the feds but my father. He's pissed off at me. How was I supposed to know some fed was driving behind me when I picked up a hitchhiker? Look at me. I'm jittery all the time and can't think straight."

"Listen, I know exactly how to calm you down. I've been watching this young kid in town, and he is just what you like."

"No, no, I, uh, can't. My father told me not to do anything that would bring attention to me. I don't want to get on his bad side again, so nothing can happen near this place."

"No problem, Dickie. Nothing will happen here at your dad's place. We can have fun at my little secret funhouse."

Flemming pulled out his cell phone and scrolled through several photos. Finally, he selected one of a young kid and showed the picture to Dickie.

"Wow, how old is he?" asked Harrington.

"He's around fifteen, I think, but looks more like eighteen. He's about five-eight, maybe one-hundred and twenty pounds, and a real knockout. I've been watching the kid for a few weeks, and I think we can have fun with him like we did last year with that run away from New Jersey."

"Yeah, he's cute, but I don't know, Randy. I'm scared shitless about this investigation. My father was furious with me when I was at his house. He told me to take a week off from work, hide at my house, and do nothing stupid."

"No one knows where my cottage is. It's hidden way off the road in the woods, so nobody will find out. Just think of how great it was last year. C'mon, cousin, you're too uptight and stressed out. You need sumtin' to calm you down, man."

Dickie considered what Randy mentioned. *Randy's right. I could use some relief. I can take the back roads to his place.* "When are you planning on doing this?"

"What's a good day or night for you?"

"What about tonight?" Dickie said hesitantly.

"That's perfect because the kid always meets his two friends at a place called Joy's on Main Street for burgers and shakes on Friday nights. Then, when they finish, the kid walks home alone. So it's a perfect situation for me to offer him a ride."

Dickie craved the thought of having fun. "Call me and let me know what the situation is. Then, maybe, but only maybe, I'll come to your place."

"That's the Dickie I know. We're in for some big-time fun tonight."

* * *

Later that night, around seven o'clock, Dickie's cell phone rang. He felt his adrenaline rising, seeing it was a call from Randy.

"Dickie, it's me, cousin. This gorgeous-looking young kid is takin' a nap on my bed. I just gave him our special drink so he'll be ready for us. So get your ass over here and release all that stress you've been carryin' aroun.' But don't take too long. I'm ready to go at him."

With his sexual urges elevating, Harrington responded, "I'm not that far from your place. I should be there in about thirty minutes, but I can't stay long."

CHAPTER
45

Following Sam's exoneration by Judge Rubino in Hartford, the investigating agents formulated an investigative strategy with Durrell and Murphy at the US attorney's office. Durrell agreed with Sam's recommendation for twenty-four-hour surveillance on Richard Harrington and Randy Flemming. However, it required manpower resources and overtime. As both the Hartford Police and ATF had limited overtime budgets for conducting long-term surveillance, Durrell requested FBI support over Sam's discreet opposition.

On Friday night, the FBI surveillance teams were late getting started, but better late than not at all. The team assigned to Flemming arrived at his small blue cape in Saundersville, MA. Unfortunately, they didn't see his pickup truck in the driveway, and there was no place to park close by without being detected.

They decided to drive through the downtown business section in hopes of spotting his pickup. Driving along Main Street, they didn't see his truck anywhere. They turned around at the end of the business district near the police station and headed back toward Flemming's home.

Senior FBI Agent Jesse Wickens was sitting in the passenger seat while his younger partner, Brett Cooper, drove. "Brett, pull into the police station parking lot, so I can let the desk officer know we're in town surveilling

Flemming's residence. I don't want the department getting pissed because we didn't inform them we're in town."

After Wickens returned to the car from the police station, agent Cooper started the drive back toward Flemming's home.

"I'll look down side streets on the right, and you take note of the side streets on the left for Flemming's pickup," said Wickens.

Cooper glanced down two side streets before slowly driving by the third. "Shit, I think I just spotted Flemming's truck. It looks like he stopped and talked to somebody. I have to turn around."

He couldn't back up with cars close behind him, and there were no parking spaces for him to turn into until the cars passed him.

Wickens feverishly pointed to a driveway. "There, up on the right. Pull into that driveway."

Cooper pulled in, waited for traffic to pass by, and pulled back onto the road. He then shifted into drive and took the next right turn. When he made the turn, the pickup was out of sight.

"Step on the gas and try to catch him. We don't want to lose the bastard," shouted Wickens.

Cooper sped around a slight curve in the road, "I still don't see him. You think he made another turn?"

"Keep going. I looked down the street on the left and didn't see the truck, so he must be up ahead."

They drove another quarter mile before heading around another curve. Wickens spotted the truck. "There he is. I'll check the plate to make sure it's our guy."

Wickens used his binoculars to get a close-up view of the license plate. "That's Flemming, all right. Someone's in the passenger seat. Any idea who he picked up?"

Cooper responded, "I have no idea, but it appeared to be a guy or maybe a kid."

Cooper slowed down to keep a reasonable distance between the two vehicles. He could feel the butterflies swarming inside of him. Being a junior agent, Cooper hadn't been involved in a meaningful criminal case as yet, especially a kidnapping case.

They continued following Flemming for several minutes before the road became more nonresidential. Before long, they crossed into Wilsonbury, Connecticut.

"We just crossed the state line. If this is a kidnapping, it just became a federal offense," said Wickens.

Several minutes later, Flemming took a left turn, heading northeast. Cooper followed onto a rural road that was heavily wooded on each side. Since they were the only two vehicles on the road, Cooper slowed down to distance themselves more from Flemming to avoid suspicion. Farther up the street, the agents saw Flemming's truck take a right turn.

"Coop, drive by the road slowly to ensure Flemming didn't stop to look for a tail."

As they drove by, they didn't see Flemming's truck.

"Shit, let's not lose him. Back up and head down the road."

Once on the road, Cooper stepped on the gas for a quarter-mile before slowing around a sharp curve.

Rounding the curve, Wickens called out. "There he is. I saw the back of his pickup taking a right turn up ahead."

As they slowly approached the road, they saw it was a narrow dirt road like a driveway. Cooper pulled off to the side of the road just past the driveway. Wickens checked the latest version of their navigation and saw that the dirt road ended at a distance of maybe a hundred yards or more. Unfortunately, the navigation didn't show the name of the road.

"There's another dirt road up ahead on the opposite side. I can establish a surveillance position there," said Cooper.

"I didn't see a mailbox telling us the address here," said Wickens.

"You think it's a driveway leading to a house or a dirt road leading into the woods somewhere?" asked Cooper.

They both examined the navigation screen again as Wickens zoomed in for a close-up view.

"It looks like the dirt road doesn't go anywhere. Maybe it's a driveway," said Cooper.

"That's what I think. Coop. Back up past the telephone pole. I want to check if the pole has a number on it as a location marker."

Cooper backed up to the other side of the pole.

"Ah, there's a number 28 on the pole," said Wickens.

Cooper looked at Wickens for instructions as to what they should do next. "Should we drive down the road?"

"No. I'm going to call the state police and ask if they know where this road leads."

Wickens grabbed his folder to look up what state police district covered the area and then called the number for the Danielson Troop. When answered, he identified himself as an FBI agent on surveillance and provided the trooper with their location at a telephone pole number 28 near a dirt road on Wilsonbury Road and no mailbox.

The state police dispatcher said he would contact the trooper who covers that area. He put Wickens on hold. Several minutes later, he was back on the line. "The trooper covering that area never encountered any issues in that remote area. He doesn't know who lives in most of the homes there. He recommended you contact the town's first selectman, who has held the office for several years and would be more familiar with the locations and residents. His name is Tom Parker. I'll give you his cell and home telephone numbers."

Cooper thought Wickens should call the lead agent. "Shouldn't you call Agent Caviello to advise him when we see anything significant?"

"I don't understand why we have to report to an ATF agent for chrissake? We're the FBI. I'll call the AUSA."

Wickens found Murphy's cell number and hit the call number.

Brian Murphy answered his cell, and as Wickens filled him in on the situation, Murphy insisted he call Caviello, who was the lead on the investigation.

"Brian, I shouldn't have to report to an ATF agent."

"C'mon, Jesse, you know Caviello is the case agent. You need to keep him informed and work together as a team without this bullshit interagency competition."

Before Wickens could say another word, Murphy hung up. Then, shaking his head in disagreement, Wickens dialed Caviello's cell number. When Sam answered, Wickens brought him up to speed.

"Did you contact the selectman?" asked Sam.

"No, I haven't contacted him yet."

"Give me his name and number, and I'll call him. Have you been in contact with the team covering Harrington?"

"Yeah, we heard from them about thirty minutes ago informing us they lost Harrington traveling near Putnam."

"Putnam is not that far from Wilsonbury. I'm heading up to meet with you. I should be there in about thirty minutes. Do me a favor, contact the Saundersville PD and determine if anyone reported a missing kid in the past hour or two. Are you parked somewhere hidden from sight?"

No, we don't know how to do our job. We're out here in the open, letting Flemming see us, Wickens sarcastically thought to himself before answering, "Yes, we know how to do our job."

Sam felt the dig from Wickens. "Great, Jesse. We don't want to blow our cover now. I suspect Harrington will join Flemming soon."

Reluctantly, Wickens called the Saundersville Police Department to inquire if any recent abductions had been reported in the town. Detective Lauren Sanders was standing next to the desk sergeant at the PD and overheard the request. The desk sergeant looked at Sanders, who shook her head no, which he passed on to Wickens.

"Copy that. We are still on surveillance, so if something comes up, please let us know. Thanks."

"What's that all about?" asked Detective Sanders.

"The FBI is in town surveilling Randy Flemming, the child molester. I guess they think Randy is on the prowl for another kid."

"Do me a favor. If any further calls on that matter come in, transfer them to me. I'll be in my office."

Driving toward Wilsonbury, Sam dialed the first selectman's number. "Tom Parker here. How can I help you?"

"Mr. Parker, this is Federal Agent Sam Caviello. I am working on a joint kidnapping investigation with the state and local police departments. We have a person of interest who we believe is in your town as we speak. We suspect he may have property on Wilsonbury Road at or near an unmarked dirt road adjacent to a telephone pole marked with the number 28."

"I'm not in my office, but I keep a town map and resident information at home in case of emergencies. So give me a few minutes to check on that area."

"I would appreciate it if you could identify the property owner's name and if the dirt road leads to a dwelling."

While on hold, Sam kept hoping he'd get something tangible in the investigation. *Please, Mr. Parker, tell me something good.* A woman's voice, probably Parker's wife, was heard in the background of the call. Parker told her the FBI was looking for information on a property on Wilsonbury Road. Although Sam couldn't make out everything the woman said, it appeared she was more familiar with the properties in town than Parker.

Parker returned to the call. "My wife remembered that Rose Walsh lived in a small cottage at the end of the dirt road marked number 28. As far as we can remember, Rose was a nice woman who kept to herself. Unfortunately, she passed away, oh, maybe three or four years ago. My wife remembered that she had left the cottage to her son. I checked my records, and it lists Randell F. Walsh as the current owner. My wife said that this Randell fella is Rose's son. Rose was married twice, and her first husband was Marty Flemming, who had a landscaping business in the area."

Whoa, thank you, Mr. Parker. You just made my day, Sam thought. "Mr. Parker, is there a property diagram or plot map for the property?"

Parker answered, "Yes, I have a plot map for the property here."

"Could you take a photo of it on your cell phone and text it to me?"

"Mmm, well, I'm not going to attempt that, but my wife knows how to do it because she is always sending photos to our kids."

Seven minutes later, the photo arrived on Sam's phone. "Mr. Parker, you and your wife have been a great help. I thank both of you. If I am ever this way again, I'd like to thank you both in person. Have a good night."

Sam pressed on the gas pedal, hoping to cut a few minutes off the time to get to the Flemming property.

Agents Cooper and Wickens were parked on the opposite side of the road on another dirt driveway about thirty yards away. They had good cover since the brush on either side of them was high but still allowed them a visual line of sight. They sat there chatting for several minutes until Cooper cracked his window to light up a cigarette.

"Not another one, man. When you get my age, you won't pass the annual physical. You might even need to carry around an oxygen tank to breathe if you're lucky enough to be still alive," jabbed Wickens.

"I'm going to give it up when the baby is born. If I don't, my wife said I'd have to live in the garage."

Wickens liked to tease his younger partner, who'd been on the job for just over a year. Cooper took it in stride without countering in kind in case his senior partner was thin-skinned.

As the joking continued, Cooper moved forward in his seat to get a better look at a car coming down the road. "There's a dark-colored car turning into that driveway, Jesse. It could be a BMW."

Wickens turned his head just as the taillights of the car disappeared. "Oh shit. I was hoping this was going to be a quiet shift. We may not be going home tonight."

Cooper urged Wickens to call Caviello and let him know.

Reluctantly, Wickens took his cell from the dashboard and selected Caviello's number. "Sam, we just spotted a second vehicle, possibly a BMW, entering the same driveway as Flemming."

"That has to be Harrington. I should be there in about ten to fifteen minutes or so. Could you call the state trooper covering this area and request his assistance? We should have a uniformed officer with us when we approach the house."

Wickens asked, "We know there's a house?"

"Yes, Tom Parker said there's a small cottage at the end of the road, and the owner is none other than Randy Flemming. So now, Harrington is showing up to join him."

Wickens considered the situation. "We're not sure it was Harrington who pulled into the driveway. We're parked maybe thirty yards away and couldn't say for sure what make of car it was other than it was dark in color. Also, at this point, do we need to get the state police involved?"

"Jesse, you saw Flemming, a registered sex offender, pick up a kid, and now Harrington, another suspected sex offender, arrived to join him. We have to confront them ASAP, and we'll need a uniformed state trooper with us."

"We're not sure who Flemming picked up. It was too dark. We only saw a male figure, but it could be an adult instead of a kid."

"Jesse, my gut tells me Flemming picked up some young kid, and he and Harrington will assault him. We need to stop them!" He ended the call.

"What did Caviello say, Jesse?"

Wickens turned to his young partner while shaking his head repulsed. "The ATF agent's gut just told him Flemming and Harrington are going to rape the kid that Flemming picked up. He wants the state police to help us confront these two guys. We're not even sure Flemming picked up a kid or if that was Harrington who drove down the driveway, but he wants us to drive down there and confront them. You believe that shit?"

Cooper thought they needed to take action to save a kid. He was excited to partake in a possible takedown of serial killers. However, he didn't want to debate the issue of what was about to happen with his senior partner.

CHAPTER
46

Wickens disagreed with Sam's approach, but he contacted the state police barracks again and asked for support for a possible confrontation with two suspects.

"You got it. I'll dispatch two troopers over to your location now."

Fifteen minutes later, Sam arrived and met with Cooper and Wickens. While waiting for the troopers to show up, Sam contacted AUSA Murphy to inform him of the situation and their plan to confront the two suspects at the house. When he ended that call, he called Agent Ziglar and had him call on all Hartford agents to be on standby to respond to his location.

Shortly after that, Trooper Alex Turner arrived, followed by the second trooper, Brooks Edwards, three minutes later. Sam brought the two troopers up to speed and showed them the plot map he received from the town's selectman, as well as photos of the two suspects.

He then detailed the plan of action. "Trooper Edwards, would you maintain security at the driveway entrance with your emergency lights on but not flashing. Nobody enters the property without authorization from me. Be ready to assist us if we call on you. Trooper Turner, I'd like you to follow agent Cooper and me to the house with your cruiser's emergency strobes on so the cottage occupants can see it's the police. Agent Cooper, I'd like you to cover the back of the house. Jesse, Trooper

Turner, and I will knock and announce our presence at the front door and demand entrance."

After putting on protective vests with police badges clearly displayed, they drove down the dirt driveway to a clearing where a small one-story gray cottage stood. An outside light above the front door was on but very dim. There were single windows on each side of the door. Parked to the left side of the front door, the officers saw Flemming's truck and Harrington's BMW.

Sam quickly noticed that the BMW no longer bore license plate DICKH 1. Instead, it had a commercial plate attached. He suspected Forster Harrington had it registered to his business. After taking a photo of the VIN through the BMW'S windshield, Sam asked Trooper Turner to check its registration.

Turner ran the check on his cruiser's computer. "There was a transfer of the registration of the BMW to a construction service company in North Haven five days ago, but no further information was available."

"Wow, political influence moves quickly and goes wide and deep," whispered Sam.

While Sam and his team were getting ready outside, inside the cottage, Flemming and Harrington, both naked, were resting before having their way with Robbie Walker, age fourteen. Walker was sobbing and barely conscious from the spiked cola Flemming gave him to drink.

Randy and Dickie were listening to loud music, utterly unaware of the police presence outside. They were drinking premium scotch and smoking weed while discussing what devious acts they would have with their young victim lying in bed. They were only waiting for the drug to take effect.

Robbie continued whimpering and cried out in a gasping voice. "Please, my dad will worry about me not being home. He'll call the police. Please, let me go home. I won't tell anyone."

In an unsympathetic tone, Randy replied, "Shut up, kid. We're going to have some fun first."

"Ha, he's not going anywhere other than in a hole in the ground," Dickie whispered.

They both chuckled and reminisced about all the past fun times they had together.

"Okay, enough drinking and babbling. Let's show this kid how to please us," chuckled Flemming.

As both were about to start the fun with Robbie, they heard a loud sound coming from the front of the cottage.

Outside, Sam knocked loudly on the door.

FBI Agent Wickens and Trooper Turner stood beside him, waiting for someone to come to the door.

"What if he doesn't open the door? You know, it could just be three friends playing cards. We're not even sure who Flemming picked up. It could be another guy, and maybe they're having a threesome, for all we know," said Wickens.

"If he's not doing anything illegal, he should come to the door and open it, don't you think?" asked Sam.

Sam was annoyed by Wickens' constant questions as he banged on the door again, this time yelling, "Police, open up!"

Flemming peaked out a slot in the wooden window shutters. "Fuck, it's the cops."

"Oh shit, now what? I've gotta get out of here," said a panic-stricken Harrington.

"Listen, the door is dead-bolted and secured with a steel bar across it. I'm not goin' to let them in. I'll hide you and the kid while I deal with these guys. You both have to be quiet, understand? Don't panic, and wait till I get back. Get the kid off the bed and keep him quiet."

Flemming took his time before stepping to the front door as he heard another loud knock and an announcement to open the door.

Flemming put his head close to the door and yelled out, "What do you want? I haven't done anything wrong!" Once again, he heard the command to open the door. Flemming vehemently responded, "Do you have a warrant? If not, get off my property!"

Flemming then rushed back to the bedroom to get Harrington and the kid secured.

Outside, Agent Wickens questioned Sam again. "Well, what do we do now? We don't have a warrant."

To be on the safe side, Sam called Brian Murphy. When Murphy answered, Sam updated him regarding the stalemate the team faced.

Murphy wanted every minute detail a judge would need before issuing a telephonic search warrant. But, Sam argued, "There's no time to get a warrant. We need to act now! They could be assaulting a young kid inside."

CHAPTER
47

The desk sergeant at the Saundersville PD moved quickly from the coffee pot to his desk to answer the phone, sounding off loud enough to be heard down the hall. "Saundersville Police Department, you're being recorded?"

"This is John Walker. My fourteen-year-old son, Robbie, was supposed to be home more than an hour ago. He met his two friends at Joy's Luncheonette on Main Street around five-thirty. I told him to be home by seven-thirty. When he didn't arrive by eight, I called his cell but only got his voicemail. I then called his friends' parents. They told me their sons were home safe and sound. I asked if I could speak to their son, who told me they left Joy's at seven and walked with Robbie to the corner of Main and Westview Road. When they walked across Westview and stopped to talk to a friend, they saw a pickup truck stop near where Robbie was walking and saw him get into the truck."

As the desk sergeant listened to John Walker, Detective Sanders walked by the lobby heading toward the front entrance. He yelled out to her. She turned and softly said, "Going to get coffee. Be back shortly."

The desk sergeant shook his head no. He put his hand over the phone's receiver. "Missing boy. You need to take this."

Sanders turned and practically jogged into the secure area where the desk sergeant handed her the phone. After listening to Walker repeat his story, she asked Walker for his son's description."

She scribbled notes on the desk incident report sheet before ending the call.

"Sergeant, you still have the FBI agent's cell number?"

He scrambled to find it among the messages on his desk. When found, Sanders punched the number on her cell phone, waiting for an answer.

On the fifth ring, Agent Wickens answered the call. "This is Saundersville Detective Sanders. You called earlier asking if there were any reports of a missing person. Well, now we have one. Two kids saw their fourteen-year-old friend picked up by a green pickup truck just after seven tonight."

"Hold on for a second. Don't hang up," snapped Wickens. He interrupted Sam on the phone with AUSA Murphy to inform him what the detective had reported. Sam repeated the message to Murphy. "We now have exigent circumstances for immediate entry."

Murphy agreed, "Get in there fast and protect that kid."

Sam ended his call, yelling out, "Does anyone have a battering ram to breach the front door?"

The trooper and Wickens both shook their heads no.

Detective Sanders, overhearing the request on the phone, yelled, "The department has one! I'll take it to you!"

Sam could hear her response and grabbed Wickens' cell phone out of his hand. "Detective, this is Agent Sam Caviello. I'm going to give you the location just over the border in Connecticut. Get here as quickly as you can with a battering ram because the front door might be barricaded. If possible, bring the biggest guy available to use the ram. There will be a state police cruiser stationed at the driveway entrance. Please hurry."

"I'll be there in about twenty minutes," said Sanders.

"Trooper Turner, could you radio Trooper Edwards to allow Detective Sanders to enter and then follow her in to assist us?"

Sam devised a plan to enter the residence with the help of the two FBI agents and Trooper Turner while waiting for Sanders to arrive. Inside, Flemming was prepared for the police to enter his cottage.

Twenty minutes later, Sam and the others heard a police siren in the background. Not long afterward, Detective Sanders arrived in an unmarked police sedan with Officer Bruce Bellinger, a six-foot, five-inch muscular SWAT member. Trooper Edwards followed them in for extra support.

After the introductions, Sam outlined the plan to enter the home. "Agent Cooper will continue to maintain coverage at the rear of the house. The entry team will consist of me, Agent Wickens, Trooper Turner, and Detective Sanders. Officer Bellinger will follow behind us. Trooper Edwards, I'd like you to cover the front area and the vehicles until called in to assist. Officer Bellinger will use the battering ram if Flemming doesn't open the door. We'll enter the cottage with two teams of two and the fifth person as their backup."

Sam then knocked loudly on the door announcing their presence and their last warning to open the door. With no response, Sam gave the order to hit the door. Officer Bellinger swung the ram as far back as possible and back into the door. The door broke open about twelve inches. The solid aluminum bar securing the door sprung away from its steel hinge bracket. Bellinger rammed the door again, causing it to break wide open and taking the lower door hinge with it, leaving the door dangling by its upper hinge.

Sam and Wickens entered, followed by Trooper Turner and Detective Sanders. Bellinger tailed in behind them as their backup. Flemming was sitting alone on the sofa in the living room with a smirk on his face as Sam entered and yelled out, "Police, on the floor now!"

Flemming just sat there looking like he didn't have a worry in the world. Sam grabbed him by his long hair and threw him to the floor, saying, "Jesse, cuff him." Sam continued moving to search the first bedroom. He quickly cleared the bedroom, assisted in clearing the bathroom, and then went to the second bedroom, where Trooper Turner and Detective Sanders had cleared. All the rooms were empty.

It bewildered the team that there was no sight of Harrington or the boy. Sanders and Bellinger searched for a basement while Sam stayed in the bedroom looking for an attic or trap door leading to an attic.

Not finding an opening for an attic, Sam went back into the main bedroom, noticed a rear window was open, and looked out into the woods. "Agent Cooper, anybody come out the window?"

"Not a soul, Sam."

Sam moved back to where Flemming lay face down on the floor and cuffed behind his back. He grabbed him by the hair again and angrily demanded, "Where's Harrington and the kid?"

"What kid? There's no kid here. It's just my friend and me, and he went out of the window."

"You're a liar. No one went out the window. Our agents saw you picking up the kid in Saundersville."

"Hey, I didn't pick up any kid, and if I had, he'd be here, wouldn't he?"

Sam cursed. "You're a worthless piece of shit."

Sanders joined Sam. "There's no basement, only a crawl space."

"Let's search the bedrooms again. Double-check for trap doors on the floor and under the bed and carpets." Sam joined Sanders and Turner to search in the smaller bedroom first.

"Nothing in here. We looked under the bed and pulled up an area rug. Again, nothing," reported Sanders. Both Sam and Sanders stared at each other with puzzled looks.

"Where could they be hiding?" questioned Sanders as they walked back to the main bedroom and heard Flemming shout.

"I told you there's no kid here. You guys were just too late to see my friend go out the window and into the woods."

Sam and Sanders ignored Flemming as they stood baffled, gazing into the bedroom. Sanders studied the bedroom, scanning the ceiling and the floor for possible loose boards. Nothing was apparent. Sam stood next to her, disappointed about not finding Harrington and the kid.

While studying the bedroom, Sanders closed her eyes and concentrated on picturing the design of most bedrooms until she thought back to her own bedroom, visualizing what she saw. Then, out of the blue, she shouts. "Oh shit." She turns to face Sam. "There's no closet in this room."

Sam looked at her, then surveyed the bedroom again. "Goddamn it, you're right, Detective. There has to be one here."

"The only place it could be is behind the entertainment center," said Sanders.

Sam affirmed her impulse and advanced to the entertainment center against the wall opposite the bed. The unit's center section had a television with two doors on both ends and four drawers at the bottom. Sam first tried pushing the unit, but it wouldn't budge. Sam opened the door on the left side, which was a narrow wardrobe closet containing a pair of old jeans, two smelly sweatshirts, and a pair of boots. Next, Sam opened the right-side glass door that held a receiver, a DVD player, and the TV cable box on two shelves with several pornographic DVDs. Above the TV, Sam found a black box with a tinted glass front on another shelf. He pulled the box down to examine it. It was a three-sided box with an open backside. Hidden behind the box was a small video camera aimed at the bed.

"Oh, I can guess what these creeps filmed on that camera," voiced Detective Sanders.

Sam took photos of the camera with his cell phone, as did Sanders. Then, Sam moved back to the wardrobe door, removed the clothing, and lit up the backside of the wardrobe with his flashlight but found nothing. He did the same with the other door and the bottom four drawers but found nothing. Finally, moving to the right side of the unit, Sam felt for a button or switch of some kind. Again, he didn't find anything.

Moving to the left side again, he felt the whole side with his fingers from the top and worked his way to the bottom. At the bottom, he felt a thin vertical line like a narrow crack at the rear base of the unit.

"Detective Sanders, can you light up the area where my hand is with a flashlight?" asked Sam.

Once lit, he realized what he had found. "I thought it was a crack, but it's some kind of lever."

He felt for the bottom of the lever, and sure enough, it lifted out a bit. He pulled it up a couple of inches, but it slipped back to its original position. He realized he needed to use more muscle to pull it entirely up. So he switched to his strong hand and pulled firmly. When he did, he heard a clicking sound as the unit moved up a bit from the floor.

"We got something here, Detective," said Sam.

He then moved to the other side of the unit and had Sanders light up the bottom with her flashlight, where he found a similar lever. Sam gripped the bottom of the lever and forced it up, causing the unit to lift. Sam stood up straight and looked at Sanders. She gave him a thumbs up.

"Come on, baby. Move and don't let us down." Sam started to push the unit straight along the wall. As he shoved the unit, it began to slide. "Show us what you're hiding," Sam said as he continued pushing until it revealed an opening in the wall, a hidden closet.

As it opened most of the way, Sam yelled, "Surprise!"

Inside the closet sat Richard Harrington on the floor, wearing only a white T-shirt and boxer shorts. Between his legs was fourteen-year-old Robbie Walker, naked, with Harrington's hand over his mouth to keep him quiet.

Sam ordered, "All right, scumbag, let go of the kid, and don't you move unless told to."

Sam gently lifted Robbie away from Harrington and placed him on the bed. He took the kid's clothes from the closet floor. Robbie was still in a partial stupor, trembling and sobbing. Sam consoled him the best he could.

"You're safe now, Robbie. We're the police. You don't have to be afraid now. We'll call your dad, and you'll be home soon."

Sam helped Robbie get dressed while asking Sanders to call for an ambulance and then take Robbie out of the house to a warm car away from the scene. Trooper Turner commanded Harrington to move out of the closet and lay face down on the floor.

Flemming, sensing he's been had, attempted to get up from the floor, but Officer Bellinger pushed his head back down to the floor hard.

"Fuck, man. That hurt. I think you broke my nose. You didn't have to push so hard. I was just trying to get up."

"No one told you to get up. If you move again, I'll smash your face down even harder."

No one wanted to help Harrington put on his trousers, so Trooper Turner handed Harrington his pants and told him to stand up and get dressed. When Harrington stood, he was off-balance, trying to place one leg through his pants. That's when Turner purposely bumped him, causing Harrington to fall flat on his ass. Chuckles emitted from all the officers. Noticeable smirks remained on their faces while fear unmistakably covered Harrington's face. Harrington's arms quivered while pulling up his trousers the best he could. Turner handed him his shirt and advised him to stay down on his butt until told to get up. Harrington was totally spooked, unable to hold himself from peeing in his pants.

Sam decided to call Brian Murphy and brief him on finding the abused fourteen-year-old boy held by Harrington in a hidden closet. "I'm going to arrest Flemming and Harrington, have them initially processed at the Saundersville PD, and then transport them to Hartford. Can you call Ziggy and have him contact the rest of the guys to head to Wilsonbury? I'll have Agent Wickens contact the other FBI surveillance team and send them here to help out? Finding these guys in the act, I recommend getting search warrants for Flemming's Wilsonbury cottage, his Saundersville home, and Harrington's summer home in Uniondale. The warrants need to include the search of the property grounds by cadaver-sniffing dogs. We'll also need forensic personnel in case we uncover remains on the properties."

"I agree, Sam. Great work. You likely saved a boy's life today, not to mention it will put two serial sex offenders away for a long time. I'm anxious to call Durrell and let her know what you found. I'll call you back shortly to get all the information we need for the search warrant affidavits."

"One more favor, Brian. We need uniformed officers to help secure the properties after we finish here. Could you contact the state police commissioner and inform him of the arrests and the need for uniformed officers to help secure the two Connecticut properties until the warrants are issued? Two troopers are assisting us at the scene from the Danielson barracks. It would be great if they could stay and get some overtime. Our way of thanking them."

When finished with his call, Sam officially arrested Harrington and Flemming and read them their rights in front of all the officers as witnesses. When the ambulance arrived, Detective Sanders volunteered to accompany the boy to the hospital and arrange to have his father brought there. She called her chief to fill him in on the events of the evening.

"Chief, I'll need assistance from another detective to meet me later at the PD. Do you want to contact Robbie Walker's father, or would you prefer I call him?"

"I think you should call the father, and I'll arrange for a black-and-white to pick him up for transport to the hospital. I'll have a day shift detective report to the PD to assist you, Lauren. Good job tonight."

Before the five ATF agents arrived, Sam heard back from Murphy. He confirmed the state police commissioner would assign state troopers to assist in the overnight security of the two properties with an ATF agent. In addition, the commissioner will contact the troopers currently at the Wilsonbury site to remain there until they are relieved.

When the ATF agents arrived, Sam assigned two agents, one in Wilsonbury and the other at the Harrington property, to provide overnight security with the state police. The following day would begin the search for any buried remains at the three properties.

CHAPTER
48

Early the following day, Forster Harrington learned of his son's arrest from the state's attorney, Frank Reynolds. Forster was appalled hearing the details of the arrest. It was a long time since he felt so helpless and ashamed. He demanded Reynolds do something to mitigate the charges against his son and get him free on bail. Reynolds, already informed of the arrest, knew he would hear from Forster. He was aware Forster donated a lot of money to those in power and expected something in return.

"Forster, the feds had surveillance on your son and his associate, Flemming. They observed Flemming picking up a fourteen-year-old boy and taking him to a cottage where he was drugged. Your son and Flemming were going to rape the kid. However, the feds and state police raided the cottage before they did, and they found your son half-naked, hiding in a concealed closet with his arms around the naked kid. As a result, the feds are getting search warrants for all property owned by your son's associate and your property in Uniondale."

"What? Why my fucking property? I didn't have anything to do with raping this kid. You told me this all happened at the other guy's cottage. Besides, they already searched my property. Can't you stop them from searching my place?"

Reynolds was emphatic in his response. "Not a chance, Forster. Your son is the prime suspect in the disappearance of another young kid, who your son picked up hitchhiking and brought to your property. Besides, it's a federal case, and it will be a federal judge who approves the search warrants. I can do nothing at the state level to intervene with federal searches. I tried helping you earlier that turned out to be a disaster. I don't want anything to come back on me."

"There must be something you can do. Don't you know anyone at the US attorney's office that could at least lessen the charges?"

"Listen, Forster, if everything is true about your kid, he's going to spend many years in jail. The best you or your attorney can do is blame your son's associate, this guy Flemming, for whatever happened to those kids after they abused them. I understand Flemming is a convicted pedophile and spent time in jail. He's on the sex offender's list. Perhaps your attorney could argue Flemming is more culpable in targeting and assaulting underage kids. The only other option is getting a good psychiatrist to say your son is mentally incapacitated and not responsible for his actions."

Harrington was offended by the lack of support he received. "I'll confer with my attorney about protecting my property against any search. I don't think it's right for them to search my home when I haven't done anything that this guy Flemming or my son did elsewhere."

"That's a decision between you and your attorney. Just be aware you may not like what they find there. I advise you not to interfere with the search. Otherwise, you may find yourself in jail along with your son."

After ending the call, Reynolds contacted Ron Freedman, the governor's chief of staff. "Ron, I just got off the phone with Forster Harrington. He's pissed and wants help to intervene and reduce his son's exposure to legal jeopardy in the courts."

"I sympathize with Forster, but his son is in deep trouble. I suggest you avoid Harrington at this point and not take his calls."

After the call ended, Freedman felt the need to call the governor to inform him of the situation. Once Freedman started to appraise the governor about Harrington's request, the governor interrupted him. "Ron, in no uncertain terms, I do not want to know a thing about it. Keep me totally out of it. The only way I'm going to find out about the arrest and what happened before it is from what I read in the newspaper. Understood?"

*　　*　　*

The US attorney's office arranged for five cadaver-sniffing canines, their handlers, and forensic technicians from the state, the FBI, and ATF to assist in searching the three properties. Their plan called for search teams of seven to eight members each, including members from ATF, the FBI, state and local police, and the US attorney's office. Durrell scheduled a briefing for the teams at the Woodhaven Town Hall at ten in the morning. After the briefing, the teams would begin searching the three properties by noon.

Team one was headed up jointly by Sam and Hartford Police Lieutenant Marcus Nelson, coordinating the search at Harrington's Uniondale property. Team two was led jointly by ATF Agent Ziglar and Hartford Detective Jenkins at the Flemming property in Wilsonbury. Durrell assigned two cadaver dogs and two forensic technicians to these two teams and a canine and two forensic technicians with team three. ATF Agent Macheski, Hartford Police Detective Griffen, and Saundersville Police Detective Lauren Sanders led team three at Flemming's Saundersville property.

Sam's team headed out to Harrington's property following the morning briefing. When arriving at Harrington's property, they observed a large dump truck parked at the end of the driveway. However, no one was inside the truck. The truck blocked their entry to the house, so Sam called the ATF agent assigned to secure the property. The agent who answered apologized, saying, "It's my fault. I had to relieve myself and drove away from the road to take a leak. That's when these guys showed up."

"Okay, we'll deal with it. Thanks."

The agent informed Sam that Forster Harrington had just shown up with his attorney and an associate and wanted to enter the premises.

"Don't allow anyone in the house or move around the property unescorted. I should be there with the warrant in a few minutes."

Sam wasn't happy the truck was in the driveway. He suspected Harrington was trying to interfere with the search, but he wasn't going to take any bullshit from him or his attorney. Sam asked Lieutenant Nelson and Troopers Curtis Simmons and Dan O'Connell to go with him on foot up to the house. He asked the other team members to remain parked on the side of the road until he could get the truck removed from the driveway. While they trudged up the driveway on foot, Trooper O'Connell noticed a black metal object within the leaves on the edge of the driveway. He bent down to pick it up.

"Wait, Dan. That could be evidence. Let's carefully brush away the leaves to see what it is first." Then, after seeing it was a flashlight, Sam added. "I'm going to call for our evidence coordinator to meet us here so she can record and secure the flashlight as evidence."

A few minutes later, Jennifer Clarkson arrived with an evidence marker, which she placed next to the flashlight and took a couple of photos of it. She recorded the finding and had Trooper O'Connell sign the evidence envelope along with her signature. Then, wearing latex gloves, she picked up the flashlight and mentioned that it appeared to contain blood spatter. Sam and the troopers glanced at the flashlight before Jennifer placed it inside the envelope. They then continued up the driveway toward the house.

When they finally approached the clearing, Sam spotted Harrington's black Lincoln with commercial plates parked in front of the garage. Three men stood on the front porch, safeguarded by an ATF agent and a uniformed state trooper. Sam approached the men and displayed his badge. "I'm Special Agent Sam Caviello. I have a federal warrant to search the property."

One of the men dressed in a suit spoke. "I'm Darren Rothenburg, Mr. Harrington's attorney. I would like to see the warrant."

After reviewing the warrant, he introduced Forster Harrington as the property owner and his assistant, Lonnie Haden. He questioned why a warrant was issued for this property since Mr. Harrington is a highly respected businessman in the state and has not violated any laws.

"We have probable cause to believe Mr. Harrington's son, Richard, committed a crime here, and we're going to search for evidence of that crime. We respect your position and any concerns you have, but I recommend you also respect ours. We are here on orders from a federal judge to search the property. If you want to observe without any interference, I'll allow it. However, any interruption or provocation from you during our search will result in your removal from the property. Do we have an understanding, Mr. Rothenburg?"

The attorney nodded his head yes while looking at his client, Forster Harrington.

"Since we have an understanding, please have the dump truck removed from the driveway entrance."

Harrington interjected. "We had plans to bring equipment up to the house for repairs, but the truck broke down and wouldn't start. We'll need to have it towed."

"I don't believe you, Mr. Harrington. You knew we were coming with a warrant. That's why you brought your attorney, right? Not to mention, I doubt you and your attorney are planning on doing repairs dressed up in five-hundred-dollar suits. The truck is impeding our investigation. I suggest you have your friend Lonnie take the keys out of his pocket, walk down to the truck, and move it."

There was silence. Sam turned his focus from Harrington to his attorney. "If you don't have the truck removed in the next five minutes, I'll have it towed away."

"Be my guest. It'll save me money from having it towed," said Harrington.

Sam looked at Rothenburg. "Is this the way you want to play it, Counselor? I'm trying to be accommodating, but if you insist on impeding our work here, I can be a real hard-ass. Not only will the truck be towed at Harrington's expense, but it will also be impounded and held as evidence after we arrest you for impeding our search. Furthermore, none of you will be allowed to remain on the property."

Rothenburg looked to Harrington, who turned his back to him.

Sam sized up Harrington's associate, Lonnie Haden, who stood six feet, three inches tall, weighed about two-hundred-and-sixty pounds and was dressed in worn-out grimy jeans.

Sam asked, "Lonnie, I assume you are the truck driver?"

"Don't answer that," Harrington told Lonnie.

Irritated, Sam pulled out his cell phone, called US Attorney Durrell, and explained the situation at the property. She asked to speak to Rothenburg.

Rothenburg took the phone and listened. "Mr. Rothenburg, this is US Attorney Debra Durrell. If your client, Forster Harrington, impedes our warrant, I'll ask the judge to rule that you and Harrington are in contempt of court. If you don't remove the truck immediately, I'll ask that you both be arrested and brought before him."

Rothenburg responded, "I understand. That won't be necessary. We'll comply." He handed the phone back to Sam, pulled Harrington aside, and whispered instructions. Sam could see the anger in Harrington's scowled face.

Fuming, Harrington said, "Lonnie, go move the truck. You can go home."

It infuriated Sam, knowing Harrington purposely lied about the truck. He realized Harrington was there to impede the search and decided he wouldn't put up with him if it continued. It took twenty minutes to clear the driveway and get the entire team to the house. Then, Clarkson, ATF Agent Sanchez, Hartford Detective Kalisha Jenkins, and Trooper Simmons began to search the house's interior.

The technicians' responsibility was to search for fingerprints, blood, and hair fibers and photograph any evidence found. In addition, Lieutenant Nelson coordinated the canine handlers searching the immediate outside grounds surrounding the house and the forest area in the front and rear of the property.

Trooper O'Connell, a Worcester ATF agent, and Sam searched the woods from the front of the house to the road. They started their search in a designated straight line, starting west of the driveway. The three men, separated about twenty yards apart, carefully searched their left and right as they slowly inspected the area while advancing toward the road. Once they reached the road, they returned toward the house, covering the rest of the site in the same manner. They did not find anything of an evidentiary nature. In the meantime, the two canines cleared the grass-covered front, side, and backyard immediately surrounding the house.

As the handlers guided the two canines into the backwoods, they noticed heavy equipment tracks leading into the woods. One handler hollered out to Nelson they found tracks leading to a suspicious section not too far into the woods. "It appears recent digging occurred here, so we'll begin the search at this spot before expanding further."

Inside the house, the lab technicians raised numerous fingerprint samples and secured hair fibers from the kitchen area, including several near the kitchen table. Also, they found a pair of trousers with what appeared to have bloodstains in a closet between the living room and kitchen. In the garage trash can, an agent found a New York Yankees baseball cap buried at the bottom of the container. The agent wondered why part of the inside liner had been removed. Knowing the missing kid wore a Yankees cap, the agent considered the section removed might have included the owner's name, so he tagged it as evidence. Forster Harrington never returned to the house to burn the contents of the trash can.

CHAPTER
49

It wasn't long afterward that Sam answered a call from Agent Ziglar, who was ecstatic. "Sam, the freaking dogs are going crazy over here at Flemming's place! The dogs made four alerts so far."

"Shit. It looks like these guys have been doing this for some time, Zig. Have the forensic technicians start digging. When they find something, call me back."

Back at Harrington's property, the canines started sniffing along the area made by the tracks deeper into the woods. Sam and Trooper O'Connell went back into the house to assist in the search. As they entered the house, Sam saw agent Clarkson arguing with Harrington and his attorney. When Clarkson saw Sam enter, she immediately complained to him.

"Harrington continues obstructing our search by insinuating the downstairs bedroom is his and his wife's room and off-limits."

Sam was exasperated. "Mr. Harrington, I'm going to say this one last time. The warrant covers the search of the entire house, the grounds, the garage, and any vehicles on the property. Seeing that your Lincoln is on the grounds, we will also search that."

Harrington immediately protested. "That's my car and not part of this search. You're not searching my car!"

Sam faced the attorney. "This will be the last time I warn you. If you insist on obstructing or harassing those searching, I'll have you removed from the property. Now, I want you two outside on the porch until we have completed our search."

Rothenburg inserted, "Mr. Harrington has a point. His and his wife's bedroom and bathroom have nothing to do with what his son may or may not have done."

Sam insisted they talk outside on the porch.

"This is my fucking house, and I have the right to see what you guys are doing here. I can't see what you are doing if I'm outside on the porch," demanded Harrington.

Sam's patience was wearing thin. "If you don't voluntarily move outside, I'll be forced to have the troopers forcefully remove you from the premises. Now move outside."

"Fuck you and the troopers. You should be in jail where you belong instead of trampling through my private home and looking through my wife's personal belongings. If you guys break or steal anything, I'll sue your asses for every penny you have, which is probably very little," argued Harrington.

Sam turned to Trooper O'Connell, standing by listening to the argument.

"Dan, please escort Harrington and his attorney outside and do not allow them back into the house."

Trooper O'Connell, a tall young muscular guy, directed Harrington and his attorney out to the porch. Trooper Simmons, also close by, joined in to back up O'Connell.

Attorney Rothenburg, recognizing they were in a no-win situation, grabbed Harrington by the arm and practically pushed him outside to the porch. Harrington wasn't happy and continued arguing with his attorney. Finally, while forced outside the front door, Harrington turned to face Sam. "And you're not going to search my fucking car!"

Sam's stress was causing a tension headache. He felt the pressure increasing along the back of his head and his neck. Hoping it would help calm his nerves, he decided to join the search of the house and get his mind off the issues with Forster Harrington. A half-hour into searching, Sam received another call from Agent Ziglar.

"The dogs have hit on six sites so far. The handlers marked the areas and gave the dogs a break while the forensic guys started digging. It's a slow process. I'll get back to you when we find something."

"Thanks, Zig. There are no alerts here yet, but I feel certain there will be. Stay in touch."

Sam felt terrible that there may be six lost souls buried at Flemming's place. His only thought was for Andy Richardson. He wished nothing happened to him, and he was alive and well, but if he wasn't, he hoped to find him here on Harrington's property. He needed evidence to put Harrington's son, Richard, away for a long time.

Sam was roused from his thoughts when he heard a handler shouting, "We have an alert."

Dammit! Sam thought. *I knew there were bodies buried here.*

Sam called Brian Murphy to bring him up to speed on the search at the Harrington property and the issues with Forster Harrington. Murphy told him Durrell was heading there now and should arrive in about twenty minutes. "I have to say, Sam, she is impressed with your work in this case. If we find bodies buried there, I bet she'll trust all your hunches in the future."

While the forensic technicians carefully removed soil from the first alert site, the other handler announced another canine alert. ATF agents and a local police officer began assisting the technicians. Everyone hoped for an outcome that would end the mayhem caused by the two predators.

Sam anxiously awaited the findings when he received another call from Ziglar reporting that the technicians had uncovered skeletal remains in two graves. Although solemn in his thoughts regarding young kids buried there, Sam couldn't help but think: *We got these bastards.*

US Attorney Durrell arrived at the site with the ATF SAC, the Hartford Police chief, and Colonel Bennett. They all proceeded to the area where the technicians carefully excavated where the canines alerted. Durrell joined

Sam and Lieutenant Nelson near the dig site as a forensic technician gave a preliminary report on what they found in the first grave.

"It appears the remains are of a young male with blond hair, buried here no longer than three to four weeks ago. I found a blue backpack alongside the body. Under a flap inside the bag, I found a college student parking permit in the name of Andrew Richardson."

Standing next to Sam, Lieutenant Nelson whispered, "It will be painful for the Richardson family. I'm not looking forward to calling them with what we found."

Sam nodded his head in agreement as he glanced at Durrell, who looked repulsed. She moved closer to Sam, whispering, "You were right all along, Sam. Your hunch was on the money. I have to hand it to you. You're a gifted investigator."

Sam turned away from her so she wouldn't see the grin on his face while giving thought to her comment. *Wow, she guessed right.*

Fifteen minutes later, the partial remains of another body were uncovered, not far from the first. The forensic technician inspecting the remains called out his preliminary findings.

"The remains are of a male who appears to have had reddish hair. Based on the decomposition, I estimate the remains have been in the ground for several months."

Sam looked at Lieutenant Nelson, whispering, "Josh Davis."

As they stood near the first gravesite, they heard the sound of the dog barking and alerting approximately ten yards from the first two.

Forster Harrington, hearing the dog barking and the commotion in the backwoods, insisted on seeing what was happening. Attorney Rothenburg asked Trooper O'Connell to allow his client to see what was happening on his property. As O'Connell stepped in front of the attorney, Harrington snuck away, moving quickly toward the back of the house. He started yelling obscenities as he neared the woods. Sam turned and saw him coming his way. He quickly moved to stop Harrington as Trooper O'Connell chased behind him. Just as Sam got close, Harrington stopped and was about to take a swing at him. Sam dove under his swing and struck him like a football lineman in the midsection, knocking him to the ground. Sam sat on top of him, whispering words Harrington didn't want to hear. "We found the bodies your son buried back in the woods. I have a good mind to throw you in one of the graves, you piece of shit."

O'Connell, joined by Trooper Simmons, took control of Harrington, who continued swearing as he struggled to get away from them and take another swing at Sam. The troopers finally put him down on his knees.

Colonel Bennett and Durrell watched as Harrington cursed and struggled to get free. Finally, Colonel Bennett marched toward the troopers as Harrington continued cursing.

"We can't put up with his behavior. Arrest him for attempted assault and interfering with an officer. Take him to the nearest barracks for processing," ordered Bennett.

Harrington's attorney pleaded with the colonel. "Don't arrest him! I'll calm him down and remove him from the property."

"Take him out of here," Bennett told the two troopers

The troopers pulled Harrington to his feet, handcuffed him, and escorted him toward the state police cruiser.

Attorney Rothenburg followed. "I'll come with my client!"

"Not with us, you're not," said O'Connell.

"But I came with him. I don't have a ride."

"Tough shit," said O'Connell while getting into the cruiser's driver's seat. He backed the cruiser up, turned, and drove down the dirt driveway. Rothenburg raised both his arms up in hopelessness.

The searches at the three sites lasted for nearly four hours before they called it off due to the fading daylight. Those searching uncovered three remains at the Harrington property and four at Flemming's Wilsonbury property. Additionally, they found the remains of one body at Flemming's Saundersville property. Agents also found several videos of Flemming assaulting and raping multiple boys and girls at his Saundersville home. Two of the videos included Richard Harrington's presence.

CHAPTER
50

U S Attorney Durrell placed a call to the US Attorney General in Washington, informing her of the horrific findings at the three properties. Durrell got the green light to schedule a preliminary press conference. She decided to meet with her assistants and the local and state command staff to prepare a short message to the public, followed by a more detailed press conference in the weeks following the examination and identification of all the uncovered remains. She decided to hold the initial press conference at the Uniondale elementary school cafeteria, a short distance from the town hall.

Durrell signaled Sam and Lieutenant Nelson to meet privately with her. "I'd like to give reporter Allison Gaynor an early heads-up on our initial press conference, as thanks for her reporting and the information she gave on Buzzy Dunnledd's connection to Harrington. Please contact and meet with her somewhere away from everybody. Give her a summary of what's taken place here, without victims' names, so she gets a head start on the news cycle."

Nelson said, "She'll want to bring a camera crew."

Durrell thought about it for a moment. "Tell her she can bring one cameraman, but you'll have to accompany them to the locations without allowing entry onto the property or near the areas searched. Let her get some location shots for her story and tell her I may answer some of her questions privately after the press conference."

Sam made the call to Gaynor. "Allison, this is Agent Sam Caviello. Can you meet Lieutenant Nelson and me at the Uniondale Town Hall within the hour?"

"What's this about? Has there been a breakthrough in the kidnapping case?" asked Gaynor.

Sam responded, "I can't say anything over the phone. But, you don't want to miss out on the scoop we will give you before other reporters learn of it."

As expected, Gaynor asked if she could bring a camera crew.

"You can bring one cameraman and have limited access to certain locations. It's imperative that you don't talk to anyone about this other than telling your boss you'll have something for the early news cycle. There will be a press conference later this afternoon. Thanks to Durrell, you'll be getting an early heads-up on the story before the other reporters. So, no leaking this out to anyone. Keep it to yourself. Understood?"

Less than an hour later, Gaynor and her cameraman pulled their van into the parking lot at the town hall. When she arrived, Sam exited his car, leaving the lieutenant seated inside. "Hi, Alli. It's good to see you again. The lieutenant and I will be your guide today."

Alli was a beautiful, slender twenty-eight-year-old, five feet, five inches tall, with deep blue eyes and long curly blond hair. When she smiled back at Sam, it looked like she winked at him, or maybe it was wishful thinking on Sam's part. Nevertheless, Sam was very attracted to her.

"No doubt this will generate the biggest news story of the year in Hartford. Let's get started." Sam opened the rear door of his car for her.

"Alli, before we begin, I need your promise and your cameraman's that what you are about to learn and see cannot be reported on the air until just before the press conference and not in front of other reporters. You also have to promise not to mention you had advance notice."

"I promise, Sam, and that goes for Joel, my cameraman."

Sam constantly looked at her in the review mirror as she asked questions. Her eyes were on him the entire time. He didn't see a wedding ring on her finger and wondered if she had a special guy in her life.

Lieutenant Nelson and Sam gave Alli a summary of the investigation, including that they uncovered several human remains on three separate properties in Connecticut and Massachusetts. Excited, Gaynor asked multiple questions, one after another. Sam tried slowing her down, explaining they were limited in what they could reveal, but Durrell would disclose more at the press conference.

"We will drive you by the search locations so you can take photos and say a few words taped on camera, but not live. Unfortunately, you will not be allowed onto the properties since the searches are ongoing. However, you can mention that two federal judges issued search warrants for the three properties. ATF agents and Hartford Police detectives began searching the properties with assistance from the FBI, the Connecticut State Police, and local police from Saundersville, Massachusetts."

"Have you identified any of the remains yet?" she asked.

"No definitive identifications of the remains have been made. However, we have arrested two suspects currently held in Hartford. We are not authorized to reveal any names," advised Nelson.

Over the next hour, Gaynor gave a recorded brief storyline at each property location. To avoid onlookers, agents had only one police vehicle visible at the end of the driveways in Uniondale and Wilsonbury. In Sandersville, the local police used construction warning signs to conceal the reason for the police presence at Flemming's home.

Each time she got back into Sam's car from a property site, Gaynor asked follow-up questions, most of which went unanswered. Finally, to appease Gaynor's quest for answers, Sam informed Gaynor that Durrell would privately answer a select number of her questions following the press conference at an elementary school.

Later, outside the Uniondale Town Hall, Sam watched as Gaynor went on-air to report the day's biggest news story. Her news station interrupted their ongoing five o'clock news program to report the headline story. It ran for seven minutes and chronicled the ongoing serial murder investigation that discovered several unidentified victims buried at three locations. After Gaynor finished her penetrating account, she made her way to Sam. "So, what do you think? How was it?"

"I thought it was superb! You were accurate but sympathetic, which is how to capture viewers' attention, yet you maintained sound professionalism. A perfect balance."

She jokingly responded, "Wow. Do they teach the elements of good journalism in agent training school?"

"Well, not exactly, but I know talent when I see it. You were clearly at ease presenting your story, and it was a very well-organized presentation."

"Thanks! It was a tragedy what they tried to do to you, Sam. I'm happy you are out of jail and back on the job. Maybe we could have a private one-on-one follow-up as this investigation unfolds."

"Hmm, how about we talk about that over dinner?"

Alli looked at her watch and saw the time was close to Durrell's press conference. She reached into her pocket and handed Sam her business card. "I would like that, Sam. My private number is on the back. Call me, and we'll set a date." She then joined her cameraman in the news van to travel to the six o'clock press conference at the school.

The press conference commenced just minutes after six as numerous reporters and cameras focused on US Attorney Durrell. She stepped up to the microphone, surrounded by the participating agency leaders.

She introduced the agency heads before outlining the events of the day. "This afternoon, search warrants signed by federal judges in Hartford and Worcester, Massachusetts, were executed at three locations by a team of federal, state, and local law enforcement officers. Our search uncovered human remains buried at each property. We have not yet confirmed the identification of any remains. Federal agents and police have arrested two suspects, Richard Harrington, forty-two, of West Glasterbury, a state employee, and Randy Flemming, age forty-three, of Saundersville, Massachusetts. The two suspects arrested were charged with several federal and state crimes, including kidnapping and murder. Also, Richard Harrington's father, Forster Harrington, was arrested at one of the search locations for attempting assault, interfering with the search, and disobeying a direct order from the state police. We anticipate additional arrests in connection with this investigation in the coming weeks."

A bit choked up, Durrell described the horrific scene at each location and how it was incomprehensible that anyone could commit such heinous crimes. She concluded the briefing by thanking the exemplary investigative teamwork of the agencies involved and said that she'd hold an additional press conference in the coming weeks as the investigation develops. Durrell spoke for only fifteen minutes and took a few questions before reporters went on air for the six-thirty news program. Later, she met with Alli Gaynor privately to answer some unanswered questions at the press conference.

CHAPTER
51

The following morning, the searches commenced at ten o'clock and continued until law enforcement leadership believed they had left no stone unturned. News vans and trucks with satellite dishes made traffic difficult at all three sites. Reporters with microphones and camera crews lined the streets as state and local police did their best to maintain some traffic flow.

By the end of the day, the searches uncovered a two-day total of twelve human remains, nine male and three females. Coroners transported them to a state facility for forensic examination. The authorities found three remains at the Harrington property, six at Flemming's Wilsonbury property, and three at his Saundersville property.

The news media coverage went nationwide, and the lead stories continued for weeks in Connecticut and Massachusetts. Two weeks later, Durrell held a follow-up press conference in downtown Hartford. Police cordoned off the block in front of the federal building, where seven news vans and police vehicles covered the block in front of the building. The conference included opening remarks by the governor, followed by Durrell, Murphy, the state police colonel, and police chiefs from Hartford and Saundersville. The reporters and attendees in the conference room waited impatiently to pump the speakers with dozens of questions. When it ended, much of the press remained in hopes of conducting personal one-on-one interviews of those on the stage, especially with Sam.

However, Sam didn't want any part of it. As the last question got answered, he left the stage and headed toward a side exit to escape reporters. Seeing Sam moving quickly off the stage and toward the exit, reporter Buzzy Dunnledd pushed and slid his way through the crowd of reporters to catch Sam as he reached the exit door. Dunnledd shouted out at him. "Caviello, was the assault at the hotel actually staged, or did the government bury it to save face with the public?"

Irritated, Sam turned to face the reporter and said loud enough for other reporters to hear. "Hey, everybody, look who it is! It's Fuzzy Dumhead, again trying to score points with his criminal friends who set me up!"

Dunnledd wasn't amused. "I don't think you're funny, Caviello, and I certainly don't have any criminal friends. My reports were from reliable sources and checked for accuracy."

Sam said his final words before he exited the side door. "We know who fed you with all the bullshit lies that you wrote. It was all fake, and you know it."

Sam then vanished through the exit and made his way toward his car when someone called out his name. He turned and saw it was Alli Gaynor.

"Hey, Sam! Just so you know, I can't stand that guy, Dunnledd. He's a bad example of professional reporting. Anyway, I was hoping we could get together for dinner."

"Alli, there is nothing I would enjoy more than having dinner with you tonight. However, I can't say much more about the investigation since it's still ongoing. The investigation may result in additional arrests or other actions that I can't comment on at this point."

"We could talk off the record. I won't report on it until you give me the okay."

"Ah, in other words, I should trust you won't report what I tell you. That could be risky for me. Tell you what, let's get to know each other and develop some trust before you quote me on the six o'clock news."

Alli paused for a moment while they looked into each other's eyes. Then, she added a smile and said, "That's fair. Where would you like to meet?"

"I have your number. I'll call you." He then walked to his car, criticizing himself. *What the hell did I just do? Am I trying to be hard to get? I could be having dinner with her tonight.*

*   *   *

Forster Harrington finally got up the backbone to face his son in jail after days of agonizing over it. He felt bitterness and resentment toward his son. He suspected for years that his son was different and was hiding his true personality from the family, but his wife dismissed it as being shy and keeping to himself.

After a security search at the jail, a guard escorted Harrington to a private room where his son was seated and cuffed to a small table. His son couldn't even look at his father as he entered the room.

Forster took a seat opposite his son. There was only silence for a minute or two before Forster spoke. "Do you know what you have done to your family and me? What you've done to your mother? She is heartbroken. She wouldn't even come out of her room and talk to me for a week. And your sister had to leave her job because she couldn't face her colleagues at work. The police arrested me trying to protect my property and you. I'm out on bail for ridiculous state charges that won't amount to a hill of beans, but it was an embarrassment to me and the business. Now, I've heard through my sources that the feds will indict me for trying to help you get out of this mess. I might have to go to jail too. The shame and embarrassment you have brought to our family and me are inexcusable. I don't understand you. Why did you have to kill those boys? How could you do this to your mother and me, Dickie?"

With his eyes swelling with tears and in a trembling voice, Dickie, still avoiding looking at his father, mumbled that he was sorry. He lifted his head slightly but wouldn't look straight into his father's eyes. Finally, he whispered, "Can you do anything to help me? Maybe get me out on bail and arrange for me to leave the country? Please, Dad, I can't survive in jail, and I don't want to die. I'll do anything you ask. I'll change. I promise."

Repulsed, Forster Harrington angrily said, "They found three bodies buried on my property. Young boys murdered so you could have your sadistic, sick fantasy with them. The feds found you in your underwear, hiding in a fucking closet with a naked and drugged fourteen-year-old kid. You're sick. You need help that I can't give you. I gave you all the help I'm ever going to give you. If I helped you escape the country, they would put me in jail in your place. Is that what you want? Well, I'm done with you. You are no longer my son."

Forster walked out of the room. He had already instructed his attorney's firm to represent his son, Dellagatti, and Garcia. Forster wanted to ensure Garcia wouldn't testify against Dellagatti and himself. He figured Garcia might get additional time in jail, but Harrington's offer was a significant payoff and a full-time job for life. It didn't work. Garcia refused the offer.

Next, Harrington had to find a way to get Flemming to admit to all the murders and say his son was unaware of what happened to the kids after their encounters with them. He thought that Flemming might confess to all the murders if Harrington's attorneys could secure a plea deal in exchange for taking the death penalty off the table. Also, they would make arrangements to protect him from harm while serving life in prison.

The attorney thought it might work but told Harrington that it would be impossible to guarantee protection for Flemming while in prison. Harrington's response was, "Who cares?"

With Harrington's approval, his attorney contacted Flemming's attorney to arrange a sit-down to discuss the defensive strategy. Flemming's attorney agreed in hopes of getting ideas from a top-notch law firm on how best to defend his client.

It turned out Harrington's plan would not have worked even if Flemming and his attorney agreed to it. Days following his dad's visit to the jail, Richard Harrington was found dead in his cell. Using a bedsheet tied tightly around his neck and secured to a crossbar on the jail cell door, he quickly slouched down, causing tightening of the bedsheet around his neck, asphyxiating himself to death.

*   *   *

At the press conference, the US attorney did not mention she had already secured several true bill indictments still under seal due to the ongoing investigation. Grand jury members voted to indict Richard Harrington and Randy Flemming for multiple counts of kidnapping, rape, sexual assault, murder, and conspiracy. In addition, the indictment included Anthony "Tony" Dellagatti, Benjamin "Benni" Garcia, and Forster Harrington for conspiracy to obstruct a federal investigation and the attempt to frame a federal agent.

The grand jury had three unindicted coconspirators listed as John Doe et al. However, their identities remained unknown to the public until further investigation. They were State's Attorney Frank Reynolds, Chief of Staff Ron Freedman, and Detective Russel Mastin.

Over the following several days, Lieutenant Russel Mastin testified under subpoena before a grand jury regarding the state's attorney's role in the attempted frame-up and his investigative negligence. After thinking his testimony would be made public, Mastin retired after twenty-five years with the state police and accepted a position as the assistant director of public safety at one of Connecticut's private colleges. His testimony was never made public, and he never faced any charges.

With mounting evidence against him, Frank Reynolds, threatened with prosecution and jail time, conceded to cooperate and testify against Forster Harrington. As part of the deal, he agreed to resign as state's attorney in exchange for written assurance that he would not face charges and that the details of his involvement would not be made public.

The government did not have sufficient evidence to charge Ron Freedman, but US Attorney Durrell met with the governor privately and outlined Freedman's involvement. She made it clear that Freedman must be held accountable, either by her office or the governor. To avoid negative publicity on Freedman from Durrell's office, the governor asked for and received Freedman's resignation.

Sam was incredibly grateful to Durrell for obtaining additional background on Buzzy Dunnledd's close association with Forster Harrington that created an undeniable and unfair bias against Caviello in his news columns. Durrell met with Dunnledd's newspaper publisher, who decided to terminate Dunnledd's employment after reviewing her report.

Zake Barnes, Benni Garcia, Jenny Chen, and Fred Asckis cooperated with investigators and gave sworn testimony in exchange for reduced charges with no jail time, small fines, and community service. Garcia still faced state charges of breaking and entering a state facility. Barnes lost his driver's license for one year other than for use as transportation to and from work. Asckis agreed to resign as a constable.

Hartford Police, ATF, and the state police interrogated Simone Schizas, known to inmates as Schitzo, at the Hartford jail. Schizas agreed to talk provided he got what the corrections officer, Rocco Marcello, had promised him. The warden approved Schizas would get extra food and dessert portions, a thicker mattress, and an extra pillow for his cell in exchange for his testimony. However, the warden rejected Schizas receiving adult magazines and marijuana. As a result, Schizas admitted Rocco Marcello promised all the extra items if he stabbed Caviello. He claimed Marcello told him that Caviello was a murderer of young children.

Believing his friend, Forster Harrington, would provide and pay for a top-notch attorney, Marcello initially wouldn't talk to investigators. However, Harrington refused even knowing Marcello when the word got out of the failed attempt on Caviello's life. Facing conspiracy charges in an attempt to murder a federal agent, Marcello subsequently agreed to testify against Dellagatti and Harrington in exchange for a lighter sentence. He told the investigators he had played football with Dellagatti and Harrington during high school, and they were lifelong friends. Nevertheless, Marcello broke down crying when describing when he met them at a café near New Haven.

"They didn't tell me the guy was a federal agent, only that Caviello had killed young kids. They said I should pick an inmate who had nothing to lose and promise him anything if he killed Caviello. Forster Harrington promised I would get twenty-five thousand dollars and a lifetime job at his construction company at a salary more than I earn as a corrections officer. It was stupid for me to get involved with them. I've never done anything like this before, and I'm sorry I did."

EPILOGUE

Sam met Alli at a small suburban restaurant outside Hartford known for its excellent cuisine. He ordered a bottle of champagne to celebrate the successful outcome of the Harrington investigation and the job offer she received from a national television broadcasting company. They toasted to their continued success and friendship.

"Alli, I appreciate your fair and responsible reporting after my arrest. It meant a lot to my son and me," said Sam.

"That's how I report the news, Sam. Besides, everyone I interviewed, including agents, police officers, attorneys, and friends, had good things to say about you. For example, the Hartford agents described you as a friend and a colleague. They never used words like boss or supervisor to describe you."

"I enjoy working with them on investigations rather than sitting at a desk reviewing reports and writing evaluations. I prefer to be part of the team versus being the boss."

"I understand, but every team needs someone to lead, whether the person is called captain, supervisor, a manager, or whatever."

"Well, I see us more like a family, with me being the father figure looking after the younger ones."

"Well, your family members certainly look up to you, even describing you as having a special talent for finding things that baffle them at times. They say you have unusual gut feelings about what to do or where to look. Is that all it really takes, a gut feeling? Are those feelings always right?"

"When I follow those feelings, they usually lead me in the right direction, but not always."

"What are gut feelings anyway?"

"Well, my gut feelings, hmm, it's, uh, just an expression, as an intuition. So let's order dinner, and I'll do my best to answer some questions you have about the Harrington case. However, I'm limited on what I can tell you since the case has not been fully adjudicated, and even then, you'll have to attribute some of what I say to an anonymous source."

"I can live with that, Sam. We'll talk business after dinner."

"That's another thing. The dinner tables here are very close together, so I feel uncomfortable saying too much here."

"We could talk more privately at my place if you prefer," suggested Alli.

"I'd be much more comfortable there," said Sam, thinking well beyond any business talk and hoping for a very special night at her place.

*　　*　　*

In the days to follow, the feds subsequently arrested Forster Harrington on numerous federal charges, including obstruction of justice and multiple conspiracy charges, including attempts to frame and murder a federal agent. He was arraigned at the Hartford federal court and released on a three-million-dollar bond and had to surrender his passport. When he walked out of the courtroom with his attorney and daughter, Rachel, he noticed Sam Caviello talking on his cell phone down the hall near the restrooms. Harrington excused himself to make a quick stop at the men's room. Sam noticed Harrington heading his way and quickly pushed an app icon on his phone before placing it in his shirt pocket.

As Harrington approached, Sam greeted him. "Having a pleasant day, Harrington? Did you enjoy your day in court? I could relate to it, as you know."

Harrington stared at Sam with hatred in his eyes and whispered, "Fuck you, Caviello. You're responsible for destroying my family, my business, and for my son's death. I'm going to enjoy paying you back for all the misery you caused my family."

He moved in closer, going nose to nose with Sam, and whispered a threat. "I know you have a son. My advice to you is to keep him safe if you can, but you'll never know when an unfortunate accident could happen to him."

"You have bad breath, Harrington, and terrible manners, so keep your distance from me."

Harrington moved away from Sam and entered the men's room.

Sam wasn't going to take the threat lightly. He was pissed. He looked around, ensuring no one was nearby. He then quietly entered the men's room, saw Harrington at the urinal, and moved up behind him. He then shoved Harrington's head hard and held it against the wall, causing Harrington's aim to miss the bowl as he pissed down his pant leg and onto his shoe. Sam pulled out his cell phone with his free hand and replayed the recording of Harrington's threat a moment ago. "I suspect the court won't be too friendly at sentencing when they hear the threat you just made to me. It could add many more years to your long stay in prison."

He pressed Harrington against the wall with more force. "If anything happens to my son, I'll know exactly who to look for, you scumbag. Just remember what goes around comes around right back at you." Sam released Harrington and turned to walk out of the men's room.

Harrington's attorney walked in as Sam was on his way out. "What's going on here, Agent?" he snapped.

Sam, with a smirk on his face, answered him. "Your client just pissed his pants. I think he's scared shitless of being in a prison community bathroom with all those criminals knowing what his son did to all those kids."

Harrington's daughter, Rachel, was waiting for her dad outside the men's room. When she saw Sam come out, she gave him a revolting look. "Our family is in shambles and will never recover because of you. I hope someone does the same to you someday."

Sam decided not to respond and walked away. The investigation was coming to a close, and Sam felt satisfaction and peace with the outcome. Although facing slander and humiliation during the investigation, he stayed the course and trusted his instincts about Richard Harrington.

Despite all that had happened, Sam continued to believe there was a mystical element in the investigation. Although not deeply religious, he thought it was miraculous that the kid's phone, lost and buried among the leaves in the woods, could emit the final ring sounds from a dying battery. Sam felt the final sounds coming from the phone were Richardson's last cry for help.

He was awakened from his thoughts when reporter Alli Gaynor appeared outside the courtroom. She waved with a big smile as he walked to meet her. Not having a serious relationship with a woman since his divorce, Sam was excited to have begun one with this beautiful reporter.

"Hi, Sam! It looks like Forster Harrington will spend a long time in jail, thanks to you."

"Yeah, it couldn't have happened to a nicer guy. It's appropriate that those involved with violating the law, or their ethics in this case, got what they deserved."

"Oh, that reminds me. Did the resignations from the state's attorney and the governor's chief of staff have anything to do with their involvement with the scheme to set you up?"

Before Sam answered, she added, "Also, Lieutenant Mastin retired and took another job at a local college, and Buzzy Dunnledd no longer works for the paper. Were their career changes a result of your investigation, Sam? You have anything to do with what happened to them?"

"Let's discuss that over dinner and champagne. After all, we should celebrate both the ending of a successful investigation and the job offer you received for your journalistic excellence."

"Oh, and I suppose you'll feel more comfortable answering the questions at my place?"

As they walked out of the building together, hand in hand, Sam replied, "It's so thoughtful of you to invite me to your apartment for dinner, champagne, and a night of —."

She interrupted him. "I know what you're thinking, Sam. So let's go straight to my place, and we'll decide where we'll dine later."

ACKNOWLEDGMENTS

First, I'm grateful to ATF for providing me with a fulfilling and rewarding public service career. ATF is a distinguished and respected federal law enforcement agency that also formed a lasting community of friends among thousands of men and women dedicated to serving and protecting the great citizens of the United States.

My thanks to John Paine, editor, who guided me in developing good characters and dialogue, and Ryan Quinn, proofreader, who revealed and corrected surface errors, ensuring every piece of the book was in its proper place. Special thanks and love to my son, Paul, who did a professional job copy editing and encouraging the importance of social acceptability in writing.

I'm indebted to my friends Dave Campbell, John Tinnirella, and Barbara Keiser for their tireless and comprehensive review and input of the initial draft of my book from a reader's viewpoint.

I also appreciate the professional support from authors Andrew Watts and Wayne Miller. They provided essential counsel, advice, and needed references in the long, tedious journey of writing, publishing, and establishing readership for debut writers.

The publication of my book would not have been possible without the teaching and counseling by my coach Geoff Affleck, a master at guiding aspiring authors in launching and promoting their books in the maze of self-publishing steps to optimize sales and readership. I couldn't have done it alone with success without his expertise and guidance.

Last, but in reality, foremost, my special thanks and love to my wife Donna and son, Paul. Paul first encouraged me to finish what I had started long ago—to write novels. With his more advanced computer knowledge, he not only guided me in its use for writing but also copy-edited my work with recommendations that improved my writing. My wife, Donna, was my constant supporter who read draft chapters nearly every day, circling errors and making suggestions on changing words, improving sentence structure, and recommending deletions. Her continuous support and encouragement were the primary incentives I needed to complete my novel. Donna and Paul's reinforcement, devotion, and love were the inspiration that drove me to write, and I love them dearly for it.

ABOUT THE AUTHOR

Stan Comforti is a thirty-year law enforcement veteran. He was a federal air marshal and then a Special Agent with the Bureau of Alcohol, Tobacco, Firearms, and Explosives (ATF). As a field agent, he worked numerous investigations against drug dealers, outlaw motorcycle and street gang members, and felons who possessed, stole, traded, or trafficked firearms, including illegal sawed-off shotguns and fully automatic weapons. Many of his field assignments involved working undercover. Subsequently, as an office supervisor in Massachusetts and Connecticut, he directed many high-profile investigations, including a murder-for-hire case where a father paid an undercover agent to kill his daughter by placing an explosive device under the car she drove. ATF arrested the father before any harm came to his daughter. Another investigation involved the unlawful sale and possession of firearms, including a machine gun that involved police officials, one of whom was also engaged in a major police exam-scam operation. Also, for seven years, Mr. Comforti was a leader of Boston ATF's Special Response Team. He led many early morning arrest and search warrant raids against drug dealers and gang members who illegally possessed and used firearms in their illegal operations.

THE SAM CAVIELLO FEDERAL AGENT CRIME MYSTERY SERIES

Book 1: *A Cry for Help*

Book 2: *Chasing Terror*

Book 3: *Finding Ena*

Available at Amazon and other book sellers.

If you enjoyed this novel please leave an Amazon review.

Connect with the author at stancomforti.author@gmail.com, or visit StanComforti.com. You also scan the QR code to reach his website.